DARK ROVER'S LUCK

THE CHILDREN OF THE GODS
BOOK NINETY-FIVE

I. T. LUCAS

Dark Rover's Luck is a work of fiction! Names, characters, places, and incidents are products of the author's imagination or are used fictitiously and are not to be construed as real. Any similarity to actual persons, organizations, and/or events is purely coincidental.

Copyright © 2025 by I. T. Lucas

All rights reserved.

No part of this book may be reproduced in any form or by any electronic or mechanical means, including information storage and retrieval systems, without written permission from the author, except for the use of brief quotations in a book review.

Published by Evening Star Press, LLC.

EveningStarPress.com

ISBN: 978-1-962067-74-4

1

FENELLA

*L*ife in the immortals' village was good, Fenella decided as she stirred a packet of sugar into her cappuccino cup. Spending a Sunday afternoon in the outdoor café with her new best friends and exchanging flirtatious smiles with hunky immortal males was a very pleasant way to pass the time.

After spending the last fifty years believing that she was some kind of anomaly and roving from place to place to avoid discovery, Fenella was now surrounded by other immortals like her, and it was all thanks to the two women sharing her table in this lovely café.

She owed everything to this mother-daughter duo.

If Jasmine hadn't arrived with an immortal and Kra-ell cavalry to free Kyra, Fenella would still be a prisoner in the hands of that monster who'd called himself a doctor.

As a shiver ran through her, she imagined pushing the horrific memories to a dark corner of her mind, closing the door on them, and throwing away the key.

There was no point in dwelling on the past. She should enjoy the present instead.

The lunch crowd was thinning out, the residents moving on to whatever activities immortals indulged in when they weren't plotting world-saving missions or running from evil Doomers and other boogeymen.

God knew there were many of those, and the monster doctor was just one example in an ocean of them.

That was why Fenella doubted that this place was as idyllic as it looked. Every inch of the village was meticulously maintained, and everyone was too bloody good-looking and cheerful. Frankly, she preferred the Kra-ell with their somber faces and pent-up violent energy. They looked dangerous, deadly even, and they didn't bother with trying to look civilized and harmless like the immortals.

"Earth to Fenella." Jasmine waved her hand in front of her face. "You've gone from looking content like a happy kitten to frowning like the sky is about to fall."

Fenella winced. "Not a good analogy given that Din is in the air right now."

The guy had had a crush on her fifty years ago, and despite every possible obstacle fate had thrown in his way, he was still adamant about reuniting with her. It was flattering, but it was also worrisome. Fenella had learned to listen when fate joined hands with intuition to warn her against this or that.

Not that it always worked. Failing to realize that the charming, good-looking guy who'd called himself a doctor was the devil incarnate hadn't been the first mistake she'd ever made. It hadn't been the second either.

There had been quite a few of them.

"Are you worried?" Kyra asked.

"I am, but that's not why I was frowning. I was just thinking how bloody nice everyone and everything here is, and that it can't be real. The funny thing is that the aliens are the ones who look normal. They are not as sickeningly saccharine as the immortals."

"You mean the Kra-ell?" Jasmine asked. "Because, for your information, we are all aliens here. Well, part aliens is a more accurate description. We are mostly human with a little godly mixed in."

Fenella waved a hand. "Of course, I mean the Kra-ell. They are the ones who look alien."

"I think you are just stressed because of Din."

Kyra took a sip of her coffee. "And I don't blame you for being anxious. I don't know much about international travel, but I've never heard of anyone encountering so much trouble to get from one place to another, and I've spent the last twenty-three years in the Kurdish resistance, so that's saying something."

Kyra was right, and Fenella knew that her irritation stemmed more from concern about Din's travel troubles than from the village being too perfect. It had been one thing after another, but the stubborn guy insisted that the universe was not trying to tell him to stay home. In his view, the universe was piling up difficulties to make him work harder to reach her, so he could prove to her that he was serious this time.

As if he hadn't been serious before and hadn't shunned his best friend for fifty years because that friend had supposedly stolen her.

It was sweet, and she wanted to believe that Din was right about the universe just testing his resolve, but that nagging churning in her stomach said otherwise. Something bad was going to happen, and her gut knew it.

"Was this the third or fourth delay?" Jasmine asked.

"It's the third." Fenella leaned back in her chair, crossing her arms. "First, it was the accident on the way to the airport, then the next flight was canceled because of some mechanical problems, and then a storm hit, and all outgoing flights from Edinburgh were canceled." She shook her head. "Though I don't understand why I'm worrying so much about someone I can barely remember." She waved a hand. "Look at all these guys. I can have my pick. Why am I waiting for a man who already has a bad track record with me?"

"You're curious." Kyra cast her a knowing look. "You need to see the guy who's spent five decades obsessing over you."

"Yeah," Fenella admitted. "I guess that's as good of an explanation as any. But enough about my non-existent love life." She gave Kyra a knowing smile. "Tell us how the meeting with your ex-husband went."

Kyra lifted her coffee cup and took a sip. "It went well. Eva's disguise worked flawlessly, making me look the age he expected me to be, and he didn't suspect anything. Poor Boris has been blaming himself for my disappearance throughout all these years, thinking that I was dead, so he was very happy to see that I was alive and well. I think I gave him closure and got some for myself." She smiled. "I felt like I couldn't really start my new life with Max before tying up that loose end. I also did it for Jasmine. She deserves to have both parents for a change, and I told Boris that I intend for us to visit him from time to time. It made him happy."

Jasmine nodded. "We all need healing. I would

love to improve my relationship with my father. We were practically estranged."

"I'm happy for you both." Fenella tore off a piece of the most delicious chocolate croissant she'd ever tasted and put it in her mouth. Groaning with pleasure, she turned to Kyra. "So, you came back to the village and celebrated by shagging Max all night long."

Kyra snorted. "You are terrible, Fenella. My daughter is sitting right here with us."

"It's okay, Mom." Jasmine put her hand on Kyra's arm. "Don't feel shy. There is nothing you can say that will shock me, trust me. Think of me as your best friend rather than your daughter."

"I'd like to think of you as both."

"Oh, that's so sweet." Fenella took another piece of the chocolatey goodness and ate it greedily.

"Let's just say that a lot of pent-up energy was released." Kyra sighed. "I'm still rediscovering it all. Max was my first consensual sexual experience in nearly two and a half decades."

The momentary darkness in Kyra's expression was an unwelcome reminder of what they'd all been through. For all the lightness of their afternoon coffee date, they'd each survived horrors that would haunt them for a long time.

Maybe even forever.

"I'm so glad I don't remember most of it," Kyra said. "I wish my sister Yasmin could be made to forget so she could be spared the grief of losing her husband. I don't know how to help her."

Jasmine nodded. "She and the children didn't even have the closure of a burial ceremony. It must be so hard for them."

"How are the children of your other sisters doing?" Fenella asked.

"All of them have been traumatized to some extent," Kyra said. "Being taken from the life they knew, however imperfect it was, and thrust into this completely foreign environment can't be easy for any of them." She shook her head. "I need to talk to my sisters about seeing the clan psychologist."

"You need to see Vanessa as well, Mom," Jasmine said.

"I know." Kyra leaned back in her chair. "If the Clan Mother can't help me with the retrieval of my memories, I might contact Vanessa. I heard that she's very busy, though, and Yasmin needs her much more than I do."

"When are you going to see the Clan Mother?" Jasmine asked.

"When I am summoned. I know she wants me to help her find her beloved, so I expect it to be soon." Kyra put her hand over the pendant she always wore. "Although I really don't know how I will be able to help her. Finding missing people has never been one of my gifts."

"I'll help you," Jasmine said. "I wasn't able to do it

on my own, but I have a feeling that together, we will be stronger than the sum of our parts."

Fenella lifted her hand. "Hey, maybe I can help too. After all, we seem strangely connected somehow. I think the Fates Max keeps talking about are trying to tell us something. Right?"

Mother and daughter regarded her with curious expressions.

"You might be onto something," Jasmine said. "Do you know that Amanda, Kian's sister, tried to get Max interested in me? He took one look at me and disliked me instantly because I reminded him of you."

Fenella waved a dismissive hand. "I heard that story, and I think it's absurd. We look nothing alike."

Jasmine was tall and curvy. She wasn't carrying extra weight or anything, but she was a big woman who occupied a lot of space. Compared to her, Fenella felt almost petite.

"We have similar coloring and the cleft in our chins." Jasmine pointed at Fenella's, which was much less pronounced than hers. "Anyway, he was mad at you for coming between him and Din."

"Men are so bloody ridiculous," Fenella muttered. "And they blame everything on women. I didn't even know Din had feelings for me, but Max did, or should have known if he considered Din his best friend. It's his fault, not mine."

"He knows that now," Kyra said, "Max has matured a lot since then."

"Yeah, he has." Fenella remembered their talk on the way back from Iran. "Max and I have sorted it out. But I still don't get why you reminded him of me. You're tall and sexy, and I'm not."

"You are beautiful," Jasmine said. "I never liked my height or the size of my hips. I would have loved to look as delicate as you."

"Delicate?" Fenella barked out a laugh. "No one who knows me would call me delicate, love. I've always compensated with my big mouth and even bigger attitude."

Smiling, Kyra nodded. "I'm starting to realize that about you. I bet that's what Din fell in love with."

"He doesn't know me, let alone love me." Fenella turned to Jasmine. "Speaking of my supposed future with him, though, you promised me a tarot reading. Now that your mum's back with the cards, I could really use your mystical guidance."

Jasmine nodded. "I don't have them with me, but we can go to my house and do it there."

"Brilliant. I hope you have decent alcohol and mixers. I can make drinks you've never even heard of."

Jasmine's eyes widened. "I forgot that you were a bartender. You should talk with Ingrid. Her partner runs the Hobbit Bar, and it's open only on weekends because he doesn't have help. You could work for him."

Fenella had worked as a barmaid during her travels, but she hadn't bartended since she'd left Scotland half a century before. Nevertheless, she still remembered many of the drinks she'd prepared back then. Besides, learning new ones was easy now that everything was accessible on the internet.

Most importantly, though, having a job meant earning money, and she could use some for when she decided to leave this place.

"I'll happily talk to the guy. What's his name?"

"Atzil," Jasmine said. "During the week, he works for Kalugal as his main chef. He cooks for all the men—breakfast, lunch, and dinner. That's why he can't open the bar midweek."

Fenella grimaced. "So, he's one of those former Doomers?"

Jasmine nodded.

"I don't know if I could work for one of them," Fenella admitted. "After what his fellow so-called Brother did to me..." She shivered.

"Atzil is the nicest guy." Jasmine leaned over and put her hand on Fenella's arm. "Don't hold his past against him. We've all done things we are not proud of, and in his case, he was born into that crap. It took tremendous will and good character to break free from the brainwashing and realize that he was working for evil incarnate."

"I guess." Fenella put what was left of the croissant in her mouth and concentrated on the sweetness to chase away the bad memories.

"So, what's going on with Din?" Kyra asked. "When is he supposed to get here?"

"This evening, but after all the delays, I have a feeling he's not going to make it today either." Fenella sighed. "I actually feel a bit less concerned than I did after the first two delays. Misfortune always comes in threes, so now that the third happened, that should be it."

She didn't really believe that, but saying it made her feel a little less anxious.

Kyra laughed, shaking her head. "You're that superstitious?"

"Says the woman who makes life-or-death decisions based on a magical pendant," Fenella shot back.

"Touché," Kyra acknowledged. "But the pendant actually works."

"So do my gut feelings," Fenella countered. "They've kept me alive this long."

2

DIN

*D*in stretched out in the wide leather seat, enjoying the upgrade to business class. Normally, he didn't splurge on luxuries like this, but this was the third time he had rebooked a flight, so he'd given in to a small indulgence. If the Fates insisted on testing him with endless obstacles on his path to Fenella, he could at least travel in comfort.

Closing his eyes, he tried to picture Fenella and what she looked like now. Since she'd turned immortal, she probably hadn't changed much, but she'd said that she was harder now, so maybe her smile wasn't so bright anymore, and her eyes didn't sparkle with mischief and amusement like they used to when she bartended. She had been so beautiful, so full of life, and for some reason, the twenty-three-year-old Fenella had intimidated him—an immortal who had lived nearly half a millennium.

Had he been afraid of falling in love with her? Probably.

He'd thought that she was just a human girl, a bright and colorful butterfly whose lifespan was but a blink of an eye in the span of his. He couldn't have known that she was a Dormant.

Hell, back then, there had been no Dormants to be found.

Knowing that they had to exist among the human population, the clan had searched for them, investigating every rumor of witchcraft and supernatural ability, hoping to find a Dormant behind it, and yet, they'd found none.

How could he have known that a Dormant was right there in front of his eyes?

How could he have realized that Fenella's pull on him was more than just a normal attraction to a pretty girl?

Was it any wonder that both he and Max had been obsessed with her?

But Max had always been the cocky one, the one who had to win every bet, to bed every woman, and this time, it had been no different.

Max had seduced Fenella, inadvertently induced her transition, and then left her without knowing that she'd turned immortal. The poor girl hadn't known what hit her, why all those changes were happening to her, so she'd left her home and started roving the world in search of answers.

It was Din's fault that she'd suffered. His and Max's.

If he hadn't been such a prideful idiot, such a stubborn fool, he would never have gone to see her after Max left her and spoken to her in the way that he had. If he had just handled things differently then, they might have been together for half a century already, and she would have been spared all the horrors that had been inflicted upon her.

The Doomer who'd done that to her was still alive in the clan's dungeon in Los Angeles, and Din had every intention of changing his life status.

Kian's permission was required for ending that vile life, and Din would have to wait until every last bit of information was extracted from the monster, but Kian would recognize Din's right to avenge his mate, even if she didn't accept him as her one and only yet.

"We will be landing soon," the pilot announced, breaking through the haze of rage that had momentarily blinded Din. "Please collect your electronic devices…"

"Are you okay?" the woman sitting next to him asked.

Bloody hell. Din could feel the armrests groaning under his fingers and forced them to loosen their grip.

"Yes," he murmured without turning toward her, and keeping his eyes closed to hide their inner glow.

His elongated fangs were a little harder to conceal, though. He had to get a hold of himself before he let the woman see his face.

"There is no shame in being scared of flying," she said. "I'm especially terrified of landings. Would you like me to hold your hand?"

He followed her gaze to where he was still gripping the armrests, not as hard as before, but his knuckles were still white. Under no circumstances could he allow her to hold his hand. He might crush hers accidentally.

"Thank you for the offer, but I'll be alright in a couple of moments. I'm trying to concentrate on my breathing exercises."

That should get her to mind her own business and stop looking at him.

"Oh, I see. I'll leave you alone to meditate then."

Thank the merciful Fates.

Soon, he would be in New York, and from there he'd fly to Los Angeles. After all the broken travel arrangements, this final leg to Fenella felt like the end of a half-century vigil.

He could almost imagine the look she would give him when he finally showed up at the village. Disbelief, maybe. Annoyance, perhaps. But under it all, he hoped for just a flicker of excitement. Or at least relief that he'd arrived in one piece.

On some level, he was glad that Fenella was so

worried about him and imagined each delay as a bad omen. It meant that she cared for him.

He could work with that.

Musings about Fenella calmed the storm he'd created in his mind, and he even started dozing off when the chime sounded, and a moment later, the pilot's calm but taut voice crackled through the cabin speakers.

"Ladies and gentlemen, this is the captain. We seem to be experiencing a mechanical issue with the landing gear. There is no need for alarm. We are working on a solution."

What kind of a solution could they come up with in the air? And how were they going to land the aircraft without landing gear?

A collective ripple of alarm coursed through the cabin.

The woman beside him gasped, her knuckles now going white on the armrests. "W-what does that mean?"

"It means that we might need to land differently than planned," Din said, trying to keep his tone calm for her sake. "The crew will do all they can to fix it."

He certainly hoped they could do that. Even immortals couldn't survive a serious plane crash. Not that a jet landing on its belly would be fatal to him unless the whole thing caught fire and exploded. Still, he could potentially open one of the emergency doors and jump out. A fall, provided that it wasn't from too high up, would injure him but not kill him.

The same couldn't be said for the human passengers, though, and he couldn't just leave them to die.

Another chime sounded. "Folks, we're working through checklists now. Air Traffic Control is clearing us for an emergency landing at JFK, but the runway might not be ideal if we can't get that nose gear down. We're exploring the possibility of putting her down on the water if needed. Please remain calm and listen to the flight crew's instructions."

The woman next to Din let out a trembling breath. "Oh God, oh God...we are going to die!"

Din placed his hand over hers. "It's all right," he said. "You're not going to die. We'll get through it."

Her eyes flickered with tears. "I can't die like this. My kids expect me home tonight."

"We won't die," he said firmly, pouring a little thrall into his words, just enough to calm her down. "Trust the pilots. They train for these kinds of emergency scenarios."

She nodded, closing her eyes and letting out a breath.

Din wished someone could do him the same favor and thrall him so he could stop running through various versions of all the things that could go wrong.

Amid the hiss of the air conditioning, the cabin seemed unnaturally quiet as if everyone were holding their breath, and then the flight attendants began a demonstration of bracing positions, offering life vests and instructing passengers to remove their shoes before entering the slides.

"Ladies and gentlemen," the captain's voice returned, "we're going to make an approach over the East River. We have partial success—one gear is locked, but the nose gear remains stuck. We plan an emergency landing on water if the nose fails to come down. The coast guard and rescue teams are on alert."

A wave of gasps swept through the cabin. The woman beside him buried her face in her hands, shoulders trembling despite the thrall of confidence he'd sent into her mind. Din moved an arm around her in a comforting gesture, though he doubted that any comfort could banish her terror right now.

The flight crew hurried down the aisle, checking seat belts and clearing away loose items. A flight attendant asked them to remove bulky clothing and to stow glasses and laptops.

Din clenched his jaw.

He'd lived for a long time and survived plenty of calamities, but some dangers still triggered a primal fear. Glancing out the window, he could see the city's skyline in the distance, so tantalizingly close, yet no assurance they'd reach it safely.

"Brace for impact!" The sudden command from the cockpit came as they began their descent.

People screamed. Din bowed forward, arms over his head, breathing methodically. The woman beside him did the same, trembling and crying. The plane lurched. The engines roared, reverberating through metal and bone.

A screeching wail cut through the hull, rattling overhead bins. Din squeezed his eyes shut, focusing on counting each second as they dropped altitude. The smell of burnt fuel tainted the air.

With a jarring impact, the aircraft skimmed across the water, the shriek of metal nearly deafening. The force knocked him forward, the shoulder harness biting into his flesh. He clamped his arm over the woman, shielding her as best he could. Everything tilted. Water splashed against the windows in tumultuous sprays.

Then they were skidding, the fuselage grinding with ear-splitting noise. A groan of stressed metal made him fear it might tear open. But by some miracle, the plane slowed. No roll, no shatter. Dimly, he registered that the overhead bins had popped open, baggage tumbling out. Another jolt knocked the breath from him.

And then…stillness.

For a heartbeat, the only sounds were ragged breathing and the faint hiss of steam rising from the engines.

The flight attendants sprang into action, unlatching emergency doors. Inflatable slides hissed open, some hitting the water, forming makeshift rafts. A wave of relieved sobbing rippled through the cabin. Outside, rescue vessels approached, bright lights strobing across the gloom.

Din let out a breath as he unbuckled, then helped the trembling woman next to him. "We've made it," he said.

She nodded in tearful disbelief.

They shuffled into the aisle, shoulders brushing other frantic passengers. Everyone was in that startled, half-panicked trance that follows a near-disaster. Din guided the woman to an exit, offering words of reassurance to others who were on the verge of hysterics.

Once out onto the rafts, they were met by rescue personnel.

An inflatable boat pulled alongside. Din helped the woman climb aboard, then followed. They made their way to the nearest barge, where paramedics were waiting.

Standing on the deck, Din took in the chaotic scene—passengers shivering in emergency blankets, rescue crews coordinating, the plane partly submerged but miraculously intact.

"Thank you," the woman whispered, hugging him briefly. "I don't even know your name."

"Din," he said, giving her shoulder a gentle squeeze. "You should call your kids as soon as you can because this will be all over the news in minutes, and they will worry."

"I will." She pulled the foil blanket the paramedics had given her tighter around her shoulders. "In a moment. I need to catch my breath. You should call your loved ones, too."

"Indeed. I'll do so right away."

3

FENELLA

*A*s Fenella's phone rang, she glanced at the screen, and when she saw Din's name, her heart did that annoying little flip.

"Speak of the devil," she murmured, then answered the call. "Din? Are you okay?"

"Yes, I'm fine, and hello to you too, Fenella." There was a hint of weariness in his tone, but also amusement.

"You sound okay, which is a great relief given your bad luck lately."

"About that." He let out a sigh. "It seems your premonitions were on target."

Fenella's stomach dropped. "What happened?"

"We've just made an emergency landing. There was a landing gear malfunction, and the pilot decided that the river was the best option, and he was right. I don't want to think what would have happened if he had tried to land on the ground with no wheels."

"Is everyone alright?" she asked.

"People are obviously shaken, but no one is seriously hurt. I just wanted to warn you before you see it on the news and imagine much worse than it actually was. All the passengers are fine, and they are putting us all up in hotels for the night. We'll fly out tomorrow afternoon."

Fenella closed her eyes, a chill running through her. "That's the fourth delay."

"I know what you're thinking, but sometimes a cigar is just a cigar, lass. These things happen."

He didn't sound at all sure of that, and Fenella had a feeling he didn't believe it himself at this point. "Four times is not a coincidence. The universe is clearly trying to tell us something."

Din chuckled. "And what would that be? That I should stay away from you?"

"Yes." Fenella didn't sound convincing even to her own ears. "Not that I want you to stay away. It's just that I don't want you to die trying to get to me. Perhaps I should fly out to meet you?"

That was actually a brilliant plan. She could get out of the village without offending anyone.

There was a pause. "I'm coming to you, love. I don't want you leaving the safety of the village for me. Maybe it's the devil who is putting all those obstacles in my way because it wants to lure you out of safety."

Her first response was to laugh, but Din hadn't sounded like he was making a joke or teasing. "Do you really believe that?"

He snorted. "At this point, I don't know what to believe. Evil is real. We've all seen it. So why not the devil?"

"Aye." She nodded. "I've seen it plenty of times wearing human and immortal skin." She glanced at Jasmine, who wasn't laughing at the exchange either. "Go to the hotel, Din, and after you shower and eat something, call me again."

"I will," Din promised, and she could hear the smile in his voice. "I'll text you my updated arrival time once I have it."

"Please do."

"Talk to you soon, Fenella."

Ending the call, she found Kyra and Jasmine watching her with identical concerned expressions.

"Is he okay?" Jasmine asked.

Fenella nodded. "I hope that this was what my premonition warned me about, and nothing worse is going to happen, but I would really like for you to do that spread for me."

"Maybe the universe is just testing his commitment," Kyra offered without much conviction.

"Or maybe it's warning me away from disaster," Fenella countered.

Jasmine shook her head. "If the universe didn't want you two together, it wouldn't have arranged for us to find you while we were rescuing my mother."

"That's true," Fenella conceded. She hadn't thought of it that way. "Although I really don't want to fall into the trap of believing in destiny or some other nonsense like that. It's like putting blinders on and pretending everything is made out of rainbows and unicorns."

That was a little ironic coming from her after all her talk about bad omens. If she believed in that, she should also believe in all the sunny crap, but in her experience, there was much more of the dark than there was of the light.

Jasmine and Kyra exchanged another one of those irritating knowing glances.

"Stop that," Fenella snapped. "You two have known me for all of five minutes. You don't get to have silent conversations about my love life or lack thereof."

"Sorry," Jasmine said, not sounding remorseful at all. "It's just that you keep protesting so loudly that it's comical. You want it to be the real thing as much as Din does."

Fenella groaned. "Don't you see? That's the problem. Neither of us should turn this into a chick flick in our heads. This is real life, and we are both adults."

"That's very mature and responsible," Jasmine said, and Fenella wasn't sure if she was mocking her or being serious. "Now, about the tarot reading you asked for."

"Yes, please." Fenella steepled her fingers. "I could use some insight, even if it comes from pieces of cardboard."

"They're not just pieces of cardboard." Jasmine glared at her. "In the right hands, the cards are tools, conduits for the initiated to connect to the Goddess, to the Mother of All Life."

Apparently, Fenella had stepped on the proverbial toe. "I believe you. Otherwise, I wouldn't have asked for a reading. Sometimes, I just say things in a way that sounds offensive. I'm sorry if I insulted your beliefs."

Jasmine's shoulders lost their stiffness. "That's okay. It's just that my father used to taunt me about the cards, so I'm a little sensitive about people mocking them."

Fenella lifted her hands. "I'm not mocking, I swear, but I've never had a magical anything guiding me, and I did fine. Well, until I crossed paths with that devil-spawned Doomer, that is." She sighed. "I thought that it was the worst thing that could ever happen to me, and it was, but on the other hand, it led me to finding out who I am and this entire world of immortals, aliens, and gods."

It had also led her back to Din, but it still remained to be seen if that was a good thing or not.

4

KIAN

Kian stood at the head of the oblong conference table that dominated the center of his office, arms folded over his chest, as he waited for the last of his guests to arrive.

He wished this meeting could be about the successful completion of the mission and the safe arrival of Kyra's family at the village, but as always, trouble was brewing, and this time its shadow was so big that he wasn't sure he could find a way out from under it.

He'd underestimated Navuh again.

"Good morning," Onegus said as he entered, looking sharp as always.

"Morning, chief." Kian motioned to the table. "Take a seat and make yourself comfortable."

Both of them had already received briefings from Yamanu, Max, and Jade, but this meeting was not about the mission they had just completed. It was about the situation they'd uncovered, which needed to be addressed.

"Is Turner joining us?" Onegus asked.

The strategist had his own security business that wasn't connected to the clan, and as much as Kian would have liked for him to dedicate his time fully to clan operations, Turner refused.

After this meeting, though, he might reconsider.

"I told Turner that this meeting would determine the future of the human race. That got him intrigued."

Onegus arched a brow. "Dramatic much?"

"I wish." Kian sighed. "But let's wait for everyone to get here so I don't have to repeat myself."

"I'm here." Yamanu entered the office. "Jade and Max are coming up the stairs. Are we waiting for anyone else?"

"Just Turner," Kian said.

Yamanu pulled a chair next to Onegus. "What's up, chief?"

"I don't know." Onegus shifted his eyes to Kian. "The boss is promising an exciting meeting today. Apparently, the future of the human race is on the line."

Yamanu frowned. "That bad, boss?"

Kian nodded. "Not yet, but if we allow it to continue on its current trajectory, we will lose the battle to the Doomers."

Once Jade, Max, and Turner were also seated around the table, Kian sat down. "Let's get started. The mission was mostly successful as far as retrieving Kyra's family was concerned, but the large Doomer presence the team encountered is worrisome, especially given their nuclear ambitions."

Onegus groaned. "Mark and his team had bought us time with that inspired virus they had contaminated the regime's nuclear program with, but with no proper follow-up from the world powers, that time was wasted on appeasement and futile negotiations. The regime has toyed with the naive Western governments, developing nuclear bombs right under their noses."

Kian snorted. "They were not naive. They've been complicit, bought and paid for, and the few who weren't for sale got their minds manipulated. We knew it was going to happen, and we haven't been proactive enough to stop it." He raked his fingers through his hair. "I have only myself to blame. I got distracted by the day-to-day business of making money for the clan, rescuing victims of trafficking, and recently, the dismantling of pedophile rings. Those are all important issues, and the human suffering is gut-wrenching, but we are not even making a dent in that, and furthermore, none of that will matter if we get overrun by the forces of darkness that the Brotherhood is mobilizing. We need to shift our focus back to the path the Clan Mother originally set us upon."

Max ran a hand over the stubble on his jaw. "That's not what I expected us to talk about this morning."

Kian nodded. "My apologies for the gloomy opening. I've gotten carried away. Let's start with the mission and your observations of the level of the Brotherhood's infiltration in Iran."

Max folded his arms over his chest. "The Doomers were waiting for us at almost every turn, or so it seemed. We changed routes multiple times, but they still showed up. They were much better organized than we'd expected, and they seemed to have information about us that was hard to explain."

"They had us pinned at multiple points," Jade added. "Someone either told them exactly where we would be, or they had another method of intercepting us." She placed her hands on the table. "It was obvious that they were working in coordination with the Revolutionary Guard."

"The Doomers showed up in places they shouldn't have known about," Max said, looking at Turner. "I hate to be the bearer of bad news, but I think your subcontractor has a breach. I don't think it was Nadim or Fatima, though, because no Doomers showed up at the safe house."

Turner nodded. "I will contact my guy and

suggest an investigation. His reputation is on the line."

"It's possible that they used hackers," Yamanu suggested. "What if they hacked the navigation systems in the vehicles?"

Turner tapped his pen over his yellow pad. "Yes, that's possible, but it means a breach at wherever my guy sourced the vehicles."

Max let out a breath. "That's the only explanation that would make sense for how they found us so quickly." He glanced at Jade. "We'd come up with a route on the fly, but if the vehicles themselves were broadcasting our location, the Doomers' actions could be explained."

"I don't think that's how they did it," Jade said. "I stole a car to get Rana's sons from school, and I had to use evasive maneuvers to lose the tail. I would have suspected trackers on the kids, but we checked them all upon arrival, and they were clean."

Onegus tapped a finger on the table. "Heavy presence in a nuclear-ambitious regime raises the stakes. If the Doomers have influence over key Iranian officials, they can direct those nuclear resources. We're no longer dealing with a small terrorist cell or a single compound. This is infiltration at the highest level."

Kian nodded. "That's why I said that the future of the human race is at stake. The question is, how do we respond? Up until now, we've tried to maintain the moral high ground and not use the same tactics as the Brotherhood to gain influence, but given the urgency of the situation, I don't think we can afford to keep doing that." He pressed a palm against the table, leaning forward. "If we do nothing, the Brotherhood will destabilize the entire world. I don't think Navuh would sanction the use of nuclear weapons, but I have a feeling that his puppets might get out of hand and act independently. His hateful rhetoric might produce unintended consequences."

"They will cause complete chaos," Jade murmured. "War or famine on a global scale. Either way, millions will die."

Kian swallowed the knot in his throat. Hearing her voice his fears so starkly made the possibility of them becoming reality all the more jarring. "We've spent many centuries trying to lead humanity toward enlightenment by promoting technological progress, human rights, and democracy. We wanted it to progress at its own pace, but we're at a tipping point. If we don't do something drastic, we will lose the battle to Navuh, and then all will be lost."

Onegus frowned. "So, what are you suggesting? That we intervene on the global stage? That we plant our people among world leaders and use mind manipulation like Navuh does?"

Kian's shoulders tightened. "Yes." He steeled himself for the wave of protest he expected. "We have to thrall, compel, and do whatever is needed to ensure humanity's survival and stop politicians from selling out their people. It goes against every principle I hold dear, but we can't stand idly by while the Doomers bring down every country and usher in global tyranny, turning the world into a cesspool of depravity and decay that they can easily dominate. Hell will seem like a pleasant vacation spot in comparison."

Max nodded. "Talk about an apocalypse."

Onegus regarded Kian with somber eyes. "You know the old saying about absolute power corrupting absolutely. Once we start thralling heads of state, or their closest advisors, the line is crossed."

"I know." Kian exhaled, slumping back in his chair. "The old adage about the road to hell being paved with good intentions keeps playing in my head. It's exactly the kind of slippery slope we've tried to avoid for so long. But what is the alternative? Sit back and watch the world get destroyed by Doomers and their cult of death?" He glanced at Turner, who wore a look of resigned acceptance.

"Kian is right. I see no other choice," the strategist said. "We are out of time. They've already poisoned entire governments, and they are not slowing down. We either respond in kind or we lose, and with us, the entire human race will fall. I don't want my children and grandchildren and so on to live in a world controlled by barbaric savages who celebrate slaughter. And I especially don't want my daughters and granddaughters to live in a world where women are dehumanized and treated like possessions. I'll fight until my last breath to prevent that from happening."

As far as Kian knew, Turner had a son and a grandson, but no daughters or granddaughters. Was he speaking figuratively, or had his and Bridget's efforts to conceive been successful?

Kian prayed for the latter. The clan needed more children.

They had been blessed to welcome thirteen new young ones just from Kyra's family, so he shouldn't be greedy and ask for more, but he would be very happy if Turner confirmed that he and Bridget were expecting.

Onegus regarded the strategist with a smile, lifting one corner of his mouth. "Are congratulations in order?"

To Kian's great surprise, Turner nodded. "Just don't let the good news leave this room. Bridget is meeting the Clan Mother tomorrow, and she wants to be the one to tell her."

"Congratulations." Kian rose to his feet and walked over to his desk. "We need to drink to that." He pulled out the whiskey bottle he kept in the drawer of his cabinet. "It's a travesty to drink such fine whiskey from paper cups, but I only have two glasses." He pulled them out, intending to give the expectant father a proper one and Jade the other.

"It's eight in the morning," Turner said.

"So?" Kian placed the glass in front of him and filled it to the brim. "Your happy news is cause for celebration. It turned a dreary morning into a jubilant one."

He walked over to where Jade was seated, placed the glass in front of her, and filled it.

"The rest of us will have to do with paper cups."

When everyone was holding a cup, Kian lifted his for a toast. "To new beginnings, to family, and to the future generations of our clan. Congratulations, Victor."

5

MAX

The news of Bridget and Turner expecting a baby hit Max in the best possible way, and it inspired thoughts of him and Kyra visiting Merlin to ask to partake in his fertility-inducing program.

She wanted another child, he knew that, and he wanted it for her, but what surprised him was the realization that he wanted that for himself as well.

Before meeting Kyra, Max had never given much thought to the possibility of fatherhood. For over five centuries, that option didn't exist for immortal males. Any child they could have with a human female would be born human, and no one wanted to create a life only to see it end. Dormants or immortal females who were not related to him were a new phenomenon, and Max hadn't really hoped to get blessed that way. Now that he had an immortal mate, though, he could allow himself to hope.

His jubilant mood didn't last long, though, as Kian went back to his depressing outlook on the future of the world.

"We either do it their way or watch the world crumble, and that's without taking into account the threat from the Eternal King," Kian said. "But I agree that it's a repugnant conclusion." He refilled his paper cup and took another long sip of whiskey. "At least Navuh is a known entity, and we know what to do even if we don't like the methods we will have to employ. The Eternal King is a much bigger shadow, but since we don't know how to handle that, we should focus on the enemy we are familiar with."

Was that supposed to be a pep talk?

It was like saying that they shouldn't worry about the volcano erupting because Earth was about to be destroyed by a giant meteor strike anyway.

"You should consult the Clan Mother," Yamanu said. "Sari should be part of the conversation as well. What you're suggesting is a serious pivot from the way the clan has operated until now."

Kian nodded. "I don't want to take any hasty steps yet, and I need to ruminate on this for a little longer. But if I come to the conclusion that this is our only option, I will talk with my mother and sisters and also call a council meeting. If any of you comes up with an alternative, please let me know. As always, I'm open to creative ideas." He let out a breath. "This affects the entire clan, and frankly, I'm not sure how we are going to pull it off."

"What about the traffickers?" Max said. "Are we going to stop going after them and the pedophiles?"

Kian shook his head. "Most Guardians are not qualified for undercover political work, so there is no reason to pull them away from what they are doing now." He took another long sip from his cup. "I need to consult Eva, Andrew, and Brandon. They each have particular skill sets, contacts, and resources that may prove essential."

"I have no doubt Eva can help," Max said. "I don't know the details about her vigilante days, but it probably involved a lot of undercover work."

"Mey was trained by the Mossad," Yamanu said. "And with her ability to hear echoes of conversations embedded in walls, she can find out what has been said behind closed doors. Jin is on another level altogether with her tethering ability. She's probably our most valuable asset. The problem is that neither one can thrall or compel. They can only find out information."

Max could practically see the wheels in Kian's mind turning, and his own were gaining momentum as well. "Females are the best for this kind of work," he said. "Especially beautiful immortal females who can thrall. There haven't been many who wanted to join the Guardian force, but there might be quite a few who would want to participate in this new effort."

Kian nodded. "The poetic justice of an all-female undercover crew foiling the plans of those barbaric women-haters is just beautiful. The more I think about it, the more I like it."

"It's an excellent idea," Jade said, turning her big, dark eyes on Kian. "I stand behind your decision. You have my support."

"Thank you." Kian nodded. "I appreciate that, especially coming from you."

She tilted her head. "Because I'm a female?"

He laughed. "No, because you are pragmatic, principled, and honorable."

She dipped her head in thanks for the praise. "I was raised as a warrior, and I understand the mind of a tyrant. Navuh is a conqueror who doesn't care how many die to fulfill his vision. China might be very happy to help him destabilize the West and bring about its downfall, but what they don't realize is that once he's done using them, he'll turn against them and overthrow them too. He won't leave any competitor standing."

Max felt a shiver of foreboding at her words. Jade's tribe had lived in China until Igor had found out about them and killed the males in her group, but until then, she'd learned a thing or two about the way the Chinese regime operated. Their global ambitions were no secret, and neither were their unholy alliances with shadow organizations. As far as the clan knew, the Brotherhood didn't have much of a foothold in China yet, and Lokan, who had been sent by his father to infiltrate and influence the Chinese regime, was in no rush to do so because his interests were thankfully not aligned with Navuh's.

Did Jade even know about Lokan and his mission in China?

Max wasn't sure, so he decided not to bring it up until he verified it was okay.

"What makes you think the CCP is working with the Brotherhood?" Onegus asked.

"I'm not suggesting they are working with the Doomers knowingly," Jade said. "The Chinese Communist Party supports any group or organization undermining the United States so that China can emerge as the lone superpower. But we know that's folly. The Brotherhood is not anyone's ally."

6

KIAN

"The problem is that no one is going to believe a random staffer popping up near a leader of a country," Onegus said. "We can't just slip our people in as top aides overnight."

Yamanu's lips quirked. "But we can thrall key aides who are already in place. That might be more discreet. Instead of forging a new identity for an immortal, we pick a staffer close to the seat of power and manipulate them."

Kian liked that idea. It was simple enough and much more doable than training people and then seeding them.

"That's crossing an even darker line," Onegus said. "But it might be necessary for certain high-value positions."

The conversation shifted into more practical logistics—who to target, how to maintain secrecy, how to ensure the thrall remained stable. Kian listened, letting them hash out the details.

He disliked every word.

The clan had rules for a reason, rules forbidding forced subjugation of humans outside dire emergencies. But then this was a dire emergency on a global scale.

He rubbed his temples, a headache starting at the base of his skull. "We also need to consider the possibility that the Doomers have done exactly that—thralling staffers around major leaders. We might be walking into a hall of mirrors where everyone is already compromised."

Jade nodded. "We need a chain of watchers, a network, not just one or two people. And that's an enormous undertaking." She shifted her gaze to Turner. "We don't necessarily need immortals for that. We can use humans."

Turner let out a breath. "My network is comprised of military operatives, not politicians. I don't think I can help with that."

"Which leads us back to how far we take this?" Kian's gaze swept over the group he'd assembled.

He hadn't intended to go into global politics in this meeting. It was definitely above Max's pay grade and probably Yamanu's as well. The Guardian had been right when he'd suggested that Kian talk it over with his mother and sisters first.

"We're possibly talking about a shadow empire,"

Turner said. "Covert watchers in every major capital. Controlling or at least influencing policy from behind the scenes." He exhaled. "That's how the Doomers operate. We'd just be flipping the board. But the logistics of that are daunting."

"Not just the logistics," Onegus said. "It doesn't feel right, but we have no choice. We are forced to do this to counterbalance Navuh's influence."

"We do it to preserve life and freedom," Kian said. "He does it to enslave and destroy. That is a key difference."

Onegus tapped the table once more. "We can do this discriminately—use mind control only to block catastrophic decisions or to weed out Doomer influences. We don't need to control every decision leadership makes, only the ones that can lead to existential threats."

"Like allowing fanatics to build nuclear bombs," Max said. "Or policies that allow extremist infiltration."

Kian appreciated the Guardian's perspective. "I like your suggestion. We can focus on critical threat scenarios." He raked a hand through his hair. "I still need to think this through and maybe brainstorm it with all the head guardians and council members. I like the idea of intervening only in the highest-stakes contexts—nuclear weapons, major war escalations, and policies that allow Doomers' influence to spread uncontrollably. I don't want us to become puppet masters."

"There's one more angle to consider," Turner said. "We keep referencing China's involvement, but it's bigger than that. We know that Doomers are playing a multi-continental game. They stir up conflict in smaller countries, pit them against each other, and distract the United States while focusing on nuclear ambitions in Iran and other places that should never have access to such devastating weaponry. This is a Hydra with many heads. Even if we cut one off, others might be sprouting in Africa or Latin America."

"It's overwhelming," Max muttered. "But we have to start somewhere."

Kian couldn't agree more.

"What about Eastern Europe?" Yamanu asked. "I bet the Doomers are also trying to get a foothold there."

Kian nodded. "We'll add that to the to-do list. Let's keep an eye on Eastern Europe, but we can't spread ourselves too thin."

The truth was that he had no idea how he would pull any of it off. The entire clan, including the Kra-ell and Kalugal's people, numbered in the hundreds, and most of them were not trained in undercover work. Even those who were, like Mey and Eva, wouldn't want to leave the comfort and security of the village to embark on missions abroad.

Kian needed a damn miracle.

"Okay, people." He pushed to his feet. "We are not going to solve the entire global mess in one sitting, and we all have things to do."

As people began to stand, he offered handshakes and pats on the shoulder in reassurance he didn't feel.

Once everyone left, he exhaled, letting the tension slip from his shoulders. He walked to the wall of windows behind his desk and looked out over the village. The café was busy as always, with people sitting around the small tables, chatting, drinking their coffees, and eating their sandwiches or pastries. Two Kra-ell children were on the swings in the playground, while their mothers sat on a nearby bench. Everything seemed so normal and serene, while the world outside their small haven was unraveling.

Kian stared at the trees, the gently waving greenery, and thought of nuclear fallout leveling entire cities. The imagery in his mind was too ghastly to contemplate, but ignoring it was foolhardy.

Such an unimaginable outcome would be the real cost of inaction. A cost none could afford to pay.

He pressed a palm against the cool glass of the window, letting the sunlight warm him from the other side, and closed his eyes, inhaling deeply.

Despite his two millennia of experience, he was

still constantly challenged with new, unprecedented, and seemingly more daunting threats.

This new chapter in the clan's history might mean stepping out from the shadows onto the global stage. Perhaps not openly, but in the same clandestine manner the Doomers had been operating for thousands of years.

7

ANNANI

Annani sat on the terrace behind her house, enjoying the fresh morning air. It was crisp, carrying the fresh green scent from the surrounding mountains, and usually it was enough to bring her peace even when her mind was troubled, but not today.

Ogidu stepped outside, holding a tray with a cold bottle of sparkling water, a tall glass with several ice cubes, and two chocolate chip cookies on a small plate. "I brought these for you to taste, Clan Mother."

"Thank you." Annani reached for one of the fragrant cookies that were still warm from the oven. "I am sure it will brighten my day."

"Is there anything else you require, Clan Mother?" he asked.

"No, thank you." Annani smiled at him. "Is everything ready?"

He dipped his head. "I have prepared a selection of juices for the children and teas for the older family members. Would you like me to bring them out here when your guests arrive?"

"Yes, please. It is a lovely day, and it would be a waste to spend it inside."

The younger children would appreciate the freedom of the outdoors instead of sitting still on the living room couch or at the dining room table, which reminded her that there was not enough seating for Kyra's large family.

"Can you please bring a blanket to spread over the grass for the children?"

"That is a wonderful idea, Clan Mother. I will do so expeditiously."

As Ogidu retreated inside, Annani's smile faded, her thoughts returning to her grandmother and her concern for the queen of Anumati.

The Eternal King had sent his wife on a so-called diplomatic tour of the Anumatian colonies, and the queen could not take Aria with her without it looking too suspicious. Ani, Annani, and Sofringhati had debated for days whether the queen should attempt to include Aria in her entourage. Still, it had been Ani's final decision not to take Aru's twin for fear of exposing her importance.

The king was far too shrewd not to suspect something, especially given the almost daily visits of the queen to the Supreme Oracle's temple.

Aru and Aria had created a bridge between worlds, enabling communication between Ani and Annani, and keeping that connection a secret was vital.

Annani had learned much about the political landscape of Anumati and the threat posed by the Eternal King. Most importantly, though, Annani had found an ally and a confidant in her grandmother.

She missed their nightly sessions, and she worried about the Eternal King's motives. When her grandfather wanted someone removed without political complications, he sent them on missions to dangerous colonies where deadly misfortune could befall a god with plausible deniability of any wrongdoing.

The king controlled the media, so news of such misfortunes was usually contained, but Annani hoped that her grandmother could not be easily eliminated without causing a major uproar. Not only was Ani loved by the people of Anumati, but she was also the representative of the noble families controlling all major manufacturing conglomerates. Even the king would think twice before daring to anger them. Those royal families were his power base, and he could not afford to lose their support.

That being said, the Eternal King was notoriously paranoid, constantly searching for traitors in his inner circle, so if he had even the slightest suspicion that his wife was plotting behind his back, he would find a way to get rid of her.

A long diplomatic trip would keep her away from the capital and out of the public eye. Even if he did not send her to the colonies to kill her, it was still a good way to kill her influence.

Annani took a deep breath, refocusing on the present and the joyous occasion of welcoming seventeen new members into her community. Kyra's extended family represented a significant and valuable addition to the genetic pool.

When she heard the doorbell, Annani lifted her hand and pushed her hair behind her ears to expose the translating earpieces. The children and their mothers would all be wearing them, and Annani wanted them to see that she had them on as well.

The sliding door opened, and Ogidu stepped out first. "Your guests have arrived, Clan Mother."

She rose to welcome Kyra, her sisters, and their children.

The youngest ones looked scared, while the older ones seemed nervous, but all were excited.

"Good morning," Annani said, extending her arms in greeting.

Kyra stepped forward first, a bright smile on her face and none of the weariness that darkened her sisters' expressions. "Thank you for inviting us, Clan Mother."

"The pleasure is all mine." Annani embraced Kyra

and then stepped back to look over the assembled family. "We have met briefly during the welcome party, but I have been looking forward to getting to know each of you in person."

"Let me introduce my sisters." Kyra motioned for the eldest to come forward. "This is Soraya, mother to Arezoo, Donya, and Laleh."

Soraya's features were remarkably similar to Kyra's. She looked older, and time had started etching fine lines around her eyes, but she was still a beautiful woman, and she carried herself with dignity.

"It is an honor to meet you face to face, Clan Mother." Soraya dipped her head respectfully but did not extend her hand.

Annani offered both of hers instead. "My skin might be glowing, but I assure you it is not radioactive."

That was what most contemporary humans suspected when they first saw her. In days past, people had thought she was an angel or a goddess, which was closer to the truth.

Soraya hesitated for a split second before placing her hands in Annani's. When nothing happened, she let out a breath and relaxed her shoulders.

Annani smiled. "Would you like to introduce your daughters to me?"

A flash of emotion crossed the woman's face. "They are my greatest treasures." She turned around and motioned for the girls to step forward. "This is Arezoo, my eldest. She is nineteen."

The girl curtsied, which was adorable. "It is an honor to meet you, Clan Mother."

Evidently, it was a line they had all prepared. Hopefully, they would have more to say once they loosened up.

Next were the younger girls, then Rana and her daughter, the grieving widow Yasmin and her five children, and Parisa and her four boys.

Rana's daughter Azadeh stood quietly beside her cousins, her intelligent eyes taking in everything with careful observation. Annani sensed a deep thinker in this one.

Rohan, Yasmin's younger boy, stared openly at Annani's glowing skin. "Are you made of light?"

Yasmin looked mortified. "Rohan! That's not—"

"It is quite all right," Annani laughed, kneeling to the six-year-old's level. "I am not made of light, but the glow is part of me. Would you like to touch my hand?"

The boy hesitated, looking up at his mother for permission. When Yasmin nodded, he reached out tentatively, then quickly pulled his hand back as soon as his fingers brushed Annani's skin.

"You're not hot!" he exclaimed with surprise.

"Of course not." Annani patted his shoulder and then turned to the others. "Please, everyone, make yourselves comfortable." She gestured toward the terrace seating. "The younger children can sit on the blanket. Ogidu has prepared refreshments."

Little Cyra clung to her mother's skirt, but she eyed the chocolate chip cookies with unmistakable longing.

"Those are for you," Annani told her. "Ogidu made plenty of them so do not be shy."

The child looked surprised to be addressed directly, then glanced up at her mother for permission.

"Go ahead," Yasmin said softly. "But just one for now."

As they settled down, the initial tension began to ease. The younger children gravitated toward the refreshments, while the teenagers remained slightly on edge, their eyes constantly flicking to Annani's glowing skin.

She could have subdued it or eliminated it completely, but since they were now members of her community, they needed to get accustomed to seeing her glow.

"Your home is beautiful," Soraya commented, probably to start a conversation. "I mean, the entire village is beautiful. It is like something from a dream."

Annani laughed. "Wait until you see my sanctuary in Alaska. That is a true dream made manifest."

"So, this isn't your permanent home?" Rana asked.

"I have two homes. I used to spend most of my time in my Alaskan sanctuary, but that was when I had my daughter Alena as a companion. After she found her mate and moved here, I found myself spending more and more time here. After all, three of my children live in the village."

Yasmin nodded. "I want to live next to my children, too, so I understand."

"What's special about the sanctuary?" Donya asked. "You said that it was even prettier than the village, but Alaska is in the north, and it is covered in snow."

"That is a very smart observation." Annani smiled at the girl. "The sanctuary is a magical place that is even more secure than the village. It is a tropical paradise that is hidden under a dome of ice. No one knows where it is or how to get there other than my Odus, and they will never reveal my secret."

The children looked at her with wide eyes.

"Do you have pictures?" Zaden asked.

"I do." Annani produced her phone from the hidden pocket in her gown and scrolled through her photos. "Here you go. You can pass the phone around. I only took pictures of the main grounds. The private chambers are nice, but they are not as special."

The oohing and ahhing was music to Annani's ears. She had designed her sanctuary herself, and the builders had made her fantasy a reality. Those humans had been thralled to forget what they had built, and none of them were still alive.

"Did you build it yourself?" Arman asked.

Annani smiled. "I envisioned it, and many skilled people helped bring that vision to life."

"How old are you?" Arman blurted out, earning a sharp look from his mother.

"Arman! That's not polite," Parisa scolded.

"Curiosity is natural." Annani smiled. "I am over five thousand years old."

The boy's eyes widened. "You are lying."

His mother nearly fainted, pulling him to her as if she expected Annani to smite him for the insult.

Annani lifted a hand to stop her, a smile still playing on her lips to show that she was not angry. "It is logical for the boy to assume that I am lying because he knows that no one lives that long." She shifted her gaze to Arman. "I am not human, my dear boy. I am a goddess, which means that I am immortal, have glowing skin, and can also do impressive mind tricks. But I cannot create things out of thin air or perform any other magic. I am just different than most of the people on Earth."

Arman nodded, but he seemed terrified of saying anything else, more out of fear of what his mother would do than Annani.

"I imagine that you have gained much wisdom," Soraya said, her voice respectful but with an underlying note of caution.

Annani understood the careful approach. These women had lived under oppression, where those in power demanded unquestioning obedience. They would naturally be wary of another authority figure, no matter how benevolent she appeared.

"I have lived long and seen much," Annani acknowledged. "But I learn new things every day. I understand your caution. You have come from a world where power was often abused, and where those with authority demanded submission. I want you to know that is not how we operate here. Your thoughts, your questions, your doubts—all are welcome. I do not demand faith or obedience. The only thing I will not compromise on is the safety of my people, and that might mean some restrictions on your freedom of movement, but only temporarily. Consider it a period of adjustment, a preparation for a new life of safety and freedom for you and your children."

Yasmin's eyes filled with tears. "My husband died to give us this chance."

A hush fell over the gathering.

"Yes," Annani said softly. "And his sacrifice will not be forgotten or wasted. Your children will grow up free, Yasmin. They will be able to become whoever they wish to be and have eternity to do so. You are all going to turn immortal, starting with the older boys."

"It's always the boys," Azadeh murmured. "Why can't it be the girls first?"

Annani was sure that the older girls had been told how transition was induced in females. "It is simpler for boys," she said. "They do not need to fall in love with their inducers."

Azadeh shrugged. "Neither do the girls. We are no longer restricted, and I am eighteen, which means that I'm free to choose my inducer."

Annani glanced at Rana, who surprised her by nodding.

"We are in the West now, and I support Azadeh's freedom of choice. I hope she chooses responsibly, but I don't expect her to get married first." She grimaced. "I wish I had had that choice. I would have never married my husband." She took her daughter's hand. "But then I wouldn't have had you, so it was worth it after all."

8

KYRA

*A*fter the children had been lured inside by Ogidu with the promise of watching a brand-new animated movie in the living room, the terrace became considerably quieter. Only Cyra remained, still clinging to her mother, and Essa, who also seemed reluctant to leave his mother's side.

"Essa, why don't you join the others?" Yasmin suggested. "We want to talk about grown-up stuff."

The boy hesitated, casting a wary glance at Annani, then turning his gaze to his mother. "Are you sure, Maman?"

"Yes," she assured him. "Go. Enjoy yourself."

With a final concerned glance at his mother, Essa nodded and hurried inside.

Kyra watched the exchange with a mixture of sadness and admiration. The boy had assumed the role of protector since his father's death, a burden no sixteen-year-old should have to bear.

"You have remarkable children," the Clan Mother said when only the adults and little Cyra remained. "Their resilience is extraordinary."

"They've no choice," Soraya said.

Kyra leaned forward. "My sisters have many questions about what the future holds for them and their children here."

"I will gladly answer them all," the goddess promised. "But some answers are better absorbed slowly. There is no rush. You have time."

"We left everything behind." Parisa's voice held an undercurrent of grief. "Our homes, our possessions, my late husband's grave." She glanced at Yasmin. "Yasmin and the children didn't even get to bury Javad. I hope his extended family has given him a proper burial."

"They did," Yasmin said, her voice shaking, but her tears held at bay. "I asked Kyra to check. Javad's older brother took care of the arrangements. Fareed and Hamid went into hiding after what they assumed were the abductions of their families, so they didn't come to the funeral."

"I understand the weight of your loss," Annani said softly. "No place, however beautiful or safe, can erase that pain."

Kyra knew that the Clan Mother was talking

from experience. Her own husband had been supposedly murdered by an insane god who had wanted the goddess for himself.

The god Mortdh had been obsessed with wedding Annani, not because he'd loved her but because she was the heir to the throne. As her husband, he would have gotten to rule by her side, and later, after he'd gotten rid of her, as a sole ruler over all the gods.

Kyra had told her sisters about the goddess's quest and what she wanted her to do, so Yasmin knew that the Clan Mother wasn't talking about the pain of loss as an observer but as someone who still bled for her lost love.

"Can we leave if we want to?" Rana asked.

The Clan Mother sighed. "I wish I could tell you that you can leave whenever you feel like it, but that would be a lie. To protect the secret of our existence, no one can leave here with knowledge of us. If you choose to leave right now, you still can because your memories of this place are fresh and can still be erased. That window of opportunity usually closes within two weeks."

"Why would you want to leave?" Kyra asked her sister.

"I don't." Rana waved a dismissive hand. "I just wanted to know if I've traded one prison for another, and apparently, I did, but at least this one is much nicer than the old one and comes with fringe benefits like immortality and all living expenses paid."

Kyra didn't know what possessed her sister to say such things in front of the Clan Mother. She was a sarcastic type, but that was just rude.

"I think you owe the Clan Mother an apology. Her people saved you from Doomers who would have forced you into becoming a breeder, and you know what that would have entailed. They almost did that to your daughter, and if not for this community mobilizing its resources and risking its fighters, they would have succeeded. These people welcomed you with open arms and offered you a cushy lifestyle with immortality as a bonus. The last thing you should be doing is complaining about your lack of freedom."

Rana hung her head. "I apologize, Clan Mother. I realize that I've become a sharp-tongued and unpleasant woman because I was bitter and hated my life, but you saved me, and I'm grateful." She grimaced. "I guess I need reprogramming."

The goddess smiled benevolently. "I understand. You need time and counseling." She swept her gaze over Kyra and her sisters. "All of you can benefit from talking to Vanessa. I know she is extremely busy, but she might be able to squeeze in a video call here and there. It is not as good as talking face to face, but it is better than nothing, and perhaps it is easier in a way."

"I don't want to sound ungrateful," Yasmin whispered, absently stroking Cyra's hair. "It's just that everything seems a little too good to be true. Maybe that's why Rana felt like she needed to cloak herself in sarcasm. It's her armor."

"That is a wise perspective, Yasmin," the goddess acknowledged. "Naturally, I do not expect you to blindly trust our every word. Unlike the fae in folklore, we are not bound by magic to speak only the truth. Although I must admit that I like those stories about the fae, and I've often wondered what prompted them." She leaned forward as if sharing a secret. "In my experience, most myths that have withstood the test of time have a kernel of truth. Like the vampire lore, angels, watchers, and gods."

Kyra smiled. "I don't think my sisters know what the fae are. It's not the kind of reading that's popular in Iran."

"Oh." The Clan Mother leaned back. "But you seem to know."

Kyra smiled. "I had access to entertainment that they didn't."

The goddess looked disappointed. "I hope that you have retained some subconscious memories from your time in the United States."

"I have," Kyra said. "My command of English, for one. He didn't erase that from my memories, and I often dreamt of a little girl, thinking it was me in the past, while all along I was dreaming of my Jasmine."

She didn't need to elaborate on who she was referring to.

Max had told her that the Clan Mother was on top of everything happening in her community. After all, she was the head of the clan, and Kian was her regent. It was his duty to keep her informed.

The goddess nodded. "We will talk about your memories and what can be done about them later." She turned to Kyra's sisters. "Time will prove the truth of my words better than any promises I could make you today."

That seemed to resonate with them, and the goddess continued. "In the meantime, explore, ask questions, and meet people. I suggest you meet with Vrog, who is in charge of our homeschooling program. There is no rush, but at some point, the children need to resume their studies. You can also decide that you want to study something new, and Vrog can help you enroll in online courses."

Little Cyra, who had been quietly observing the adults' conversation, suddenly slipped from her mother's lap and walked over to Annani. The adults fell silent, watching as the four-year-old stood before the Clan Mother, studying her solemnly.

"You are very pretty," she said.

"Thank you." The goddess cupped her cheek. "So are you."

Cyra shook her head. "Not as pretty as you." She lifted her tiny hand and put it on the Clan Mother's exposed wrist.

"Your skin is pretty." She ran her hand over the goddess's forearm. "So soft." Then the child stunned everyone by lifting both her arms in a clear invitation to be lifted into the goddess's lap.

The Clan Mother smiled brightly and didn't hesitate even for a moment before picking the girl up and setting her on her lap. "I adore children." She kissed the top of Cyra's head. "I have a son and three daughters, sixteen grandchildren, and many great-grandchildren, and I cherish each and every one. In fact, most expectant mothers used to travel to my sanctuary to deliver their babies there, and they stayed with me until the girls turned immortal, and the boys were a little older and not as fragile. But nowadays things are different. Most of the recent births were babies born to mothers who have immortal mates and feel safe in the village."

The goddess's grandmotherly gesture, followed by her monologue, released some of the invisible tension, and as Kyra's sisters relaxed, the conversation started flowing more easily.

Eventually, the movie ended, the children returned to the terrace, and it was time to leave.

"We've taken up too much of the Clan Mother's time." Kyra rose to her feet. "We should go."

As her family began to gather themselves to

depart, thanking the goddess for her hospitality, the Clan Mother handed Cyra to Yasmin and walked over to Kyra. "Can you stay? We need to talk."

"Of course," Kyra said. "I'll just escort my sisters to the bridge to make sure they don't get lost on their way home. I'll return right away."

9

ANNANI

When Kyra returned, Annani gestured for her to follow. "Let's talk somewhere more private."

She led Kyra past the living area into the bedroom that she had turned into a study. There was a small desk that she could move into her bedroom if she needed the room for guests, and the bed had been cleverly built into a bookcase and could be pulled down when needed. Two comfortable chairs faced the backyard with a round table between them for her morning tea and biscuits.

Usually, Annani did not bring anyone into this private space, but for some reason, she felt like inviting Kyra. Perhaps it was because she believed that Kyra would help find Khiann, and if she did, she would forever have a place in Annani's inner circle.

Possibly, though, it was the kinship that she felt

with the woman, and the inner connection she could not explain.

"Please, sit," she gestured to one of the armchairs, then sat on the other. "You have a lovely family. I believe they will find happiness and purpose in our community. They just need time."

Kyra smiled. "My sisters are a handful, but I love them even more for it. I love it that they are strong individuals with their own opinions and beliefs. It's not easy for women living under the mullahs' oppressive regime. But then, the Iranian women are the proud daughters of Persia, and they are not easily silenced and marginalized. They are fighters."

"That they are." Annani leaned forward, ready to move to the real reason she had asked Kyra to stay behind. "I know that Syssi has spoken to you about her vision."

"She did." Kyra pulled her pendant from beneath her blouse and let it rest against her chest. "She even saw me wearing this."

Annani regarded the amber stone and the symbols etched on it. The shapes reminded her of the old language of the gods, but she could not decipher the writing, and she doubted it carried any meaning. It was most likely an attempt to mimic the style, but she wondered about the artifact that had inspired the artist who had created this piece.

"What does it do?" Annani asked.

"It warms up in warning or in confirmation,

depending on the situation, but lately it hasn't been reliable. I made a mistake on the mission, insisting that we should get Soraya first, and it did nothing to warn me that it was a bad decision. Max and Yamanu kept telling me that we should get my sisters who had children first, and they were right. The Doomers went after Yasmin. If I hadn't relied on this stupid thing, I might have listened to them, and we could have saved Javad."

"The Fates had other plans, child. Do not blame yourself."

Kyra shook her head. "I should have listened to those with experience. Relying on magical objects is not wise."

"Perhaps." Annani leaned back. "Syssi requested a vision about my husband, asking if he was still alive, buried in stasis somewhere in the Arabian desert, but instead of showing her my Khiann, the Fates showed her you and your pendant. I know it is significant, and I suspect that it was their way of hinting that you will help find him."

"But I don't know how to use it that way," Kyra protested. "It warns me of danger, sometimes guides my decisions, but I've never used it to locate anyone."

"Not consciously, perhaps," Annani acknowledged. "You might not have discovered all of its abilities yet. Besides, your daughter believes that objects don't possess inherent power. They're merely conduits that assist the gifted practitioner in channeling her power."

Kyra put her hand on the pendant. "So, it was me all along making those intuitive decisions?"

Annani nodded. "Never discount your gut feelings, which is another way to say your intuition. I always listen to mine, and it is telling me that you will somehow help guide me to my Khiann."

"What would I need to do?" Kyra's fingers closed around the stone pendant. "Where do I start?"

"I am not sure," Annani admitted. "Perhaps you should consult with Jasmine. She guided a team to find my brother and sister, Ell-rom and Morelle, and she found them in the nick of time. I have a feeling that you will need to combine your powers, and maybe even Fenella has a part to play in this. I find it hard to believe that she was in the right place at the right time by chance. The Fates have been busy again, and they have plans for her."

Kyra frowned. "Fenella didn't mention having any powers. How is she supposed to help?"

"That remains to be seen. The Fates rarely bring people together without a purpose. Your paths converged for a reason. It was not a coincidence."

"I'll help in any way I can," Kyra said. "Just point me in the right direction."

Annani sighed. "I will probably need to request another vision from Syssi because I do not know what to tell you."

"Do you wish me to speak with her?"

Annani shook her head. "I will do that. Now let us see what we can do about those lost memories of yours."

Kyra swallowed. "Right now?"

"If you would rather wait, we can do it some other time."

Annani had a feeling that Kyra was too scared of what her memories could reveal.

"I'm not sure I want them," Kyra admitted. "Bad things happened to me, and I would rather not remember them. I would like to remember my childhood, growing up with my sisters, coming to America, meeting Boris, falling in love, and having Jasmine. But none of the other stuff." She lifted her eyes to Annani. "Can you do that?"

"I am not sure I can get any of your memories at all. It was a very long time ago, and I have a feeling that they are covered with a thick layer of metaphoric scar tissue. At best, I will be able to learn some truths about your past and tell you about them. I do not believe I will be able to bring back the memories from your subconscious. Truthfully, you will probably have better luck talking to Vanessa. She specializes in trauma."

Kyra did not look disappointed. She looked relieved. "I will contact Vanessa." She rose to her feet and bowed her head. "Thank you for welcoming me and my family with such open arms. It's more than I could have ever expected. You are giving us a new life."

Smiling, Annani stood up as well and put her hand on Kyra's arm. "I am glad to be in the position that allows me to be generous, but I am not doing it out of pure altruism. I meant it when I said that your family's enrichment of our genetic pool is invaluable."

She walked Kyra to the door. "Be well, Kyra. We shall speak again soon."

The woman bowed her head. "Goodbye, Clan Mother."

Hopefully, Kyra held the key to finding Khiann, perhaps not alone, but with the help of Jasmine and maybe Fenella, and possibly another vision from Syssi.

10

DIN

*A*s Din waited at the arrival gate in LAX, shifting his weight from one foot to the other, the memory of the emergency water landing kept replaying in his mind. Given all the obstacles that had popped up on his way to Fenella, trying to keep him from this moment—the traffic accident, the canceled flight, the storm, and finally the landing gear malfunction—it felt almost surreal to have finally made it.

Well, almost.

He was at the airport, but he still needed to get to the village, and someone was supposed to pick him up, but he didn't know who. Naturally, he hoped it would be Fenella, even though she'd said nothing about it when he'd called her earlier to let her know he'd landed safely.

He still hoped that she wanted to surprise him

and had been on her way over when answering his call.

Scanning the faces of the people waiting for the arriving passengers, his eyes landed on a familiar figure, and his heart sank.

Max stood there, hands in his pockets, as cocky and as self-assured as ever, but with a welcoming smile. They had seen each other not too long ago on the clan's wedding cruise, but they had mostly ignored each other then, as they had for the past few decades. After the fiasco with Fenella, Max had tried to rekindle their friendship, but getting the cold shoulder from Din time and again discouraged him from making any further attempts.

Not that Din could blame him. He hadn't expected Max to keep trying. In fact, he'd been relieved when Max had finally stopped.

"Din," his old friend called, raising a hand in greeting.

He approached cautiously, unsure of what to expect. "This is a surprise."

Max extended his hand. "It's been too long, my friend."

Din didn't hesitate before grasping Max's hand, and he didn't fight him when the guy pulled him into a brotherly embrace and clapped him firmly on the back.

He felt something loosen in his chest, a knot of resentment he'd been carrying for so long he'd almost forgotten it was there. "It's good to be back," he said, meaning more than visiting the village again. "I held on to this grudge for too long."

Apologizing had never been easy for him, and he couldn't say the word sorry even now. Hopefully, what he'd said would be enough for Max.

"Water under the bridge now," Max said with a dismissive wave. "Or should I say, plane on the river?" He grinned at his own lame joke.

"Too soon to make jokes about that."

Max had always been terrible at coming up with funny things to say, and his jokes were often inappropriate, not because they were vulgar or nasty but because they were just bad. Still, Din couldn't help smiling.

Max helped him with his luggage, which, fortunately, had been retrieved from the downed plane with no water damage.

While leading him toward the parking area, he said, "I asked for a few hours off just so I could pick you up. Thought it might be good for us to clear the air before you see Fenella."

"Does she know that you're here?"

"She has no clue. I told her that someone was going to pick you up, but I didn't say who that someone was." He led Din to a sleek sports car that gleamed under the parking garage lights.

"An Audi R8. I'm impressed."

Max patted the car's hood affectionately.

"Melinda is my baby. A V10 engine, top speed of 205 miles per hour, and zero to sixty in 3.2 seconds."

"Nice ride." Din slid into the passenger seat. "I assume you had her modified to meet the village security requirements?"

"Of course." Max started the engine, which purred to life with a sound that was almost indecent.

As they pulled out of the airport and onto the highway, Din started to relax. The atmosphere between them was surprisingly comfortable, the decades of silence somehow smoothing over the jagged edges of their broken friendship.

"That landing looked pretty intense on the news." Max glanced over at him. "Was it as bad as they made it out to be?"

Din considered this. "At the time, it didn't seem so terrible. The pilot was calm and professional. It wasn't until afterward, when I saw the footage and heard the commentary, that I realized how dangerous it was and how lucky we were." He ran a hand through his hair. "Water landings don't often end well."

Max nodded solemnly. "Thank the merciful Fates. They were looking out for you."

Din chuckled. "Those Fates have a strange sense of humor, and they are vengeful. They wanted me to struggle to prove that I was sincere about Fenella, or maybe they were punishing me for missing the opportunity they'd given me fifty years ago and screwing Fenella's life over."

Max shook his head. "If they wanted to punish you for that, they would have done so a long time ago. Besides, your punishment was self-inflicted. You lost not only fifty years with your best friend but possibly also with your mate."

"You were never one to mince words." Din let out a breath. "I see that hasn't changed over the last five decades."

"Why would it?" Max cast him an amused look. "Neither of us was a young lad back then, and for better or worse, our personalities were set. You are probably still the same judgmental grudge-holding asshole you were back then. Still, I loved you despite your rotten personality, and I'm willing to love you again." He batted his eyelashes.

Din laughed. "You're no less of an asshole than I am, just in different ways. I loved you, too, until you crossed the line."

"I thought we were done with that." Max tilted his head. "I'm a mated male now, and I no longer chase after every desirable female in my vicinity. I'm also working on my other shortcomings. You should work on yours, meaning being less judgmental and more forgiving."

"Touché." Din let out a breath. "So, what am I walking into? You know Fenella better than I do."

Max's expression grew somber. "She's been

through hell, Din. That bastard—" He cut himself off, his knuckles whitening on the steering wheel. "Fenella is tough, and if you thought that she was a ball buster before, then get ready for the new and improved version."

That was a very diplomatic way to describe what Fenella had endured and how she'd survived. Still, Din felt his fangs itch and his venom glands fill up.

"I'd expect nothing less after what she endured, and I'm ready for whatever she will throw at me."

"Just be patient with her," Max said. "She acts like nothing fazes her, but it's mostly bravado. I don't know what she's ready for, if anything."

Din nodded. "I'm a patient male. I'll wait as long as it takes."

Max looked satisfied with his answer. "I'm glad you're here for her, and not just because it resolves the guilt I've been carrying around. She needs someone who sees through her defenses but respects them anyway."

"She might not want me at all," Din pointed out.

"True," Max conceded. "But she's curious and she's willing to give you a chance. That's a good start. Did she tell you she wanted to fly out to you instead? After your plane incident?"

"She did, but I thought it was just talk."

"She meant it, but I suspect she wanted out of the village more than she wanted to see you." Max cast him an apologetic look. "No offense, it's just that

Fenella is a rover. She feels cooped up in the village. If the two of you hit it off, and you want to make her happy, expect to travel a lot."

That wasn't good news given his job, but a mate came first, and he would find a way to make it work. Instead of teaching, he could actually start taking part in digs, but not as the onsite archeologist because that would bore her as well. A consultant job would be perfect.

They rode in silence for a while, the landscape passing in a blur as Max navigated his sleek car with the care and devotion of a lover.

"I've arranged for you to stay with Thomas," Max said. "He was my roommate until recently. Good bloke, keeps to himself mostly."

"Until recently?" Din asked, raising an eyebrow. "You and Kyra moved in together, I take it?"

Max grinned. "We did. We live across from Jasmine and her mate. It's nice."

"That sounds so domestic. I'm happy for you."

"Kyra is extraordinary," Max said with such naked adoration that Din had to look away. Max in love was a different male from the Max he used to know.

They fell back into comfortable silence as the city gave way to winding mountain roads. Din grew nervous when they entered the tunnel leading to the village, and when they parked and stepped out of the car, he was once again disappointed that Fenella wasn't there to greet him.

"Where is she now?" he asked as they entered the elevator. "Fenella, I mean."

"I don't know. She could be at her place or with Kyra or Jasmine or both. The three of them have become good friends." Max looked him over. "I can call her to find out, but the question is, do you want to freshen up first or go see her straight away?"

Flying from New York to Los Angeles wasn't the kind of journey that required a change of clothing, but Din needed a moment to compose himself. After fifty years of building Fenella up in his mind, the reality of seeing her again was more daunting than he cared to admit.

"I think I'll freshen up first," he decided. "Then perhaps we can meet at the village café."

Max nodded. "She'd probably prefer that. Baby steps."

"We need to go through the entire courtship dance, and I'm actually looking forward to it." Din smiled. "I'm not just old-fashioned. I'm old, and I kind of miss the days when the hunt required skill and finesse. It's too easy these days, making the whole thing meaningless and less satisfying."

Max shrugged. "I quite enjoyed the ease of conquest until I met my one and only, but if you like your balls slow-cooked, I have no problem with that."

11

FENELLA

"Din landed." Fenella put the phone down. "We need to hurry up."

Jasmine looked up from the deck of cards she was shuffling with her dexterous fingers. "Relax, we have plenty of time. With rush-hour traffic, we have at least two hours before he gets here."

That was good to know. Fenella wasn't ready to meet Din yet, and she wanted to know what the cards said, even if it was stupid.

"I'd rather get this over with before he arrives."

Jasmine's lips quirked in a knowing smile as she shaped the deck of cards into a neat stack and then started shuffling them again. The cards moved fluidly between her slender fingers, making soft whispering sounds that somehow added to the atmosphere.

"You don't need to pretend for my sake. It's okay to be a little nervous."

"Please." Fenella rolled her eyes. "I've faced down far worse than a lovelorn Scotsman." She leaned back and folded her arms over her chest. "Speaking of lovelorn men, where is Ell-rom?"

A shadow crossed Jasmine's face. "Training."

"Training for what?" Fenella asked. "Martial arts? Sword fighting? Target practice?"

"It's confidential," Jasmine murmured, thumping the deck into shape on the wooden table between them with a bit too much vigor.

Fenella raised an eyebrow. "Does it have anything to do with the Doomers in Iran?"

Yesterday, she'd heard Kyra telling Jasmine that the clan planned to look into Doomer activity there.

Jasmine shook her head. "As I said, it's confidential. Let's focus on your reading, shall we?"

It seemed like Jasmine was adamant about keeping her mate's activity a secret, which was fine. Everyone had their secrets, and Fenella had her share. Besides, she was curious about what the cards might reveal, even if it was all nonsense. It was a nice way to pass the time and get rid of the nervous energy coursing through her.

"Let's. You promised me insights about Din, and I can't wait to hear them, even if it's all hogwash."

Jasmine cast her a mock glare. "And that's what you'll get, ye of little faith."

Fenella waved a hand dramatically. "Work your witchy magic, oh high priestess of the Mother of All Life."

Jasmine smiled at that. "What exactly are you looking for guidance on? Your relationship with Din? His intentions? Or your future together?"

Fenella hesitated. "Is he trouble?" she asked finally. "That's what I want to know. Am I making a mistake by letting him back into my life?"

Jasmine nodded. "Think about that question and hold it in your mind as you cut the deck into three," she instructed, handing her the cards.

Taking the deck, Fenella divided it into three piles, trying to keep her mind focused on Din and the question she'd asked. She felt ridiculous, but also tense, as if these pieces of cardboard might actually hold some truth.

Jasmine gathered the piles, reassembled the deck, and began to lay out cards in a pattern that looked vaguely like a cross.

"This is your present situation," she said, turning over the first card to reveal a figure carrying ten wands. "The Ten of Wands. You're carrying a heavy burden—past experiences, suspicions, fears. They weigh on you, but you're determined to manage them alone."

"Doesn't take mystical powers to see that," Fenella muttered.

Jasmine ignored her, turning over the next card, showing a man and a woman exchanging cups. "This card represents a challenge you're facing. The Two of Cups. Interesting. The challenge is about partnership, connection, and mutual exchange of emotion. You're struggling with the possibility of letting someone in."

She turned over a third card, placing it above the cross. "This crowns you—it's what you're aspiring for." The card showed a woman sitting on a throne, holding a cup. "The Queen of Cups. Emotional fulfillment, intuitive wisdom. Even though you pretend otherwise, part of you wants to trust your feelings."

"Well, there is nothing surprising or—" Fenella began, but Jasmine was already turning over the fourth card.

"This is beneath you—the foundation." She placed the card at the bottom of the cross, revealing a woman bound and blindfolded, surrounded by eight swords. "Eight of Swords. You feel trapped by circumstances, by your past. But notice how the bonds are loose—the limitations are self-imposed."

Fenella shifted uncomfortably. She didn't like how accurately Jasmine was reading her, cards or no cards, but then it wasn't difficult to deduce for someone who knew the circumstances of her life.

"This is behind you," Jasmine continued, placing a

card to the left. "The Five of Cups. Loss, regret, focusing on what's been spilled rather than what remains." She looked up at Fenella with a gentle expression on her beautiful face. "You've lost much over the years."

"Haven't we all?"

Jasmine placed the next card to the right. "This is coming in the immediate future." She turned it over to reveal a ship sailing away. "The Six of Swords. A journey away from troubled waters toward something calmer. It often represents a physical journey to a distant place."

"A journey?" Fenella perked up. "I just got here, and I don't think they will let me out to travel the world anytime soon."

"The cards don't always mean what we think," Jasmine said cryptically, turning over the next card and placing it at the bottom of a new column she was forming. "This represents you in the situation."

The Fool looked back at them—a young man about to step off a cliff, a small dog at his heels.

"The Fool represents new beginnings, innocence, taking a leap of faith."

"I'm hardly innocent," Fenella scoffed.

"It can also mean inexperienced, and it applies to you regarding trusting people." Jasmine placed the next card above The Fool. "This is your environment, external influences." The card showed a beautiful garden with nine cups. "The Nine of Cups represents wish fulfillment, contentment. The village offers you safety, prosperity, and the possibility of emotional satisfaction."

"And this," Jasmine said, placing the next card above that one, "represents your hopes and fears."

The Empress stared back at them, a fertile, maternal figure surrounded by nature's abundance.

"The Empress embodies creation, nurturing, abundance," Jasmine said. "Perhaps you fear settling down, creating roots. Or perhaps you secretly hope for it."

Fenella said nothing, but the card made her uneasy. She had never wanted children, had never even considered it a possibility. But immortality changed the equation.

"And finally," Jasmine said, reaching for the last card, "the outcome."

She turned it over, and as she placed it at the top of the column, her expression changed, a furrow appearing between her brows.

"The Tower," she said.

The card depicted a tall tower being struck by lightning, with figures falling from its heights.

"What does it mean?" Fenella asked.

"Sudden change. Upheaval. The breaking down of false structures," Jasmine said. "It's not necessarily negative. Sometimes we need to break down the old before we can build the new."

"Breaking down," Fenella repeated flatly. "Sounds fantastic."

Jasmine studied the spread, her eyes moving from card to card. "There's a journey ahead of you—both physical and emotional. Din's arrival is just the beginning. You'll face challenges, upheaval, but also the possibility of real connection."

"So, is he trouble or not?" Fenella returned to her original question. "I didn't get a clear answer from your cards."

Jasmine looked up with a serious expression. "The cards don't see him as the source of trouble, but trouble surrounds this connection. The Tower doesn't appear for minor disruptions. Perhaps it means that you will face challenges together."

"Well, that's comforting," Fenella said with a sarcastic edge.

"The cards aren't meant to comfort," Jasmine said. "They're meant to illuminate."

They were nonsense, a parlor trick meant to entertain when done for free and defraud when done for money.

Fenella stood up and stretched. "Thanks for the reading," she said, trying to sound dismissive. "It was interesting."

"You don't have to pretend with me," Jasmine said. "I can see that it has affected you."

"No offense, Jasmine, but it's a bunch of hogwash." Even to her own ears, the protest sounded hollow. "Pretty pictures and vague interpretations that could apply to anyone, and in my case, you knew too much about me to do an impartial reading. You might have even guided the results with your preconceptions."

Jasmine didn't look offended as she began gathering the cards. "It's possible that I influenced the results with what I knew, but it's also possible that I didn't."

Fenella paced across the living room, trying to shake off the unease that had settled over her. Why was she allowing herself to get worked up over a deck of cards she didn't believe in?

It was ridiculous.

And yet, her intuition prompted her to believe what the damn cards had shown her, and she knew better than to doubt her gut feelings. Every warning sign she'd gotten so far in regard to Din had proven accurate, and she wasn't sure that the emergency landing was what they'd been warning her about. It all might be pointing to something wrong about this reunion with him.

And now The Tower. Upheaval. Destruction.

Her phone buzzed with another text. She picked it up, half-expecting another message from Din, but it was from Max.

Got Din. Showing him to his temporary quarters. All good.

Fenella stared at the message, confusion and irritation rising in equal measure. Why had Max picked up Din? Had he wanted to warn him about her? They'd probably spent the entire drive gossiping about her.

"What's the matter?" Jasmine asked.

"Max picked up Din at the airport," Fenella said.

"That's good, isn't it?" Jasmine asked. "Those two should rebuild their friendship, and the sooner the better. They have fifty years of catching up to do."

"I suppose," Fenella conceded. "I just hate the thought of them talking about me, which I'm sure they are doing right now. Maybe that's why I was so antsy."

Jasmine grimaced. "Well, I won't tell you that's not what they are doing. Men gossip as much as women do, but I don't think they would say anything unkind about you, so you shouldn't get upset."

Fenella loosened a breath. "You are probably right."

Her eyes drifted back to where the tarot cards had been. The Tower's image lingered in her mind—the lightning strike, the crumbling structure, the falling figures.

Din had overcome many obstacles to reach her, and according to Jasmine's cards, they were headed for some kind of cataclysm.

She ran a hand through her hair, feeling the familiar knot of anxiety tightening in her chest.

She'd survived half a century by trusting her instincts and recognizing when something was off, and everything about this situation felt like a giant warning sign.

Din might not be the source of the trouble, as Jasmine had said. But trouble was coming all the same.

12

DIN

As Din and Max rode the elevator up to the pavilion, Din couldn't help but notice how settled his old friend seemed. That was new. Love, apparently, did that to a man provided that it was reciprocated.

Max felt safe with Kyra.

"Thomas is a nice guy. Do you remember him?" Max asked.

"Vaguely." Din followed him out of the elevator. "What did he do before returning to the force?"

"He was a bricklayer."

"Good paying job," Din said. "I did that for a while, then I thought about studying architecture, but somehow found myself drawn to archeology." He stopped by the new display of artifacts that had been placed around the glass pavilion. "I should have a talk with Kalugal about his digs." He turned to Max. "Are you close to the guy?"

Max shook his head. "I'm just a lowly Guardian. Kalugal now sits on the council and is chummy with Kian and Toven and the rest of the elite."

Din cast him a sidelong glance. "Do I detect resentment?"

"Not at all." Max turned onto a walkway that was flanked by flowering shrubs. "I have no problem being 'just' a Guardian. I have zero political aspirations, but given who I'm mated to, that might change." He smiled. "Kyra is a rebel, and she fights for those no one else is fighting for. If she asks me to help, I will in any capacity I can."

"As you should." Din was impressed with the transformation his old friend had undergone. He couldn't imagine him saying something like that fifty years ago. "Kyra's changed you for the better."

"I know." Max knocked on the door, and moments later it swung open to reveal a tall, lean man with sandy hair and smiling eyes.

"Max," Thomas greeted with a nod, then shifted his gaze to Din. "Welcome to my humble abode, Din."

Din extended his hand. "Thank you for your hospitality. I hope I'm not imposing."

Thomas took his hand in a firm grip. "Not at all. Max's old room has been gathering dust, and it'll be good to have someone in it again. I don't like how empty the house is." He gave Max an accusing look. "No one sings in the shower with an open door or tells stupid jokes anymore."

Max laughed. "I thought you'd be glad to get rid of me."

"I thought so too, but now I miss the noise you used to make. Would you like to come in for a glass of scotch?"

"Thank you, but I will have to take a rain check. I need to report back for duty." He turned to Din. "Do you want me to come back later? I can escort you to wherever you and Fenella decide to meet."

Din shook his head. "No need. The village isn't that big, and I remember my way around well enough."

"You sure? It's been a while since you've been here."

"I'm sure," Din said.

He'd spent enough time with his old friend today to last him for a while. Din had forgotten how talkative Max was, and that his high energy was tiring after some time. Besides, he didn't want to be shepherded around like a lost tourist.

Max surprised him by pulling him into another brotherly embrace. "It's good to have you back, Din. I missed having my best friend."

The warmth in Max's voice caught Din off guard,

and he returned the embrace. "It's good to be back. Thanks for the lift, Max."

Max pulled back and turned to Thomas. "Don't let him brood too much in that room. He's inclined to get lost in his own head."

Thomas chuckled. "I'll do my best, but I'm hardly one to talk about brooding."

"Two peas in a pod, then," Max said with a grin. "I'll see you both around." With a final wave, he headed back down the path.

Thomas led Din inside, showing him the features as they headed toward the room Din would be staying in. The interior was clean and comfortable, and there were books stacked on nearly every surface. It reminded Din of his own flat in Edinburgh, though with considerably better weather outside the windows.

"Max's old room is this way." Thomas led him down a short hallway. "Well, I suppose it's your room for the time being."

The bedroom was spacious, with a large window overlooking a small private garden. A writing desk sat against one wall, and a comfortable-looking bed against another. The room had been recently cleaned, the scent of lemon polish still lingering in the air.

"I tidied up a bit when I heard you were coming," Thomas said, almost apologetically. "Max left it in decent shape, but it's been empty for a couple of weeks."

"It's perfect." Din set his roller suitcase by the door. "Thank you."

Thomas lingered in the doorway for a moment. "I'll let you get settled. Bathroom's through that door. Feel free to take anything in the kitchen, though I don't keep much on hand besides coffee, tea, and whiskey."

"I appreciate it," Din said.

With a nod, Thomas left him alone, closing the door behind him.

Din sat on the edge of the bed and rubbed his face with his hands, his beard rough against his palms.

A shower. That's what he needed first. Then he needed to call Fenella.

Standing under the spray, the hot water cascading over his shoulders, Din let his thoughts drift to the series of obstacles that had nearly prevented him from reaching the village. The traffic accident on the way to the airport in Scotland. The flight cancellation due to mechanical issues. The storm grounding all flights. And finally, the landing gear malfunction that had resulted in a water landing that could have ended far worse than it had.

Fenella's words about bad omens echoed in his mind.

The universe had seemed determined to keep

him from reaching her. But why? Was it really to test his resolve, as he'd suggested to her? Or was it trying to warn them both away from each other?

Din wasn't superstitious.

Five centuries of existence had made him pragmatic about most things. But even he had to admit that four near misses in a row stretched the coincidence theory to a breaking point.

Yet here he was, in the village, just minutes away from seeing Fenella again. Whatever forces had attempted to prevent their reunion had ultimately failed.

That had to count for something.

As he toweled off and dressed in clean clothes, Din wondered what Fenella would be like now. Max had warned him that she'd changed, that she was harder now, more defensive, wary of connection. But then the young woman he'd fallen for half a century ago had already possessed a certain steel beneath her charm.

He remembered her behind the bar, effortlessly handling rowdy customers with a sharp word and even sharper wit. The way she'd thrown her head back when she laughed was unselfconscious and genuine.

How her eyes had followed Max whenever he'd entered the room…

Din pushed the memory away. That was the past,

and dwelling on it would only poison whatever chance he had at a future with her.

Dressed in dark jeans and a navy button-down shirt, Din reached into his suitcase and withdrew a small wooden box, its surface smooth from years of handling.

He sat on the bed and opened it carefully.

Inside, nestled against faded velvet, lay an antique Scottish brooch. The silver had tarnished slightly over the decades, but the Celtic knotwork pattern remained intricate and beautiful. At its center sat a small amber stone that reminded him of whiskey caught in sunlight.

He'd purchased it for Fenella shortly after meeting her, imagining the moment he'd present it to her. In his mind, she would accept it with that bright smile of hers, perhaps wear it on the woolen scarf she'd sometimes draped around her shoulders on chilly evenings. But he'd never gotten the chance. Max had moved faster, more confidently, and Din had been left holding a gift that would never be given.

After she'd chosen Max over him, Din had made a bitter vow to give the brooch to the first girl he befriended next, but despite the plentiful dalliances over the decades, he'd never met anyone he'd wanted to offer it to. It had remained in its box, sometimes forgotten for years at a time, only to be rediscovered during moves or spring cleanings.

When he'd found it again while packing to move to his Edinburgh apartment, something had compelled him to bring it along, though he'd had no reason to believe Fenella was even alive, let alone that he'd ever see her again.

Din ran his thumb over the amber stone. He'd never been one to believe in fate or destiny, yet here he was, carrying a fifty-year-old gift to a woman he'd been sure was lost to him forever.

Perhaps there was something to this destiny business after all.

His phone buzzed from the bedside table, breaking his reverie. Replacing the brooch in its box, he checked the message from Max:

Did you call Fenella yet? She's probably pacing a hole in Jasmine's floor waiting for you.

Din shook his head. Typical Max, micro-managing everyone around him, but he had a point, and he knew Din. As always, he'd been procrastinating, hesitating over a task he found unnerving and delaying the inevitable.

Taking a deep breath, he dialed Fenella's number.

She answered on the second ring. "Din?"

Her voice sent an unexpected jolt through him—the Scottish lilt he remembered was still there, though muted by decades away from her homeland.

"Hello, Fenella." He was surprised at how steady his own voice sounded. "I'm here, in one piece as promised, and I can't wait to see you."

"I know," she said. "Max texted me. I hope the two of you had a pleasant drive. Plenty to catch up on after fifty years, I imagine."

There was an edge to her tone that Din couldn't quite interpret. Wariness? Jealousy? Or simply the natural awkwardness of their situation?

"Surprisingly, it was not awkward," he admitted. "Though we barely scratched the surface."

"Mmm." The sound was noncommittal. "So, when do you want to meet?"

Direct as ever. Din smiled despite the nervousness fluttering in his stomach.

"Whenever you want," he said.

"How about the café in half an hour?" she suggested. "It's usually quiet this time of day."

"The café sounds perfect." He hesitated, then added, "I've been looking forward to seeing you, Fenella."

There was a pause on the other end, long enough that Din wondered if she'd hung up.

"I would have preferred to meet you at the Hobbit Bar, over a stiff drink, but it's only open on weekends. Have you been there yet? I hear that it's quite new."

Din chuckled, relieved that she hadn't rejected his sentiment outright and also because of the unexpected shift in conversation. He'd forgotten that she used to do that. "We'll have to save that for a Friday night date, then."

Her laugh was short and sharp. "That's very confident of you to think that we're going to last that long. It's only Monday."

The words stung more than Din cared to admit. He swallowed, forcing lightness into his tone that he didn't feel. "I'm sure that I can convince you to see me every day from now until Friday. I'll do my best not to bore you."

"I'm sure you will," she said, and there was something in her voice he couldn't read. Regret? Discomfort? "I'll see you in half an hour, Din."

"I'm looking forward to it," he said, but she'd already ended the call.

Din lowered the phone, staring at the blank screen. That hadn't gone exactly as he'd hoped, but what had he expected? A warm, enthusiastic welcome? Fenella had never been the effusive type, even before whatever horrors she'd endured at the hands of that Doomer.

He slipped the phone into his pocket and picked up the wooden box again. Should he bring the brooch with him? Would she see it as presumptuous, or worse, pathetic?

After a moment's hesitation, he put the box in the bottom drawer of the nightstand. He wouldn't give it to her today—that would be too much, too soon.

A knock at the door pulled him from his thoughts.

"Come in," he called.

Thomas opened the door, hovering by the threshold. "I'm heading out to the gym. Make yourself at home."

"Thanks. I'm meeting Fenella at the café soon."

Thomas nodded. "Good luck."

After he left, Din spent a few more minutes gathering his thoughts. He'd been so focused on overcoming the seemingly endless obstacles to reach Fenella that he'd given little consideration to what would happen once he finally saw her.

What if she took one look at him and decided the reality wasn't worth the fifty years of buildup?

Din looked at himself in the mirror, straightening his collar. He was being ridiculous. He was five hundred years old, and he could handle Fenella.

You couldn't fifty years ago, a nasty voice said in the back of his mind.

"I'm not the same male I was then," he said to his reflection in the mirror. "I will never again let something I want slip through my fingers."

With that, he left the house and walked the gravel path toward the village center.

His phone buzzed in his pocket just as the café came into view, and he had a sinking feeling that Fenella was texting him to cancel their date.

Pulling out the device with dread, he was relieved that it was a message from Max.

Worked some magic for you. I traded concert tickets with a friend who had reservations for Callie's tonight, so you can take Fenella out for a nice dinner. If things don't work out between you two, I will take Kyra there instead, so let me know. The reservations are for seven o'clock.

Din had heard how difficult it was to get reservations at Callie's, and he was beyond grateful.

Thank you, he wrote back. *I owe you.*

The answer returned almost immediately. *Consider us even.*

13

FENELLA

Fenella ended the call with Din and tossed her phone onto the couch, annoyed with herself. Why had she made that cutting remark about not lasting until Friday? The hurt in his voice had been palpable, though he'd covered it well with that confident response.

"That was unnecessarily bitchy of me," she muttered.

Jasmine, who had been pretending not to eavesdrop from the kitchen, returned with two glasses of water. "What happened?"

"Din suggested we go to the Hobbit Bar on Friday, and I basically told him he was being presumptuous to think we'd still be speaking to each other by then." Fenella took the water and gulped it down. "I don't know why I said that. It just spilled out."

"Defense mechanism," Jasmine said with a knowing smile. "You're scared."

"I'm not scared of anything," Fenella snapped, then caught herself. "Okay, fine. Maybe I'm a little nervous." She pushed to her feet. "I should go home and change."

Not that she had anything fancy to change into.

All she had were the few items that Jasmine had ordered for her, and she hadn't wanted to order anything else if she couldn't pay for it. She couldn't keep relying on Jasmine's generosity.

"I need to get a job and start earning money so I can buy myself some nice things."

"You said that you will talk to Atzil about bartending at the Hobbit."

"Yeah, but I haven't had a chance to do that yet. Besides, if the bar is only open on weekends, I won't be making much even if he hires me." She smoothed a hand down her shirt. "Until then, I'll have to make do with what I have."

Jasmine pouted. "You can borrow something of mine. I have a large closet packed with things, and I know my way around a curling iron and makeup brushes."

Fenella stared at her with incredulous eyes. "You're at least half a foot taller. Nothing you own would fit me."

"Not true," Jasmine said, already walking toward her bedroom. "I have skirts and dresses that would look perfect on you. They might be a little loose, but nothing some pins and tape won't fix."

"I don't want to wear something that has pins in it," Fenella protested, but Jasmine was already ducking into her bedroom.

There was something infectious about Jasmine's enthusiasm, and despite her reluctance, Fenella followed. She hadn't played dress-up with a girl-friend in so long that she'd forgotten how much fun it was.

Jasmine's walk-in closet was stuffed to the brim. Clothing of every color hung in orderly sections, with one entirely dedicated to shoes. It was the kind of feminine indulgence Fenella had always scoffed at but secretly envied.

"This is obscene," she said, running her fingers along a row of silk blouses. "No one needs this many clothes."

"I'm an actress." Jasmine grinned. "That's my excuse, and I'm sticking to it. The truth is that I'm a hoarder, and I can't part with anything, so a lot of these outfits no longer fit me." She rifled through a rack of summer dresses, pulling out one with a vivid floral pattern in blues and greens against a white background. "This would look stunning on you. It's a bit short on me, but it should hit you right at the knee."

Fenella eyed the dress skeptically. It was prettier

than anything she'd worn in recent memory—flowing, feminine, with thin straps and a fitted bodice that flared into a full skirt. "It's a bit girly, isn't it?"

"That's the point," Jasmine said with a wink. "Try it on."

Against her better judgment, Fenella took the dress and retreated to Jasmine's bathroom to change. The fabric was soft against her skin, lighter than she expected. When she looked in the mirror, she had to admit that it looked good on her. The dress accentuated her curves, the light colors contrasting with her dark hair.

Still, she emerged from the bathroom feeling self-conscious. "The dress is gorgeous, but I don't have the right shoes to go with it." She pointed to her Skechers.

Jasmine assessed her with a critical eye. "You're right. Hold on." She disappeared back into the closet, returning moments later with a pair of leather flip-flops in a caramel color. "These should work. They might be a tad big, but they'll do the job."

The sandals were indeed a bit large, but they matched the dress far better than her old shoes. Heels would have been better, but to wear Jasmine's, Fenella would have to stuff the toes with cotton like she'd used to do when she'd borrowed her mother's shoes as a teenager.

"You look great." Jasmine assessed her with a critical eye. "Now for hair and makeup." She steered Fenella to a vanity setup that would have made a professional stylist envious.

Fenella sat down on the stool. "My hair is not wet, and when it's dry, it won't hold the curl no matter how strong your curler is."

"Don't worry about a thing. You're dealing with a pro here." Jasmine plugged in a curling iron. "Once I'm done with you, you will blow Din's mind."

Fenella couldn't argue with the appeal of that. "Fine. Do your worst. I mean best."

Jasmine worked quickly, styling Fenella's hair into a loose updo with a few tendrils framing her face, then applied makeup with a light touch—just enough to enhance her features without looking overdone.

"There," she said, stepping back to admire her work. "Take a look."

Fenella turned to the mirror and blinked in surprise. The woman staring back at her looked soft, feminine, almost vulnerable—a far cry from who she really was.

"I look like the sweet girl next door," she said with a laugh. "Which couldn't be further from the truth."

"Maybe not, but you can play the part and see how it fits. That's what I did for years. I tried on different personalities until I found the one that fit me best."

Fenella raised an eyebrow. "It's a bit weird to change personalities like outfits, don't you think?"

Jasmine shrugged. "It's what actors do. We explore different facets of ourselves through the characters we play. Sometimes you discover pieces of yourself you didn't know were there."

The idea wasn't as ridiculous as it at first seemed. Hadn't she done the same over the years? Adapting, blending in, becoming whoever she needed to be to survive?

"I'm not trying to become someone else," she said, more to herself than to Jasmine. "I just want to look nice." The admission felt vulnerable, almost embarrassing. She quickly added, "You know, for myself. Finding my style and all that rot."

Jasmine's knowing smile made it clear she wasn't fooled. "Of course. It has nothing to do with wanting to dazzle Din or make him fall in love with you all over again."

"That's a silly, girly fantasy," Fenella protested, but the denial sounded weak.

"After everything you've been through, you're allowed a few silly, girly fantasies," Jasmine said softly, her expression suddenly serious. "Everyone deserves a little happiness, Fenella. Even stubborn, independent rovers like you."

The simple kindness in those words threatened to undo her.

Fenella swallowed hard, blinking back an unexpected sting in her eyes. "Well," she said, her voice slightly hoarse, "I suppose it doesn't hurt to look dazzling from time to time."

Jasmine glanced at her watch. "We should head out if you want to be just fashionably late."

"You don't need to escort me there. I can find my way to the café."

Jasmine looked offended. "It's late, and I don't want you to get lost and be rudely late."

It finally dawned on Fenella that Jasmine was curious to see Din and that was why she wanted to accompany her.

She narrowed her eyes at the female. "Admit it. You want to meet Din and see what all the fuss is about."

"Guilty," Jasmine admitted with a grin. "The man carried a torch for you for fifty years. That's got to be some kind of record."

"Or some kind of pathology," Fenella muttered, but there was no bite to her words. "Alright, you can come. I'd appreciate your opinion of him, actually."

"Really?" Jasmine looked surprised.

"Don't look so shocked. I value your judgment." Fenella stood and smoothed down the sundress. "Besides, if he turns out to be a complete wanker, I'll need someone to complain to afterward."

"That's what friends are for," Jasmine said.

As they left the house and walked into the golden afternoon light, Fenella grew increasingly nervous with each step. What if Din was disappointed when he saw her? What if she didn't live up to the fantasy he'd built up in his imagination? What if the reality of the sharp-tongued, difficult woman she'd become was a major letdown?

When the café came into view, it was relatively quiet, with only a few patrons still lingering as the place was about to close.

"I don't even remember what he looks like," Fenella admitted, scanning the tables. "It's been fifty years, and we barely spoke to each other back then."

"There," Jasmine said, nodding toward a man sitting alone at a corner table. "I think that's him."

As if sensing their attention, the man looked up and stood, raising a hand in greeting.

Fenella froze, momentarily breathless.

She wouldn't have recognized him. The Din she vaguely remembered had been a quiet presence in the background of Max's boisterous personality—a shadow she'd barely noticed. The man waiting for her now commanded attention without even trying.

He was tall, with broad shoulders tapering to a lean waist. His dark hair was swept back, giving him a distinguished look that suited his strong features. He had high cheekbones, a strong jaw that was softened by a neatly trimmed beard, and eyes that even from this distance seemed to smolder when he looked at her.

"Bloody hell," she murmured. "He's gorgeous."

Jasmine chuckled beside her. "I have to agree."

For the first time in her life, Fenella was speechless, lost for words, and confused. Din was watching her with an expression that stunned her. He looked like a man seeing a ghost, or a dream come to life.

"Remember," Jasmine whispered as they neared the table, "you're allowed to be happy."

Easy for her to say, Fenella thought. Jasmine had found her truelove mate, her other half. She had a mother, a family, a place in this world. Fenella had spent half a century convinced she belonged nowhere and to no one.

And yet, as Din's eyes met hers, something inside her—something long dormant and carefully guarded—stirred to life.

He was real. He was here. And despite her best efforts to remain indifferent, Fenella realized with a jolt of alarm that a small, treacherous part of her wanted very much for this to work out.

The Tower card from Jasmine's reading flashed in her mind—upheaval, destruction, the breaking down of false structures. Perhaps the structure being dismantled was the wall she'd built around her heart.

As they reached the table, Din's smile deepened, revealing a small dimple in his right cheek that Fenella found unreasonably attractive.

"Hello, Fenella," he said, and his voice—deep, Scottish-accented, warm—sent an unexpected shiver down her spine.

Fifty years was a long time to wait for someone.

As Din pulled out a chair for her with old-world courtesy, Fenella couldn't help but wonder if maybe he might have been worth it after all.

14

DIN

*D*in's heart hammered against his ribs as he saw Fenella.

She wore a colorful sundress, her hair was swept up in a casual updo, a few strands escaping to frame her face, and her bare feet were in simple flip-flops, one dangling half-off her foot in a way that was inexplicably captivating.

As their eyes locked across the café, the background noise seemed to fade. She was just as beautiful as he remembered—perhaps more so, with the confidence and character that the years she'd lived added to her gaze.

The young barmaid's softness had been replaced by something more defined, more knowing.

Din forced himself to breathe and keep his face from betraying the storm of emotions churning inside him.

He stood as Fenella approached with the woman beside her in step. He had no doubt that it was Jasmine, not Kyra, mainly by her statuesque figure and her slight resemblance to Fenella.

"Din," Fenella said, his name a soft exhalation that somehow carried over the café's ambient noise. "I'm so glad you made it here in one piece." She offered him her hand. "After all the trouble you've gone through, I was afraid of what might befall you on the way from the house to the café."

Her welcome was a little biting, but Max had prepared him for her sharp tongue, and he had a feeling that she used it as a sword to protect herself when she felt threatened. Though why she would feel that way toward him, he couldn't begin to guess.

"The Fates seemed determined to put obstacles in my path," he said, his Scottish brogue sounding thicker to his own ears. "But I think they are done testing me. I didn't encounter any obstacles on my way from Thomas's house to here."

The woman beside Fenella cleared her throat, breaking the moment. "Hello, Din."

"This is Jasmine," Fenella said, gesturing to her companion. "My new bestie and Kyra's daughter. Kyra is Max's mate."

"I know." Din offered his hand, studying Jasmine with interest.

Max had mentioned a resemblance between the two women, and it was there, but it was superficial.

They shared the same dark chestnut hair color and olive skin tone, and even had matching clefts in their chins, but the similarities ended there.

If he had to compare them to desserts, Jasmine would be a chocolate cheesecake with too much mousse on top—rich, complex, and a bit overwhelming. While Fenella was more like a delicate vanilla crème brûlée, seemingly simple but with hidden depths, perfectly balanced between sweetness and sharp edges.

"It's a pleasure to meet you," Jasmine said, her warm smile revealing perfect teeth. "Max has told me a lot about you."

"Good things, I hope."

Jasmine laughed. "You know Max. He's almost as sharp-tongued as Fenella."

"Ouch." Din winced. "Now I hope that he didn't paint me in too gloomy colors."

"He didn't." Jasmine cast him a charming smile. "I should leave you two alone to catch up on old times. It was lovely to meet you, Din. I hope your stay in the village is long and fruitful."

There was something in her tone, a slight emphasis on the last word, that made Din wonder what she meant, but before he could ponder it further, she was turning to Fenella.

"Call me later?" she asked.

Fenella nodded, and the two women exchanged a

look that seemed to contain an entire private conversation.

"Good luck," Jasmine added with a smile that encompassed them both, and then she was gone, weaving through the tables with a graceful sway of her hips.

Din had been worried that Jasmine might stay, creating a buffer between him and Fenella during their first so-called date. While he understood Fenella might not want to be alone with him after everything she'd been through, it would have been disappointing to have a chaperone in the very public setting of the café.

"Shall we sit?" He pulled out a chair for her.

"Yes. Definitely." She sat down and adjusted her sundress with a casual flick of her wrist.

"What would you like?" he asked. "We should order quickly before the place closes."

"A cappuccino would be nice." Her eyes drifted to the display case. "And one of those almond croissants."

"Coming right up." He walked up to the counter and placed the order for two cappuccinos and two almond croissants.

The truth was that he could have waited for the waitress to approach their table, but he needed a few moments to collect himself after the shock of seeing Fenella again.

She was even more breathtaking than he remembered. The years had added character to her beauty, but there was a certain wariness in her gaze that hadn't been there before. She carried herself differently too, with the watchful readiness of someone who had learned the hard way to always be prepared for trouble.

It made his heart ache to think of what she must have endured.

He returned to the table with their cappuccinos and pastries, setting Fenella's down in front of her.

She broke off a corner of her croissant. "So, you're a professor now? Of archaeology?"

Din nodded, wrapping his hands around the warm cappuccino cup. "At the University of Edinburgh. I fell into it by accident, to be honest. I started with night classes to pass the time, and then I discovered that I had a knack for it."

Fenella studied him. "I can picture you hunched over ancient relics, piecing together forgotten histories."

"You make it sound more romantic than it is." Din chuckled. "Most of my time is spent grading mediocre papers and attending dull faculty meetings."

"Still, it somehow suits you." She took a sip of her cappuccino, leaving a small foam mustache that she quickly wiped away with her napkin. "Teaching is better than tending bar, I imagine."

"I'm not sure. It depends on your character. You always enjoyed being around people. I didn't.

Frankly, I'm surprised at myself at choosing to teach. I thought I would be spending my days in dusty digs."

"Why don't you?"

He shrugged. "Sometimes the Fates lead you somewhere you never intended to go, but you discover that they were right."

Her eyes darted away, her fingers fidgeting with the handle of her cup. "I barely remember my bartending days," she admitted. "They seem like they happened to someone else."

"In a way, they did," Din said. "You were a different person back then."

"I was just a girl," Fenella agreed. "Naive. Sheltered, despite thinking I was so worldly and wise."

"And now?"

Her eyes met his, sharp and assessing. "Now I know better. The world isn't safe, or nice, or fair. It's a dog-eat-dog world and evil lurks everywhere." She shivered. "I had no idea how bad it could get. I wish I could go back to being naive and not knowing."

He leaned over and placed a hand over hers. "There are many good people out there, Fenella. Don't judge the entire world by its bottom feeders."

"It's hard to tell the difference sometimes," she said. "Indifference is almost as bad because it allows evil to flourish. Most people just want to live their lives and not be bothered, and I get it because I was the same way. But eventually the rot reaches them as well, and then they have no choice and are forced to join the fight. Only then, it's often too late."

An awkward silence fell between them, heavy with unspoken histories.

"I'm such a downer." Fenella forced a smile. "Enough of this doom and gloom. Tell me about your work instead. Have you ever taken part in a dig?"

Din took the lifeline, grateful for the shift to safer territory. "I have. Quite a few. I once took a group of students to Jordan. It was fascinating—a Bronze Age settlement near the Dead Sea, virtually untouched. We found pottery with intact pigments, tools, and even some jewelry. The preservation was remarkable due to the arid climate."

As he spoke about his work, he watched Fenella gradually relax, her posture becoming less rigid, her eyes softening. She asked intelligent questions, showing interest in his discoveries.

"You've traveled extensively," he said during a lull in the conversation.

"Necessity rather than choice," she said with a shrug. "Never staying in one place too long was safer."

"Was there anywhere you enjoyed? Somewhere you might have stayed if circumstances were different?"

Fenella considered his question, absently tucking a strand of escaped hair behind her ear. "Greece," she said after a moment. "The islands, not the mainland. There's something about the quality of light there, and the people mind their own business." A faint smile touched her lips. "I rented a room in a little whitewashed house on Naxos for almost a year. Longest I ever stayed anywhere."

"Why did you leave?" Din asked.

The smile vanished. "A tourist recognized me from a bar I'd worked at in Vienna years before. I went by a different name, of course, and I claimed no knowledge of the barmaid he was talking about, the one who looked exactly like me, but it was time for me to leave. It's amazing how small the world seems when you want to disappear."

Din wanted to reach across the table and take her hand again, but he resisted the impulse. "It must have been exhausting," he said. "Always being on the move, looking over your shoulder."

"I adapted," Fenella said with a shrug that didn't quite achieve the casualness she was aiming for. "Speaking of adapting, how are you handling your job and your unchanging appearance?"

His smile wilted. "It won't last. At some point, I will need to disappear and return as someone else in a different university. The clan is very good at arranging for alternative identities, including titles. Naturally, it's better to live in the village or back in Scotland in our castle and only venture out on assignments like Max does. There is much less risk of exposure that way."

"Ah, yes, Max," Fenella said. "You two seem to have patched things up rather quickly. Fifty years of not speaking, and suddenly you're best buddies again?"

"Not quite," Din said. "But life's too short—even immortal life—to hold on to old grudges. Especially when there are far more important things at stake."

"Like what?"

"Like making amends for my part in what happened to you," Din said quietly.

Fenella's eyes widened. "Your part? You weren't even there when Max..." She trailed off, unable or unwilling to finish the sentence.

"I didn't know you were a Dormant," Din said. "But there was something about you that I should have identified as more than just an attraction to a pretty girl. If I weren't such a colossal ass, I wouldn't have said all those horrible things to you, lashing out in anger without thinking. I would have stuck around and found out what was happening to you when you transitioned. Imagine all the grief I could have saved you. Instead, I was so caught up in my rivalry with Max that I lost sight of what mattered."

Fenella stared at him, her expression unreadable. "So, you think that this is all your fault?"

"Not entirely," Din said. "I could have handled the situation much better, and I offer my deepest and most heartfelt apology for how I acted, but the blame for what happened ultimately lies with Max and with the monster who hurt you. Still, I could have prevented it, and I didn't. And that is my greatest regret."

She looked away, her throat working as she swallowed. "It's in the past," she said dismissively, though her voice had a slight tremor. "Water under the bridge, as Max would say."

"Is it?" Din asked. "Because it seems to me that you're still carrying it with you."

Her eyes flashed back to his, suddenly fierce. "Don't presume to know me, Din. A few memories of who I was half a century ago don't give you that right."

"True," he conceded immediately. "I apologize."

She exhaled slowly, some of the tension leaving her shoulders. "It's fine. Just... let's not rehash the past, all right? It is what it is."

"Fair enough," Din agreed, taking a sip of his now-cooling cappuccino. "What would you rather talk about?"

"Tell me about Scotland," she said after a moment. "Is it still as dreary and beautiful as I remember?"

"That sums it up perfectly," Din chuckled. "The Highlands are still wild, the cities still full of history and whiskey. Edinburgh's changed, though, and not for the better. But the heart of it is the same."

"I miss the rain sometimes," Fenella admitted.

"Everything's so bloody sunny here. Perfect weather, perfect surroundings, perfect people with perfect teeth and perfect lives." She rolled her eyes. "It's kind of boring."

Din laughed. "I keep forgetting that this is all new to you, and that you didn't know immortals existed until a couple of weeks ago. It's always jarring to come home from my flat in the city and see how perfect everyone looks in comparison to the humans."

Fenella leaned forward, her eyes lighting up with the pleasure of being understood. "It's like living in a glossy magazine spread. Even the bloody squirrels look well-groomed."

"At least the coffee's good," Din said, lifting his cup in a small toast.

"The coffee's excellent," Fenella agreed, clinking her cup against his. "And the security's top-notch, I'll give them that."

"Have you thought about what you'll do here?" Din asked. "Any plans, or are you taking it day by day?"

"Jasmine mentioned that the Hobbit Bar is looking for help. The owner only opens it on weekends because he works for Kalugal during the week."

"Ah, Kalugal." Din nodded. "The wayward Doomer prince."

She arched a brow. "Why do you call him a prince?"

"Because he is. He's Navuh's son. Has no one mentioned it to you?"

She shook her head. "Who is Navuh?"

Din snorted. "They didn't tell you much, did they?"

"I guess not. So, who's Navuh?"

"He's the founder and leader of the Doomers. Evil incarnate himself. He's the son of Mortdh, the one who killed all the gods and murdered the Clan Mother's beloved husband."

Her eyes widened. "And yet your people invited his son to live with them in the village?"

Din shrugged. "I have nothing against the bloke. He's not his father, and he managed to escape with a platoon of soldiers who were loyal to him."

"Max said that Kalugal and his men never believed in the Brotherhood's twisted ideology," Fenella said, though she didn't sound entirely convinced herself. "That's why they defected."

"People can change." Din smiled, lifting his cup as if to toast his statement.

"Speaking from experience?" Fenella asked, her head tilting slightly.

He met her gaze steadily. "I'd like to think I've changed for the better over the centuries. Grown wiser, at least. More patient."

She laughed. "I'd say. You were patient enough to wait fifty years for me when you had no reason to believe that I was still around."

Din considered how to answer. "I should have searched for you," he said.

"Yes, you should have."

"I thought that you didn't want to be found."

Her eyes never left his. "That's a convenient way to absolve yourself."

"Convenient, but not entirely untrue," Din countered. "Would you have welcomed me if I had found you in, say, that house on Naxos?"

Fenella considered this, her fingers tracing patterns in the condensation on her water glass. "Probably not at first," she conceded. "But getting an explanation for what happened to me would have been welcome."

He nodded. "I know that I'm a little late, but how about now?"

Her eyes were guarded but not cold. "I already know what I am and what happened to me, but I'm here, am I not?"

It wasn't much, but it was something. A starting point, perhaps.

"You are," Din agreed. "And I'm grateful for the chance you are willing to give me."

A small smile tugged at the corner of her mouth. "Don't get ahead of yourself, professor. I'm still deciding whether you're worth the trouble."

"Fair enough." He was unable to suppress a smile. "Take all the time you need. I've waited half a century. I can wait a bit longer."

"Ever the patient Scotsman," she said, a hint of her old teasing manner returning.

"Only for things that matter."

Their eyes held for a long moment, something unspoken passing between them—not quite trust, but perhaps the possibility of it.

Somewhere in the background, he noticed that the serve-out counter had closed and that the other patrons had left, but he paid attention only to Fenella, aware of the subtle shift in her demeanor from wary to cautiously receptive.

It wasn't perfect, this reunion. There were still walls between them, histories unshared, wounds unhealed. But it was a beginning, and after fifty years of wondering, of regretting, of imagining this moment, Din would take it.

For now, it was enough that she was here, that she was safe, that she was willing to give him a chance to know the woman she had become.

15

FENELLA

Fenella glanced around the café, noting that most of the patrons had left, and the window at the serve-out counter was closed.

"Soon we will be the last ones here," she said.

Din looked up as if surprised. "So it would seem."

He'd been so focused on her the entire time that it was almost uncomfortable. She'd never had anyone look at her and listen to her so intently. Din was treating every word that left her mouth as if it were gospel. It made her self-conscious, made her think twice before saying anything, and then made her rethink what she'd just said.

It was flattering, but it was also unnerving.

Fenella wasn't used to such intense scrutiny, and she didn't like it.

Was that what other women craved? Was that what they meant by wanting to be seen?

Fenella wasn't sure she could tolerate such intensity for long. Ironically, she would have preferred Max's flippant attitude because then she could have been just as flippant back, and she wouldn't have to allow any emotion to penetrate deeper than the surface.

"Would you like to go on a walk?" she suggested. "We could explore the village together."

Perhaps shifting some of his focus to the sights would ease the burden he was placing on her.

"Of course." He rose to his feet and collected their cups and plates. "I'll just drop these at the bin."

She watched him walk over to where the café staff had left a bin for dirty dishes, admiring his taut backside and fluid walk.

His students must be salivating over him, and she could just imagine how many he had bedded. Now that she knew that voracious sexual appetite was part of what it meant to be immortal, she realized that Max hadn't been the anomaly she'd thought he was back when they had been together.

It also explained her promiscuity during her travels, even when such behavior had endangered her. That incessant drive had been killed by that Doomer, though, and nowadays the only way she could even think about sex was when it didn't apply to her.

He'd killed that part of her, and she hadn't even properly mourned its loss yet.

Well, truth be told, she hoped for a miraculous healing and for her soul to regenerate and return to what it had been before the last shard of faith in humanity had been beaten out of her.

"Ready?" Din appeared at her side, offering his hand to help her up.

"Yes." She forced a smile and took his hand.

The electrical current she'd hoped for didn't happen, but at least she hadn't felt revulsion either, so it was a step in the right direction.

He let go of her hand as soon as she was up. Standing beside him in her flip-flops, she realized how tall he was. She felt tiny in comparison, and that only added to her feelings of awkwardness.

"I've been to the village a couple of times before," Din said. "But I don't remember where everything is, so we might have to ask for directions on the way."

She waved a dismissive hand. "Or we might just make up designations for what we see on the way."

He frowned, looking confused by her suggestion. "Give me an example."

She pointed at the café. "This could be the outdoor dining hall where meals are served for the entire clan throughout the day." Next, she pointed at the office building. "This could be the school, and the clinic could be the art center."

He looked unsure about the game she suggested, but he nodded nonetheless, and Fenella smirked under her breath.

Men were so easily manipulated, especially during the stage of impressing a woman. After, when they were secure in having captured her affections, they were usually much less accommodating.

Walking beside Din along a winding gravel path, Fenella was conscious of the careful distance he maintained between them—close enough for conversation, but not so close that they might accidentally brush against each other. He was treating her like a skittish colt, which was understandable given what she'd been through, but he was overdoing it.

She wouldn't have minded him holding her hand.

"This path leads to the meditation garden." Din gestured ahead where the trail curved around a stand of trees. "Not many people use it, which makes it perfect if you need a quiet moment to yourself."

She wasn't sure if this was part of their game or if the meditation garden was for real, and the lone bench sitting under the tree didn't help solve the puzzle.

"Do you often need quiet moments to yourself?" she asked.

Din gave a small, self-deprecating smile. "Certainly. Especially at the university. Sometimes I lock the door to my office and pretend that I'm not there."

She grimaced. "I can imagine how hard it must be for a young-looking professor like you to fend off all the female attention to stay out of trouble."

He nodded, not even trying to refute her statement. "I think it became a sport for them." He chuckled. "Who can seduce the professor, that sort of thing."

She arched a brow. "And? What's their success rate?"

"Zero as far as my students go. It's against the rules, and I make it very clear that I follow them and don't engage with my students."

"What about students from other departments?"

Why was she pushing the issue? It was none of her business, and she had been far from celibate even before her transition.

Din smiled. "There are no explicit rules about that."

They reached a fence, which she hadn't seen anywhere else in the village, and the houses on its other side were a lot different from the ones on their side.

"What's over there?" she asked.

"That's Kalugal's part of the village. He paid for the construction, but the clan provided the land."

Fenella tensed. The former Doomer's name had come up several times since her arrival in the village, often spoken with respect and even admiration, but she still couldn't reconcile that with what she knew about the Brotherhood.

"You don't approve of him," Din observed.

"I don't know him," Fenella hedged, trailing her

fingers over the fence. "Everyone speaks of him respectfully, even fondly, and he was invited to join this community, but given what his kind did to me, you can't blame me for being disturbed by him and his men being here. I look at every male I see, and I wonder if he's a clan member or a former Doomer." She took a deep breath. "I'm scared, and it's not easy for me to admit. It's like having been bitten by a rabid dog and then being afraid of all dogs that look like it even if they are the kindest and sweetest creatures."

"That's completely understandable, and for what it's worth, I initially shared your reservations, but I trust Kian. If he decides that Kalugal and his men are trustworthy, then I accept his judgment. Also, the Clan Mother compelled everyone in our community to cooperate and never strike against each other, so you really have nothing to fear."

"What about the things they did before joining the clan? If they raped, slaughtered, and pillaged, is all of that just going to be forgiven because they'd turned over a new leaf?"

He hesitated before answering. "I don't think that they did any of those things. Kalugal was always different, and he chose the right kind of men for his platoon, freeing them from Navuh's brainwashing and keeping them assigned to places where they were just regular soldiers."

Fenella snorted. "Right. Nice story. Do you have proof of their so-called innocence?"

"I don't," he admitted.

She threw her hands up in the air. "Why are good people always so bloody gullible? You think that because you are good and would never do such horrible things, everyone else, with the exception of a few monsters, is motivated by the same principles? That's simply not true. There are entire cultures that are built on evil underpinnings, and the few good people are the exception."

Din smiled as if she'd just proven his point. "Then you admit that there are exceptions, and even an evil society like the Brotherhood can have a few good people who are worth saving."

He got her there, but she was not willing to concede defeat yet. "Sometimes there are none to be found. Take Sodom and Gomorrah as an example. That story is told just to warn naive people like you that some places are so rotten that they are beyond redemption."

He stopped walking and turned to face her. "I understand your anger and frustration. What was done to you was unforgivable. If I ever get my hands on the one who hurt you—"

"You'll what?" Fenella challenged. "Kill him? He's already in your clan's dungeon, being pressed for information."

His eyes blazed with inner light. "I hope they take

their time with him, and when they are done, I'll ask Kian's permission to finish him off."

The vehemence in his voice gave her perverse satisfaction. It seemed he understood the depth of what had been done to her, and she appreciated that he didn't try to minimize it or suggest she should forget it and move on.

"That's nice of you, but you'll have to take a ticket and stand in line. Max said the same thing. He wants revenge for what the monster did to Kyra."

Din bared a pair of impressive fangs. "I'm willing to share."

Finally, he was showing his true colors, the kind that Fenella could feel good about. She didn't like the reserved professor. She liked the warrior hiding under the thin veneer of civility.

"That's very gallant of you." She threaded her arm through his, surprising him. "Shall we continue?"

Looking down to where her arm rested on his, he nodded. "There's a viewpoint a few minutes' walk from here. If it's not taken, we could sit on the bench and watch the sunset."

"Sounds lovely."

The viewpoint was beautiful, even though it was just a patch of grass with a bench, a few trees that provided shade, and several shrubs. What made it special was the unobstructed view of the ocean in the distance.

"I'm surprised that no one claimed this spot," she

said as she sat down. "Now that I know it's here, I will try to make it every day at this time to see the sunset."

He looked at her with that intensely focused look again. "I will join you for as long as I'm here."

"Oh, that's right. You need to get back to the university. How long is your vacation?"

"I took two weeks off, claiming a family emergency, but I can always call to say that the emergency continues, and I can't return yet. It's not like I depend on that job for a living. It's just something I enjoy doing."

That was a concept she couldn't wrap her head around. Everything she'd done during her adult life had been about survival, about earning enough to pay for food and a roof over her head. It would be nice not to have to worry about mundane things like that. It would also be boring. No wonder that Din chose to keep himself busy doing something he liked.

"Tell me about your work," Fenella said. "Is there more to it than having easy access to a horde of beautiful young girls?"

A smile lit Din's face, transforming his serious features. "My young students are a nice perk, but that's not what drew me to archeology. There's nothing quite like unearthing something that hasn't been touched by human hands in thousands of years and then trying to piece together the information that can be deduced from it. I see it as a connection across time, and for an old immortal like me, it's especially significant because so much of our past is guesswork."

"With how old you are, you've lived through so much of human history. You must know things no one else knows." She leaned closer to him. "We all know that what's written in the history books cannot be trusted. So much of the information has gone through the sieve of the writers' prism. None of it is objective."

He nodded. "My life might seem long to you, but I've witnessed a mere sliver of human history firsthand." He shifted on the bench, inching closer to her. "Last year, I led a dig in northern Turkey, and we uncovered a series of clay tablets with a writing system no one's been able to decipher yet. Pre-dates Linear A by at least a thousand years." His eyes had taken on that distant look people get when talking about something they're passionate about. "There are entire civilizations, entire languages that have been lost to time. Sometimes I think about all the stories that will never be told, all the knowledge that's simply gone."

"That's depressing," Fenella said.

Din chuckled. "I suppose it is. But it also makes the discoveries all the more precious."

The breeze ruffled his dark hair, and Fenella had a sudden, inexplicable urge to smooth it back into place. She clasped her hands in her lap instead.

"What about you?" Din asked. "You said you spent time in Greece. Where else did your travels take you?"

Fenella hesitated, sorting through which parts of her nomadic half-century she was willing to share. There were dark chapters she preferred to keep to herself—desperate times when she'd done things she wasn't proud of to survive.

"I moved around a lot," she said finally. "Europe mostly, though I spent a few years in Southeast Asia. Bangkok, then Cambodia for a while. Morocco for almost two years. I waited tables, served drinks in bars, cleaned hotel rooms—whatever would pay cash with no questions asked. And I played poker to supplement my income, but I had to be careful with that. A girl alone winning games is perceived as an easy target."

"That must have been difficult," Din said softly.

Fenella shrugged, aiming for nonchalance. "I adapted. The hardest part was never staying long enough to form attachments, but I got used to that as well. Though perhaps that was for the best. Attachments complicate things." She put a hand over her chest. "It's nice to have calmness here when it's quiet and there is no turbulence. That's practically impossible when there are other people in my life to complicate matters."

Din studied her face for a moment. "I know what you mean, but what's the point of living forever without feeling anything in here?" He touched his chest. "It's an empty kind of life. Ask me how I know?"

She tilted her head. "Are you lonely, Din?"

"Yes, and like you, it's by choice. But I often reflect on my decisions and wonder about their validity. Avoidance is not a recipe for happiness, and even though relationships are messy and sometimes painful, it's better to experience them than not."

Fenella looked away, uncomfortable with the direction the conversation was taking. "There was a monastery in Tibet," she said, deliberately changing the subject. "I stayed there for almost six months, high in the mountains where the air was so thin it made my lungs ache. The monks took me in, no questions asked." She smiled faintly at the memory. "Talk about choosing avoidance. I was the calmest I've ever been but also bored out of my mind."

He chuckled. "I can't picture you in a monastery."

"I would have stayed longer despite the boredom, but I couldn't stay anywhere for long. It's not just the non-aging that gives us away. It's the little things like hearing or seeing something that shouldn't be possible for a human or healing too fast from scrapes and bruises. We just can't live with humans without risking exposure."

"So, you ran again," Din said.

"It's what I do or rather did. I'm not sure what I'm going to do, now that I'm here."

"Whatever you want," Din said. "That's the gift of this place—the freedom to choose a path without constantly looking over your shoulder."

16

DIN

*D*in credited his years at the university with his newfound ability to communicate with people and especially women, which was now helping him with Fenella.

She was slowly opening up to him.

He hadn't had the skill fifty years ago, and talking to a woman with an explosive personality like hers had seemed daunting. Paradoxically, it was the type he was most attracted to.

Her volatility and unpredictability stirred something inside of him. She excited, challenged, and forced him outside his comfort zone and into uncharted, unscripted territory.

She alleviated the boredom and drudgery of over five centuries of existence.

"I need to catch that guy Atzil," Fenella said. "I

need to ask him about a job at his Hobbit Bar. I was good at bartending back in the day, and I enjoyed it."

"I remember," Din said with a smile. "You had a way of making even the most sullen patrons feel like they belonged, like they were part of the cool club."

She laughed. "Are you talking about yourself? You were always skulking around, watching me from dark corners like a stalker, looking angry and dejected."

He looked surprised. "You noticed that?"

"Of course. You are not the only one with observational skills."

He frowned. "I hope I didn't scare you."

"You didn't. Somehow, I knew that you were harmless. I just assumed that you were going through some crap in your life that made you unhappy." She patted his arm. "I'm not one of those idiots who expect everyone around them to be smiling all of the time, or who think that every frown is about them. Life is full of misfortune, and when it slaps people around, they often come to the bar to drown their sorrows. I never held that against my customers, and I was always willing to listen if they wanted to talk about it, but I never pushed. That's why I didn't ask you what your problem was. Maybe if I had, I would have saved us both a lot of hardship."

"Don't ever blame yourself. It was all my fault." He rubbed the back of his neck. "It was easy to blame

Max. He is guilty of being an insensitive jerk, but I shouldn't have shrugged off responsibility for what happened. My cowardice cost us fifty years." He sighed. "Instead of just watching and skulking in dark corners, as you so elegantly described it, I should have said something."

An awkward silence fell between them, the ghosts of their shared past hovering over them like a physical presence.

"We should head back." Fenella rose from the bench. "I'm getting hungry."

Din stood up and smiled. "I pulled some strings and got us a reservation at Callie's." It had actually been Max who had done that for him, and he should have given the guy credit, but right now he wasn't in the mood to lavish praise on Max.

Fenella's eyes widened. "That's wonderful. I heard that Callie's is exceptional, but that the waiting list is so long that there is no chance of getting in for months."

Now he had no choice but to confess. "To be honest, it was Max who pulled the magic. He traded concert tickets with one of his Guardian buddies for his reservation at Callie's."

"Oh, wow." Fenella looked down at her flip-flops. "Do you think it's okay for me to show up there looking like this?"

"You look perfect." He draped his arm around her

middle and held his breath, expecting her to flick it off.

She didn't, leaning into him instead.

He released the breath. "Now the challenge will be to find Callie's. I think it's in the newest section of the village that I haven't shown you yet."

She looked up at him. "We can ask for directions."

"Let's try to find it first on our own. The reservations are for seven, so we have plenty of time."

Fenella waved a hand. "Lead the way."

The pathway was deserted as they headed toward where he remembered the new section was. Fenella would have no doubt preferred the bustle of other people around them, the buffer of public space diluting the intensity of their one-on-one interaction. Still, Din loved having her all to himself and gently, attentively, demolishing the barriers she'd built around herself.

Well, truth be told, it wasn't he who was doing the demolition work. Fenella was doing it all on her own, the safer she felt with him. It hadn't escaped his notice how comfortable she seemed with him, reining in her formidable tongue. It had been nearly fifteen minutes since her last cutting remark, which was a great achievement. She also no longer seemed to feel the need to fill the quiet between them with meaningless chatter or to maintain a façade of breezy indifference.

It was remarkable progress given the short time they'd spent together so far.

They found Callie's quite easily, and as they entered, Callie herself welcomed them with a bright smile.

"It's lovely to see you two here. Please, take a seat." She motioned to a small table for two, one of about twenty in the entire place. No wonder it was booked months in advance. "The menu is on the table, but it's for information only. There is no ordering in my place." She chuckled. "It's like showing up for dinner at your mom's. You eat what's served."

"I love the concept," Fenella said. "Does the selection change every day?"

Callie nodded. "It's a very long rotation, so months can pass before items repeat, but I still try to innovate as much as I can."

As they sat down, Din noticed Ingrid's platinum updo, which could rival Dolly Parton's, and sitting next to her was a guy who looked like the younger version of the colonel from the movie *Avatar*. Atzil was so muscular that his biceps were straining his dress shirt, with close-cropped light blond hair, and a jaw that could cut glass.

"Talk about serendipity." He motioned with his chin toward the couple. "Ingrid and Atzil are here."

Ingrid turned around and flashed him a bright smile. "Did I just hear my name spoken?"

Din nodded. "I pointed you out to Fenella. She wants to speak with Atzil about a job in his bar."

That got Atzil to turn around. "Come join us." He motioned with his hand.

Din wasn't happy about sharing Fenella with others, but he knew she wanted this. Maybe even needed it.

"Are you sure this is okay? We don't want to intrude."

"It's perfect," Atzil said.

Din rose to his feet and pulled his chair next to Ingrid and Atzil's, and then did the same for Fenella's.

"You should bring the table as well," Ingrid said. "Once Callie starts serving the meal, we won't have enough space on this small table for four plates."

"Good point." Din lifted the small table and pushed it closer to theirs.

"So, Din," Atzil said after Din sat down. "I hear that you are visiting us from Scotland. How long are you going to stay in the village?"

Din cast a sidelong glance at Fenella. "That depends. The plan is for two weeks, but I might extend my stay."

Ingrid sighed dramatically. "I wish all of you would move here. The clan is too small to be divided, and we have enough space in the village even with the Kra-ell."

Atzil chuckled. "I'm just glad that most of the

Kra-ell don't need reservations at Callie's or it would have been impossible to get a table."

"Right." Fenella pushed a strand of hair behind her ear. "I was told that the purebloods and even some of the hybrids only drink blood."

"Not exclusively." Atzil leaned over as if to whisper a secret in her ear. "Even the purebloods drink alcohol. They're some of my best customers."

17

FENELLA

"Fascinating." Fenella's interest was piqued. "What do they like to drink?"

"Mainly hard liquor, but they like mixing it with some sweet juices that they can tolerate to an extent. It's not good for their digestion, but then it's not good for humans either, but they still like to drink."

Atzil seemed like a nice guy, and Fenella had a feeling that she would like working with him.

"Do you have anyone helping you in the bar?" She threw the bait, hoping he would bite.

"No, which is why I only open on weekends," Atzil said. "During the week, I cook for Kalugal and the rest of our men."

"A chef and a bartender." Fenella leaned back. "That's an interesting combination."

Atzil smiled, something rueful in the expression.

"Food and drink make people happy, and I like doing both."

A young waitress, who couldn't be older than Arezoo and looked like she had some Kra-ell in her, brought over two bottles of wine, a red and a white. Fenella opted for a glass of red.

"I should tell Kyra's older nieces about Callie's. I'm sure they would love to have a job in the village, and it looks like Callie needs help here."

"She does." Ingrid sipped on her red wine. "I would love for her to move to a larger place and cook enough for the entire clan. Maybe then Kalugal and his men will come eat here, and Atzil will be free to open the bar every day of the week."

"I can help with that." Fenella seized the opening. "I mean in the bar. I have a lot of experience bartending, and I need a job."

Atzil leaned forward. "What's your specialty? Classic cocktails? Modern mixology? Or just pulling pints and lending an ear?"

"All of the above. I've worked everywhere from dive bars to five-star hotels. I can mix a perfect martini while breaking up a fight and balancing the till."

Atzil laughed, a rich sound that transformed his serious face. "Impressive resume. When can you start?"

"I'm available whenever you need me," Fenella said. "And I just want to add that I can run the place on my own while you are busy cooking for Kalugal. I can keep the bar open every night."

Atzil looked intrigued. "How about you stop by the Hobbit tomorrow afternoon? I'll show you around, and we'll discuss particulars."

"Perfect." Fenella beamed, feeling an unexpected surge of optimism.

When their food arrived, it temporarily diverted the conversation to appreciative comments about the meal. The pasta was excellent, simple but perfectly executed with fresh ingredients and a light, flavorful sauce.

Once the main meal was over and it was time for dessert, Fenella leaned back with her coffee and leveled her gaze at Atzil. "From what I was told, Kalugal and a number of Brotherhood members escaped during WWII, but I was wondering what you did after you escaped."

"The Brotherhood had been deeply embedded in the Imperial military structure," Atzil said. "They were using it as cover for their operations in the Pacific. When the nuclear bombs were dropped in the area where we were stationed, we used it as a perfect opportunity to disappear. Not even immortals can survive a nuclear blast, so we were presumed dead. Getting to the United States wasn't difficult for a guy who could compel and a group of soldiers who could shroud and thrall. We arrived in New York with nothing, and establishing ourselves wasn't easy. We had no resources, no identities in the modern sense. Kalugal made difficult choices to ensure our survival."

"What kind of choices?" Fenella asked, though she suspected she already knew.

Atzil met her gaze steadily. "He used thralling and compulsion on Wall Street traders, extracting insider information that allowed us to build a financial foundation. Not ethical, certainly not legal, but necessary at the time and super effective. We were practically swimming in money, and then he moved to investing in technology. Our boss is very smart."

The guy obviously worshiped the ground Kalugal walked on, and she couldn't blame him. His boss had saved him from a horrible life in the Brotherhood's ranks and then ensured that his men were well provided for.

"I've done worse to survive," she said. "Much worse."

The admission hung in the air, raw and honest.

"I wish white-collar crimes were the only ones I needed to confess to." Atzil sighed. "They are just the easier ones. We all have lines we never thought we'd cross. Until we did."

"And then you have to live with it," Fenella said, thinking about those crimes that Atzil didn't want to talk about.

"Yes," Atzil agreed. "But you also get to choose who you become afterward. That's the gift of a long life—the chance to reinvent yourself, to atone, to do better."

Fenella found an unexpected resonance in his words. She had been running for so long—not just from external threats, but from the parts of herself she wasn't proud of, the compromises and sacrifices that had kept her alive but chipped away at her soul.

"Is that what you're doing here?" she asked. "Atoning?"

Atzil smiled faintly. "In my own small way. Feeding people, mixing drinks—it's hardly heroic, but there's a simple goodness in it. In creating moments of pleasure for people I care about." He swept his arm in a wide arc. "That includes everyone in this community. They are all my peeps, as the young humans like to say."

When the conversation shifted to lighter topics like Atzil's favorite mixes and which drinks were the most popular in the village, Fenella felt more at ease than she could remember. It could have been the wine, or the food, or the good company, or all of the above.

"We should get going," Ingrid said at some point, picking up her fashionable handbag. "This was lovely. We should do it again soon."

"Definitely." Fenella nodded, turning to Atzil. "What time do you want to meet tomorrow?"

"Three o'clock is good for me. It's the lull between lunch and dinner at Kalugal's."

"Perfect." She shook his hand. "I'm looking forward to it."

"What did you think of him?" Din asked after Ingrid and Atzil left.

"I liked him a lot. He's a good guy." She lifted the small cup of coffee to her lips and took a sip. "After what was done to me, I wanted to hate anything connected to the Brotherhood, but I can't hate Atzil. He's just too nice."

"Do you trust him, though?"

The question gave her pause. Trust was something Fenella had rationed carefully over the decades, extending it rarely and often regretting it when she did.

"My gut tells me that I can trust him, but I can't help being cautious and reserving judgment."

"That's progress, I guess," Din said.

"Of a sort." Fenella drained the last of her coffee. "I should head back before Shira starts to wonder if I've been kidnapped."

"I'll walk you home," Din offered while swiping his card over the scanner.

"I can find my way there," Fenella said automatically, the instinct for self-reliance too deeply ingrained to ignore. "The village is super safe, right?"

"It's not about safety. I would just like to walk you home, if that's okay with you."

"Of course it is." She flashed him a broad smile.

If she was being honest with herself, she wasn't quite ready for the evening to end either.

When they stepped out of the restaurant, it was nearly completely dark outside, and with no illumination allowed in the village, she had to rely on her excellent night vision.

"It's beautiful here." Fenella threaded her arm through Din's. "Almost too beautiful, if that makes sense."

The night air was pleasant, carrying a clean, earthy scent that reminded her of how it smelled after rain.

"It's like a dream," Din agreed. "One you're afraid to wake from."

She was surprised that he understood. This place belonged to him even though he didn't reside here. He could move into the village anytime he wanted, and there was no reason for him to dream about it when it could be his reality.

Following that logic, though, it was true for her as well. The boss of this place had invited her to stay, even insisted on it.

As they reached the front door of Shira's house, Fenella turned to face Din, suddenly aware of the awkwardness of this moment at the end of what had essentially been a date. Not that either of them had called it that, but that didn't change the fact that it was.

"Thank you for today," she said. "I had a very good time with you."

"It was my pleasure."

He stepped closer, and Fenella felt her heart rate increase. Was he going to kiss her? Did she want him to?

Din's hand rose, gently tucking a strand of hair behind her ear, the gesture so tender it made her breath catch. He leaned forward, his intention clear in the tilt of his head, the softening of his eyes.

At the last moment, Fenella chickened out and turned her head, so his lips landed on her cheek instead of her mouth. It was a reflex, an instinctive protection of a boundary she wasn't ready to cross yet, even as part of her yearned to do exactly that.

Din pulled back, no hint of frustration or disappointment on his face. "Goodnight, Fenella," he said. "Sleep well."

"Goodnight," she replied, her voice slightly unsteady. "I'll see you tomorrow?"

It came out as a question, uncertain in a way she rarely allowed herself to be.

"Sure. Do you want me to come with you to meet Atzil?"

The relief she felt made her weak at the knees. "I would love that."

"I'll pick you up at two-thirty so we can enjoy a leisurely stroll over to the bar."

"I'm looking forward to it."

He waited as she stepped inside, raising his hand in a final farewell before turning to walk away.

Fenella closed the door and leaned against it, her fingers rising to touch the spot on her cheek where his lips had been. The house was quiet, with Shira apparently still out for the evening.

Why had she turned away? Din had been nothing but respectful, patient, and attentive all day. He had shown no signs of pushing boundaries or expecting more than she was willing to give. Unlike most men she'd known, he seemed content to move at a snail's pace and let her set the terms of their interactions.

And yet, when the moment came, she had pulled back, some deep-seated instinct for self-preservation overriding the warmth that had been building between them all day.

Fenella walked through the dark house to her room, her thoughts churning. Fifty years she'd spent running, hiding, guarding herself against threats both real and imagined.

It was difficult to adjust to her new reality, slow down, and stop seeing everything and everyone as a threat.

18

KYRA

Kyra sat at the island, cradling a steaming mug of coffee between her palms as her daughter sliced fruit for their breakfast.

"Did Fenella call you last night after her date with Din?" Kyra asked, taking a careful sip of her hot coffee.

Jasmine shook her head, her knife moving rhythmically through a ripe, juicy mango. "Not a peep. I was expecting at least a text, but nothing. Must have gone either really well or catastrophically bad."

"I'm betting on well," Kyra said. "She was trying to hide her excitement, but I could see right through it. She's at least intrigued, and she's willing to give him a chance."

"Can you imagine?" Jasmine placed the sliced mango on two plates, then reached for a bunch of grapes. "Carrying a torch for someone for half a century? That's dedication."

"Or obsession," Kyra countered, then softened. "Though I think in Din's case, it's the romantic kind. He didn't even know she was alive, and yet he hadn't forgotten her."

Jasmine paused with a bunch of grapes hanging from her hand. "I escorted her to the café to meet him, and there were definitely sparks between them." She chuckled. "The fact that she let me style her hair and apply her makeup in preparation for the date is telling. She even agreed to borrow a dress from me."

Kyra laughed. "Did she complain the entire time and try to make it look like she was doing you a favor?"

"No. She was quiet and introspective." Jasmine finished plucking the grapes from the bunch and placed them on the plates.

"I hope it works out for them." Kyra speared a piece of mango with her fork. "After everything she has been through, Fenella deserves her happy ending."

"We all do," Jasmine said, settling onto the stool beside Kyra with her own plate. "But we already got ours."

Kyra smiled at her daughter. "So true. I have Max, I have you, I have my sisters and their children safe in the village. I've never imagined having even a fraction of such good fortune."

Jasmine nodded solemnly while chewing on a piece of fruit.

"Max traded some highly coveted concert tickets he had for a dinner reservation at Callie's, so Din could take Fenella somewhere nice," Kyra said. "Secretly, I hoped they would decline so Max and I could go."

Jasmine lifted an eyebrow. "That was very nice of him. Getting a reservation at Callie's is almost as difficult as getting one at *By Invitation Only*, which is another exclusive restaurant that is not located in the village but belongs to a clan member. I've only eaten at Callie's once, and that was with Brandon pulling strings." She popped a grape into her mouth. "There is no menu, and you get what you get, but the food is divine. If you get a chance to go, don't pass it up."

"Max promised to take me there sometime," Kyra said. "After all the excitement dies down."

"So, never?" Jasmine teased. "According to Kian, we only enjoy small breaks between one emergency and the next, and his advice is to take full advantage of them while they last."

Kyra laughed, the ease of it still sounding unfamiliar to her own ears. Laughter had been a rarity during her years with the resistance. "Well, at least we have a respite now."

"Not for long." Jasmine leveled a pair of eyes on Kyra that were an exact replica of hers. "We need to find the Clan Mother's husband."

That was the actual purpose of their meeting this morning, but Kyra couldn't let the opportunity to have breakfast with her daughter slip by. These quiet moments with Jasmine were precious beyond measure. Twenty-three years of her daughter's life had been stolen from her, and Kyra treasured even the simplest interaction.

"I've been thinking about what the Clan Mother said about my pendant." Kyra set down her fork. "That she thinks it's a key to finding her husband." She touched the amber stone at her throat. "I don't trust it as I used to. It failed me during the mission."

"You keep saying that, but I don't think it's fair. It has guided you well far more times than it failed you, which makes me think that maybe it wasn't wrong. Maybe there was a good reason for it not warning you against contacting Soraya first. Who knows what would have been the unintended consequences of that choice?"

"Or maybe it's just a piece of amber with some symbols etched on it, and I've been ascribing it powers it doesn't have."

Jasmine shook her head, pushed her plate aside, and leaned forward. "It's a conduit for your natural intuitive abilities. It's like a prism, a focus point that helps you tap into something that's already inside you."

Kyra nodded. "The Clan Mother said something similar."

Jasmine stood up and walked to a bookshelf. "It's similar to how I use this." She lifted what looked like a polished wooden stick about eight inches long. "This is my scrying stick, and it's just a piece of a fallen branch, but it helps me focus my energy when I'm trying to locate something or someone." Jasmine returned to her seat, holding the stick out in front of her. "It doesn't always work, but maybe it will cooperate now that I want to demonstrate how I use it."

She closed her eyes, her fingers wrapped loosely around the wooden implement. For a moment, nothing happened, and then Kyra noticed that the stick in Jasmine's hand began to vibrate, gently at first, then with increasing intensity until it looked like it would leap from her grasp.

It was pointing straight at Kyra, or rather, her pendant.

"Your pendant," Jasmine said. Then the stick abruptly stopped vibrating, and Jasmine blinked. "It confirmed that it's crucial to finding Khiann."

"What just happened?" Kyra asked. "How did you do that?"

"I asked my stick to point me in the direction of Khiann, and I held his image in my mind. It pointed at you and your pendant."

Kyra suppressed a shiver. The same thing had happened to Syssi when she'd asked for guidance to find Khiann. The vision had shown her Kyra.

What if Khiann had died after all, and she was his reincarnation?

That thought was beyond disturbing, and not just because Kyra couldn't imagine herself as a male. The Clan Mother would be devastated.

"What does Khiann look like?" she asked, afraid of hearing that she shared some physical characteristics with the god.

"Gorgeous like you'd expect a god to be. The Clan Mother has a portrait of him that she commissioned from a forensic artist who drew it from her descriptions."

"I would like to see it." Kyra's hand closed around the pendant. "If this thing has any mystical powers, it would help if I could do what you just did and hold Khiann's image in my head when I'm asking it to find him."

She could also see whether the image evoked any sense of familiarity.

Kyra sincerely hoped that it wouldn't.

"I'll ask Ell-rom to ask his sister for a copy. I still don't feel chummy enough with the goddess to approach her directly."

"Where is he?" Kyra asked. "Is he still in bed?"

"Oh no." Jasmine waved a dismissive hand. "He and Morelle are training this morning."

By now, Kyra knew better than to ask what kind of training. Jasmine just clammed up every time she asked.

Instead, she returned to the issue at hand. "You seem very proficient with that stick. How did you get that good?"

"Practice. Lots and lots of practice." Jasmine placed the stick on the counter, letting out a breath. "I had to learn fast when I was searching for the Kra-ell stasis pods in the Himalayas."

"You still didn't tell me how you found Ell-rom and Morelle." Kyra leaned forward. "How did the whole thing even start? You owe me that story."

"It's a really long one," Jasmine said with a smile. "And we should focus on doing what we set out to do. Practice first. But when we take a break, I promise to tell you all about it."

"I'm even more curious now," Kyra said. "But you're right. We should practice first." She touched her pendant again. "So, how do we start?"

"Let's try something simple first," Jasmine suggested. "I want you to clear your mind and focus on the pendant. Don't think about what you want it to do or how it might work. Just feel its presence against your skin."

Kyra nodded and closed her eyes.

She took a deep breath, then another, letting her awareness narrow to the spot where the amber rested against her sternum. It felt warm, as it often did, but not with the intense heat that signaled danger.

"Good," Jasmine said. "Now, I want you to think of something you've lost or misplaced. Nothing significant, just a small item."

Kyra thought for a moment. "My hair clip. The silver one. I had it at dinner yesterday, but I couldn't find it this morning."

It was a worthless trinket, but she liked how it looked, so perhaps it had some value that way.

"Perfect," Jasmine said. "Keep your eyes closed and picture the clip. Remember its details—the shape, the weight of it, the texture. Now, while holding that image, ask yourself where it is. Not out loud, just in your mind."

Kyra did as instructed, visualizing the silver clip with its delicate filigree pattern. As she mentally formed the question of its whereabouts, she felt the pendant grow slightly warmer. Not hot, not a warning, but a gentle pulse of heat like a heartbeat.

"It's warming up," she murmured.

"That's good. Now follow that feeling. Let it guide your thoughts."

Images flickered through Kyra's mind—the bathroom counter, the bedside table, the floor under the bed. None of them felt right. Then suddenly, she saw the pocket of the jeans she'd worn yesterday, folded and draped over a chair in the bedroom.

"The pocket of my jeans," she said, opening her

eyes. "Left front pocket. But that was nothing magical. I just focused and went over every possible place it could be until I figured out where I left it."

"That's the whole point." Jasmine smiled. "The pendant helped you focus your inner eye, so to speak."

It sounded like a bunch of nonsense to her, but right now, Jasmine was the authority on everything supernatural, so if she said it was the pendant that helped find the clip, Kyra was going to suspend her disbelief.

"How did it feel?" Jasmine asked. "Was it different from when the pendant warns you of danger?"

"It was more subtle." Kyra tried to articulate the difference. "When there's danger, it's like a sudden flare of heat. This was more like a gentle nudge in a certain direction."

"I think that's the key," Jasmine said. "The pendant reacts differently based on what you need from it. A warning is urgent, so it's intense. Finding something lost is less critical, so the response is gentler."

"But how would this help us find Khiann? I don't know where he is or even where to start looking for him. There is nothing for the pendant to focus on."

Jasmine picked up her scrying stick again, running her fingers along its smooth surface. "Maybe combining our abilities might help. My scrying is more targeted—I can search for specific things or people if I have a connection to them. Your pendant seems to respond to broader intuitions or dangers."

"What kind of connection would you need to find Khiann? Will his portrait help?"

"I doubt it. Ideally, I need something that belonged to him, or at least an object he touched, but I've already tried it with a piece of jewelry he'd gifted the Clan Mother and gotten nothing from it."

Kyra frowned, considering. "So, we're at a dead end?"

"We still have Syssi and her visions. She might give us another clue. Something clearer than what she's seen so far."

Jasmine handed the scrying stick to Kyra. "Here, hold this and see if you feel anything."

The moment Kyra's fingers wrapped around the wooden implement, she felt a strange resonance between it and her pendant. The amber stone grew warmer, and the stick seemed to vibrate ever so slightly in her grasp.

"They seem to be responding to each other," she said. "It's like they are saying hello through me because I'm touching them both at the same time."

Jasmine's eyes widened. "That's unusual. But since the stick is just a conduit for my powers, it might have absorbed some of them or is just responding to yours."

Before they could explore the phenomenon

further, both of their phones chimed simultaneously with incoming messages.

Kyra put the stick on the counter to check her message.

"It's from Bridget," she said, reading the text. "She wants us to come to the clinic at ten-thirty."

Jasmine checked her own phone and nodded. "I got the same message. Any idea what it's about?"

Shaking her head, Kyra glanced at the time on her phone. "That's in less than half an hour." She looked up at her daughter. "It's a five-minute walk to the clinic, so it's not like we need to rush. I'm just worried what it might be about."

"Either way, we should get ready." Jasmine dried her hands on a kitchen towel. "We'll continue this later. And I promised to tell you all about my adventures in Tibet and how it all started." She smiled. "Perhaps the preamble is even more exciting than the search itself. I was kidnapped and trafficked to a cartel boss along with Margo, who later became one of my best friends."

Kyra gaped at her daughter. "You can't just drop something like that on me and not tell me the rest."

Jasmine laughed. "Fine. I'll tell you on the way."

19

FENELLA

Fenella padded into the kitchen, rubbing sleep from her eyes. The aroma of fresh coffee and something sweet filled the air, making her stomach growl.

Shira stood at the stove, her flaming red curls piled atop her head in a messy bun that somehow looked artful rather than chaotic. Several loose tendrils framed her heart-shaped face, emphasizing her porcelain skin that was dotted with freckles.

So pretty, so perfect, but her flawless beauty no longer annoyed Fenella.

"Morning." Fenella made her way to the coffee pot. "That smells divine."

Shira turned, her face brightening with a smile that revealed perfect teeth. "I'm making French toast, and I was about to knock on your door to see if you wanted some."

"God, yes." Fenella poured herself a generous mug of coffee. "I'm absolutely famished, and that's strange given how much I ate last night at Callie's."

"How was it?" Shira asked.

Fenella took a long sip of coffee before answering, savoring the rich, dark flavor. "Fabulous. Callie's is great. I wish I could eat there every night and sample the different dishes she makes. Have you eaten there?"

Shira shook her head. "The waiting list is months long, and I'm terrible at planning ahead. I like doing things spontaneously." She chuckled. "Not a trait most would associate with a librarian, but I'm very different at work from who I am outside of it. How did you manage to get a reservation?"

"I didn't. Max did. He traded some highly coveted concert tickets for the reservations."

"That was nice of him." Shira cast Fenella a curious look. "Was it as a favor for you or for Din?"

"Both, I guess." Fenella sat on one of the barstools at the kitchen island. "He still feels guilty about what happened fifty years ago in Scotland."

"Oh, yeah?" Shira flipped the French toast, the golden-brown slices sizzling in the pan. "What happened?"

Fenella was surprised that there was anyone in the village who didn't know the story yet. The place was a hive of gossip, and rumors spread at the speed of light.

"It's a long story. The gist of it is that Din had a crush on me, but he was bashful, and Max, who was supposed to be Din's best friend, didn't realize how obsessed Din was with me and rushed to seduce me instead. In my defense, I had no idea that Din was besotted with me because he never made a move. Anyway, long story short, Max inadvertently induced my transition, and here I am today, trying to figure out what I have missed out on with Din."

Shira shook her head. "I'm missing a lot of puzzle pieces, but I get the picture." She transferred the French toast to two plates, adding a generous dusting of powdered sugar and a drizzle of maple syrup before sliding one plate in front of Fenella. "So that's what the date with Din was about? Checking out what you'd missed out on?"

Nodding, Fenella cut into the French toast. She hadn't intended to discuss Din with her roommate, whom she barely knew, but looking at Shira's eager, open face, she realized that she actually wanted to talk to someone about it.

Strange how quickly the human need for connection reasserted itself once safety was secured.

"He seems different than the guy I remember skulking at the bar I served drinks in." She took a bite of the toast, which was delicious—crisp on the outside, soft and custardy within. "He's more confident now, which is kind of absurd since he wasn't a kid back then. He's over five hundred years old."

Fenella shook her head. "I'm still trying to wrap my head around that number. Then again, I'm seventy-three, and I still feel as young as I look, just less naive and more dejected. The world sucks, you know."

Shira nodded, but her expression indicated that she disagreed.

Great, she was rooming with an optimist.

It wasn't that Fenella had anything against them, but it was even more heartbreaking to see them crashing on the shores of reality than those who had been expecting it.

The way she saw it, life sucked, bad things happened, and when something good came along once in a while, it was a fortunate and pleasant surprise rather than the expected norm.

Oh well, it wasn't her job to teach Shira that the world wasn't made of rainbows and unicorns. One day, she would discover how awful it was outside the village and the library where she worked.

Still, Fenella had to admit that the evening with Din had been one of those surprisingly pleasant, rare occurrences. Din had been attentive, with just a little bit of overbearing intensity, and he had been interested without asking intrusive questions.

The only thing that cast a shadow over their date was the almost-kiss at the door, which she regretted spoiling by chickening out at the last moment. Their date should have ended differently, and she intended to correct that today somehow.

"I don't remember Din," Shira said. "What does he look like?"

Tall, broad-shouldered, dark hair, intense blue eyes that seemed to see right through her. "He doesn't look like he belongs on the cover of a magazine, but he's good-looking in the football captain sort of way." She chuckled. "I haven't seen a bad-looking immortal yet, male or female. This village looks like a computer game with fake, pretty people with some aliens thrown in for interest."

"That's true," Shira said, her green eyes dancing with amusement. "We are blessed with pleasing features. When are you seeing Din again?"

"Today. He's coming with me to meet Atzil at the Hobbit Bar. I might have a job there."

"That would be brilliant! I've only been to the Hobbit once, and I loved it, but I need to warn you that it gets a little rowdy in there."

Fenella laughed. "I've tended bar in Scotland. Rowdy doesn't bother me."

Shira smiled. "I know what you're talking about. I was born in the new country, as we called it for the longest time, but I visit Scotland from time to time."

Fenella studied her roommate over the rim of her coffee mug. "Is it rude to ask how old you are?"

Shira tilted her head. "Normally, yes. I don't know why, but immortals are sensitive about their age, and most of us don't even celebrate birthdays.

But I'm still young, so I don't mind. I'm one hundred twenty-eight."

That explained a lot. Born into the clan's protection, Shira had never known the fear and desperation that had defined so much of Fenella's existence. She'd never had to run, to hide, to reinvent herself in strange countries with nothing but her wits to rely on. Never had to fight off predators, human or otherwise. Never had to make the kinds of choices that had kept Fenella awake at night, wondering what the purpose of it all was, and why God was punishing her to live endlessly like that.

"You're lucky," Fenella said.

Shira turned from the sink, soap suds clinging to her slender forearms. "I know," she said. "My mother keeps telling me that. According to her, it wasn't always easy for our community, and I'm lucky to grow up in the new country and all of its conveniences."

It was strange. Even though Fenella was technically younger at seventy-three, she felt ancient in comparison to Shira. The weight of her experiences had aged her. She'd been quite naive as a human, although she hadn't known that at the time, but after her transition she'd been forced to grow up fast, and the subsequent decades on the run had made her harder and more disillusioned.

"I'm not the girl Din knew fifty years ago," she said. "I'm not sure I even remember how to do this—

dating, relationships. Heck, I didn't even know how to do that then. It was all about having fun. I was young and carefree, and I was not looking for my forever guy. It feels like speaking a foreign language, and I can't find a good course to teach me about it."

"You'll learn," Shira said. "The language of love is universal, and it doesn't require translation earpieces. Just look at Jasmine and Ell-rom or Jade and Phinas. Their love crossed species. Yours only has to cross decades."

That sounded so reasonable, and yet it didn't quiet the unease in Fenella's gut.

"Maybe you are right," Fenella conceded, though she wasn't convinced.

The ability to speak the language of love, as Shira had put it, required a solid foundation and an unburdened heart. But those parts of her had been broken, perhaps beyond repair. The ability to trust, to allow someone close enough to hurt her—she wasn't sure those pieces could be reassembled.

"He waited a long time for you," Shira said. "That's patience and dedication."

"That's the part I don't understand." Fenella waved a hand. "Who carries a torch for that long? Especially for someone they barely knew and thought was probably gone?"

Shira shrugged. "Immortals have a different perspective on time. And maybe Din just couldn't find anyone else who evoked such strong feelings in him." She settled her luminous green eyes on Fenella. "Did he tell you about fated mates?"

A jolt that felt like an inner earthquake shook Fenella. Din hadn't mentioned it, but Jasmine, Kyra, and even Max had talked about that enough for her to know what it meant for immortals.

"Forgive me for sounding like a heretic, but I don't believe in all that Fates nonsense."

"Oh, it's real." Shira put the rag aside and came to sit next to Fenella at the counter. "Fated mates are real, and that might have been what Din felt for you all those years ago. He didn't know that you were a Dormant, so he couldn't understand the pull, but it would explain why he's never forgotten you and why he flew over here as soon as he heard that you'd been found. Don't you feel the same pull toward him?"

Before Fenella could formulate a response, her phone buzzed with an incoming text. She glanced at the screen, frowning.

"Everything okay?" Shira asked.

"It's Bridget," Fenella said. "She wants me to come to the clinic at ten-thirty."

Shira looked concerned. "Why?"

"I don't know," Fenella muttered, but a cold tendril of fear slithered through her stomach. "She didn't say."

What if Bridget had found something during her examination when Fenella first arrived at the keep?

She'd taken a lot of blood samples, and not all the results had been available immediately.

What if it was something the Doomer had done to her?

Something that was permanent damage or worse, a progressive disease that would undo her immortality and make her human again?

Fenella had been subjected to countless indignities and abuses during her captivity, most of which she didn't remember and others that she tried not to think about.

"It's probably just a follow-up to your initial screening," Shira said.

Fenella nodded, but the knot of anxiety didn't ease. "Yeah. You're probably right." She looked at the time on her phone. "I should shower and get dressed."

"Do you want me to walk with you to the clinic?" Shira offered. "I don't start work until noon."

The offer was unexpectedly touching. Fenella wasn't used to people looking out for her without wanting something in return.

"Thanks, but I'll be fine," she said, forcing a smile. "I know how to get to the clinic."

As she headed to the bathroom, Fenella tried to convince herself that she had nothing to worry about but failed.

The hot water of the shower did little to wash away her anxiety, and as she let it cascade over her back, her thoughts oscillated between Din and Bridget's summons.

Din's face appeared in her mind's eye—the way he'd looked at her when they'd said goodnight, the gentle press of his lips against her cheek when she'd turned at the last moment. Why had she done that?

Part of her had wanted that kiss, had been curious about what it would be like to be kissed by him. Yet something in her had pulled back, erected a barrier at the crucial moment.

Sighing, Fenella turned off the water and wrapped herself in a towel, studying her reflection in the foggy mirror. Her face was youthful, unmarked by the passage of time, but her eyes told a different story. They'd seen too much, those eyes.

Pushing those thoughts aside, she dried herself briskly and thought instead about meeting Atzil at the bar. That was something concrete she could latch on to that didn't require adjusting her feelings or anything complicated like that.

Bartending was simple. She knew how to do it, had done it countless times before, and she was good at it.

Once Fenella was dressed, she sat on the bed, pulled out her phone, and googled Din's name on a whim to distract herself. To her surprise, several hits came up—a university faculty page, publications in archaeology journals, a couple of articles about an excavation in Turkey that had made minor waves in academic circles.

Dinnean MacDougal, PhD. The formal name looked strange to her, almost like it belonged to someone else. The faculty photo showed him in a tweed jacket, looking scholarly and serious. It was hard to reconcile this academic figure with the immortal who had bared his fangs last night at the mention of avenging her.

She closed the browser, unsettled by the glimpse into Din's other life. He was established and respected in his field. He had a career, colleagues, and students who depended on him.

What was she bringing to the table?

A half-century of drifting, of survival, of running from shadows. No roots, no achievements, nothing to point to with pride except the bare fact of her continued existence.

The thought was sobering.

20

KYRA

As Kyra arrived at the clinic with Jasmine, she was surprised to see Fenella heading their way.

"Looks like we're not the only ones summoned." She nudged Jasmine and waved at Fenella, who quickened her pace when she saw them.

"You two got called in as well?" Fenella asked as she reached them.

Kyra nodded. "Any idea what this is about?"

Fenella shook her head. "Not a clue, and it's making me nervous. I keep thinking Bridget might have found something wrong with me, something bad that the fake Doomer doctor did to me."

Kyra's heart constricted as her own fear echoed Fenella's. She was very familiar with the lingering dread and the way it made her constantly brace for the next blow, the next revelation of damage.

"I doubt it's that," Jasmine said. "Otherwise, Bridget wouldn't have asked me to be here as well. I didn't suffer at the hands of that monster."

That made a lot of sense, but then Bridget could have thought that Kyra and Fenella would need emotional support, and that was why she'd included Jasmine in her summons.

Still, Fenella seemed to relax at this logic. "Good point."

"Only one way to find out." Kyra pushed open the clinic's door, and the three of them stepped into a bright waiting area.

Unlike most medical facilities, there was no receptionist gate-keeping access to the doctor. Instead, Bridget waved at them from a small office that was adjacent to the waiting room.

"Come on in, ladies," Bridget said, her slight Scottish accent lilting pleasantly. "Please, have a seat," she gestured at the chairs on the other side of her desk.

It was a bit crowded for the three of them in the tight space, but they weren't strangers, and rubbing elbows and thighs wasn't a problem.

"What's this about, doctor?" Kyra asked.

Bridget folded her hands in front of her. "As part of our standard protocol, we run genetic screenings on all new arrivals to the village. It helps us track family connections, the matrilineal being of utmost importance because of the taboo of inter-mating within the same maternal line."

Kyra's stomach twisted. "I hope we don't share a line with the Clan Mother."

If that was the case, she couldn't be with Max, and Fenella couldn't be with Din. Jasmine was probably fine with Ell-rom because he came from a different maternal line, and that was a relief.

"You don't," Bridget said. "But that was only one of the concerns behind the testing, and not just because of the need to eliminate the possibility that new members are genetically connected to the Clan Mother through some ancient ancestor. So far, we haven't had incidents like that, and frankly I don't anticipate them, but there is always a slight possibility of a lost member producing offspring. The other consideration is that, sometimes, people who join us discover that they are distant relatives of existing members."

Kyra let out a breath. "You had me worried for a moment there. If I were from the same maternal line as the Clan Mother, my relationship with Max would have been considered taboo."

"I can imagine." Bridget smiled reassuringly. "Perhaps I should have opened with that to save you the scare. Anyway, the reason I asked all three of you to meet me together is that something unexpected came up when I ran the tests on Fenella's samples. I repeated the analysis to be certain, and then I pulled samples we had on file for Kyra and Jasmine to compare." She paused, looking at each of them in turn, a smile tugging at the corners of her mouth. "The results are quite definitive. You three are related."

A stunned silence fell over them.

"Are you serious?" Fenella was the first to speak. "How is that even possible?"

Kyra wanted to know that as well. Fenella was from Scotland, and she was from Iran. She doubted that any of her ancestors had ever been to Scotland, let alone come from there. But then she didn't know much about her family and where they'd hailed from. Her sisters should know more, though, and she planned on asking them later.

Bridget tapped on her tablet, bringing up a series of diagrams. "It's a maternal connection. Let me explain the testing process so you understand what we're looking at."

She turned the tablet so they could all see the screen. "There are several ways we can analyze genetic relationships. Autosomal DNA tests can trace relationships back five to six generations on both sides of a family, but they have limitations. The random nature of DNA inheritance means that after about ten generations, only a small fraction of ancestors contribute directly to one's DNA, making precise relationship determinations difficult for distant relatives."

"But you sound quite certain about our connection," Kyra said.

"That's because I didn't just run autosomal tests," Bridget explained. "I also analyzed your mitochondrial DNA, or mtDNA. This is a special type of DNA that's passed only from mother to child, and only daughters can pass it on to their own children. It creates an unbroken matrilineal chain—from mother to daughter to granddaughter, and so on."

Fenella frowned. "I don't understand. My mother was Scottish. Kyra's family is Iranian. How could we possibly share matrilineal DNA?"

"That's the fascinating part," Bridget said, her eyes bright with excitement. "Mitochondrial DNA is remarkably stable over time. A person's mtDNA is likely to be identical to that of their direct maternal ancestor from many generations ago. Mutations are very rare, which is why mtDNA testing can trace matrilineal ancestry back thousands of years."

"So, you're saying we share a common female ancestor who could have lived hundreds of years ago?" Jasmine said.

Bridget nodded. "Based on the specific markers and haplogroup designation in your mtDNA, your shared maternal ancestor likely lived in what is now northern Iran or the Caucasus region, possibly around 700 to 800 years ago."

Kyra felt a strange tingling sensation, starting at the base of her neck and spreading through her body. Her family was growing, and the thought was overwhelming.

From a lone wolf, so to speak, to a clan of her own.

That was a fortune beyond measure.

"But how did my ancestor end up in Scotland?" Fenella asked, her voice uncharacteristically small.

"Human migration patterns are complex," Bridget said. "Trade routes, invasions, slavery, displacements—people have been moving across continents for millennia. The Mongol conquests, the Silk Road, later migrations to Europe—there are countless ways your maternal ancestor could have traveled from the Caucasus to Scotland."

Kyra was struggling to process the information. "So, Fenella is what—my distant cousin?"

"You are very distant cousins through your maternal lines," Bridget confirmed. "The exact degree of cousinship is difficult to determine without more genealogical information, but based on the mtDNA patterns, I'd estimate your common ancestor lived approximately twenty-five to thirty generations ago."

"That's incredible," Jasmine breathed. She turned to Fenella with a look of wonder. "No wonder we felt such a strong sense of connection when we met. Family recognizing family on some instinctual level."

Fenella seemed frozen in place, her expression a mix of disbelief, hope, and vulnerability that Kyra had never seen on her face before. "That's unbelievable," she finally said. "How reliable are the results of those tests?"

"The mtDNA match is definitive," Bridget said. "You three share a direct maternal ancestor."

Kyra watched as Fenella's carefully maintained composure began to crumble. Her lower lip trembled, and her eyes grew bright with unshed tears.

"That's incredible. After I turned immortal and was forced to leave my parents' home, I thought that I would never have a family I could actually interact with." Fenella wiped her eyes. "I couldn't let them see that I wasn't aging."

Kyra knew how it felt to discover that you were not alone in the world, and the emotion in Fenella's voice struck a chord. She reached over Jasmine's lap to take Fenella's hand. "You're part of our family now, and you are welcomed with love."

"Our family just keeps growing." Jasmine placed her hand over theirs. "First, I found Mom, then she found her sisters and nieces and nephews, and now we've found you."

A tear slipped down Fenella's cheek, followed by another. She made no move to wipe them away, staring at their joined hands as if they were something precious and fragile.

"I thought I would ask my sisters if anyone in our family history came from Scotland," Kyra said. "But given that our shared ancestress lived twenty-five generations ago, that's irrelevant."

"Your common ancestor was almost certainly from the Caucasus region," Bridget said. "Her descendants might have moved slowly westward over the generations."

"Still, it's quite amazing to think about," Jasmine said. "This woman who lived centuries ago, who probably never traveled more than a few miles from her home in her lifetime, has descendants scattered across the globe who've somehow found each other."

Fenella snorted. "The bloody universe does have a sense of humor after all. I've been running from place to place, never putting down roots anywhere, and it turns out I had family halfway across the globe."

"No wonder I was obsessed with freeing you," Kyra said. "My rebel friends thought that I was crazy for risking my life that way for a stranger."

Jasmine frowned. "Based on that logic, you should have felt something about the girls who were imprisoned in the same facility."

"They must have been brought in after I was captured." Kyra closed her hand over her pendant. "I was constantly drugged, and he took my pendant. I had no conduit for my intuition."

"Blood calls to blood," Bridget said. "I know this sounds very unscientific, but there's more to familial connections than we can explain with science alone."

21

FENELLA

"Bloody hell." Fenella looked up at the ceiling to contain the sniffles. "I'm not just part of the clan now. I'm part of an actual family. How am I supposed to ever leave this sodding place?"

Jasmine leaned away from her. "I didn't know that you had plans to leave."

Fenella shrugged. "I'm still making my mind up. The village is lovely, but it is claustrophobic. I need room to breathe." She sighed. "But I like having cousins." She reached for Jasmine's hand. "Even remote ones like you. Blood is blood, right?"

"Definitely," Kyra said. "And we take care of our own."

"Well, in this case," Fenella rose to her feet, pushing her chair back, "I think it's time for a group hug." She pulled Kyra and Jasmine to their feet and into a fierce embrace.

The three of them stood, arms wrapped around each other, foreheads touching, creating a circle of connection that felt ancient and new all at once. Fenella held back tears, but Jasmine had no qualms about shedding them openly.

Kyra, the quintessential warrior, somehow managed to remain dry-eyed.

For Fenella, the moment was surreal. Just weeks ago, she'd been alone, expecting to die in captivity with no one to miss her, let alone mourn her. Now here she was, embracing distant cousins she hadn't known existed and dating a guy who might be her fated mate.

"I still can't believe it," she murmured, her voice muffled against Kyra's shoulder. "I've spent most of my life drifting, and now I'm part of something. It's a strange feeling."

"Now you're stuck with us," Jasmine said with a watery laugh. "The ever-expanding Persian clan."

"Does this mean I have to learn Farsi?" Fenella pulled back to look at them both.

"Absolutely," Kyra deadpanned. "It's a family requirement, but since Jasmine doesn't speak it either, I think we will make do with the translation earpieces for the near future."

Bridget stood and collected her tablet. "I'll leave you three to process the good news."

"Are you okay?" Kyra asked Fenella after the physician left. "You look a little green."

"I do?" Fenella patted her cheeks.

Kyra laughed. "No, not really. Just a little dazed."

"Can you blame me? It changes everything and nothing," she said. "I'm still me, with all my baggage and complications. But knowing I have family, real blood family, feels like finding an anchor after drifting for decades."

"That's how I felt when I found Jasmine," Kyra said. "Or rather, when she found me. And then again, when I found out that the girls were my nieces, and again when I got my sisters and their kids out of Iran. It's like pieces of myself that had been missing were suddenly returned to me."

"I've always wanted a sister," Jasmine said with a smile. "But I'll settle for a cousin, even a ridiculously distant one who's technically older than me."

"Cheeky," Fenella said, but she was smiling too.

"We should tell the others," Kyra said. "My sisters will be thrilled. More family is always cause for celebration in our culture."

"God, what a day," Fenella sighed, running a hand through her hair. "First, I agree to go on another date with Din, then I find out I'm part of your family. What's next? Am I secretly a princess too?"

Jasmine laughed. "I wouldn't rule it out. Did I tell you about my quest for a prince and how I found Ell-rom, my real-life prince?"

Fenella shook her head.

"I promised Mom I would tell her the entire story, and you are welcome to join us. We can do it over coffee and pastries at the café."

"That's a great idea." Fenella glanced at the time on her phone. "Din is picking me up from Shira's place at two-thirty, but I have plenty of time until then."

With the café being right outside the clinic, it took about fifteen steps for them to find a table and sit down.

"The Clan Mother seems to think Fenella might help us find Khiann," Kyra said. "This blood connection might have something to do with it."

Fenella arched a brow. "How do you think I can help?"

"I don't know," Kyra admitted. "But the Clan Mother raised an important point. You and I were discovered together for a reason. She does not believe in coincidences, and frankly, I agree with her on that. What were the chances that you would be caught in that part of the globe by the same monster that caught me, and then we would be rescued together? And all of that happened after Syssi saw me in Tahav in a vision, although she could have seen you. We look similar enough for someone who doesn't know us to confuse us."

Fenella had no choice but to agree. The whole thing had fate's fingerprints all over it. "I don't have any paranormal talents other than a good sense for poker."

"Perhaps you haven't discovered them yet," Jasmine said.

Kyra nodded. "When Jasmine and I practiced with her scrying stick earlier, there was a resonance between the stick and my pendant. Maybe having a blood connection amplifies whatever abilities we have."

"You two share much more blood than I share with either of you." Fenella folded her arms over her chest. "I wish I had an ability, but if I did, don't you think I would've discovered it by now?"

"Your survival instincts, your gut feelings—those could be manifestations of the same intuitive abilities that my mother and I channel through the various tools we use. For me, it's the tarot cards and the scrying stick, and for my mother, it's the pendant."

Fenella looked skeptical. "I think you're reaching. I survived because I was careful and lucky, not because of some mystical power."

"Maybe," Kyra said. "But I've learned not to dismiss unusual connections too quickly. We will find out what your special talent is."

"Amanda needs to test you," Jasmine said.

Fenella didn't want to be tested or take part in experiments. She'd had enough of those to last her a lifetime, even as long as hers was supposed to be.

It was time to change the subject, and hopefully, Jasmine would forget about Amanda and the testing.

"I was promised a story," she said after Aliya had taken their orders.

Jasmine smiled. "Indeed." She leaned back in her chair. "It all started with a scumbag named Alberto…"

22

DIN

*D*in stared at his laptop screen, his eyes glazing over as he read through yet another student paper on Mesopotamian pottery styles. He had already graded fifteen essays that morning, and they were beginning to blur together in an endless stream of mildly plagiarized paragraphs and enthusiastic but uninformed theories about ancient civilizations.

"The distinctive red slip seen on vessels from the early fourth millennium BCE shows clear influence from neighboring regions..." he read, sighing as he marked another grammatical error, even though those would not affect the final grade he gave on the paper.

He wasn't an English teacher, but it was sad to see that the student struggled with basic writing skills despite being a third-year archaeology major.

He wasn't the exception either.

Din had promised his department chair that he wouldn't fall behind on grading during his absence, a commitment he now regretted. The last thing he wanted to do after reconnecting with Fenella was to immerse himself in undergraduate essays, but duty called, and five centuries of existence had taught him the value of honoring commitments.

The front door opened, and Din glanced up to see Thomas entering with a grocery bag in hand. His temporary roommate gave a casual nod of greeting as he headed toward the kitchen.

"I thought you'd be out with Fenella." Thomas set his bag on the counter.

Din stretched his arms overhead, feeling the satisfying crack of his spine after hours of hunching over his laptop. "I'm only picking her up at two-thirty, and until then, I have to grade these bloody papers."

"I admire your dedication," Thomas said. "Especially since you don't really need the job. Do you enjoy doing what you do?"

"I enjoy most of it, but not grading papers," Din admitted. "But if I fall behind now, I'll have twice the work when I return." He closed his laptop and stood, rolling his shoulders. "What about you? Don't you have work today?"

Thomas pulled a carton of eggs from his grocery bag, placing it in the refrigerator. "I'm going on a mission tonight, so my day is going to start at four o'clock for the briefing." He arranged a few other items in the fridge. "I'll probably be back by morning."

"Anything serious?" Din asked.

Thomas shrugged. "Routine stuff. Yet another trafficking cell to bust, and more victims to rescue. Nothing exciting."

"I'd say it is very exciting." Din leaned back in his chair and crossed his arms over his chest. "It must be heart-wrenching."

"Not nearly as bad as what the Avengers are doing. I'm very happy to be on the Savior teams."

Din frowned. "I'm not familiar with either designation. What's the difference?"

"The Saviors continue to do what we've been doing for a while, which is busting trafficking cells, rescuing the victims, and bringing them to the sanctuary for rehabilitation. The new Avengers division is in charge of busting pedophile rings. Imagine what they have to face."

Din shivered. "I prefer to be blissfully ignorant. Which one does Max serve on?"

"The Saviors, but right now he is in charge of the keep's dungeon and the collection of scumbags Kian keeps there. Don't ask me what's happening there because I don't know. I haven't been stationed in the dungeon for a while."

"I heard that the Doomer who tortured Kyra and Fenella is there, being interrogated."

Thomas nodded. "It's supposed to be confidential, but since you already know, there is no harm in my confirming that."

"Why is he still alive?" Din asked. "I'm sure they've had enough time to get every last bit of information out of him by now."

Thomas shrugged. "Don't ask me. As I said, I'm not part of that operation." Thomas closed the refrigerator door and turned to face Din with a mischievous glint in his eye, which didn't fit the conversation they'd just had. "So, how did it go with Fenella yesterday at Callie's?"

"Better than I expected. As I mentioned before, we're meeting again later today."

"A second date. That's promising."

"It's not exactly a date," Din clarified. "She's meeting with Atzil about a job at the Hobbit Bar, and I offered to go with her."

"Ah," Thomas nodded. "It's still a date or could turn into one."

Din leaned against the kitchen counter, crossing his arms. "I'm in no rush. I waited fifty years for her, I can wait as long as it takes."

Thomas gave him an approving nod. "Well, since I'll be out tonight, you'll have the place to yourself, and if you want, you could invite your lady for dinner."

Din shook his head, though he appreciated the thought. "We're not at that stage yet. Probably won't be for quite some time."

"Fair enough, but there aren't many options for eating out in the village." Thomas gave him a calculating look, walked over to the freezer, and opened it with a flourish. "Unless you want to dine with Fenella at the café with vending machine fare after hours, you might want to consider cooking her a meal here."

He gestured toward the freezer's contents—an impressive array of neatly stacked steaks, ribs, and other cuts of meat. "*Mi casa es su casa*, as they say. You can impress your lady with a home-cooked dinner."

Din peered into the freezer, considering Thomas's generous offer. He could grill a decent steak, and there was something appealing about the intimacy of a home-cooked meal.

"That's actually not a bad idea," he admitted. "I just hope she won't assume that I'm inviting her here to seduce her."

"Perhaps she'll hope you are." Thomas winked. "I do know a thing or two about wooing women." He pulled out a package of thick ribeye steaks. "These will do nicely. Pair them with some roasted potatoes, a salad, maybe a good bottle of red..." He placed the steaks on the counter. "No pressure, no audience, just good food and conversation."

Din could almost picture it—Fenella sitting across from him at the dining table, the soft glow of candles between them, the comfort of privacy that a public setting couldn't provide. Not for any hidden agenda, but simply for the chance to talk without constantly looking over their shoulders.

Then again, candles could send the wrong message, so maybe a simple meal at the kitchen counter would be better.

He nodded. "It would be nice to spend time with Fenella, get to know her better. For the first time, actually."

"That's as good a starting point as any." Thomas pointed to the steaks. "Consider it my contribution to the cause of romance. I don't have a large selection of wines in the bar, but there should be a couple of bottles to choose from, and as a former bartender, Fenella might appreciate fine whiskey. I have a few interesting brands."

"I owe you," Din said. "I'll get you a good bottle of whiskey and refill your freezer."

Thomas waved away his thanks. "Just doing my part in bringing fated mates together. The Clan Mother would approve."

"Fated mates?" Din laughed, setting the steaks to thaw on the counter. "I wouldn't go that far. I think you're getting a bit ahead of yourself."

It wasn't that the thought hadn't occurred to him,

but it was too early for that. He was too excited about the opportunity the Fates had given him to think clearly, but more importantly, Fenella wasn't ready to hear that.

"Perhaps," Thomas conceded, then glanced at his watch. "I should get some rest and relaxation before tonight's mission. I'll be out of your hair by the time you get back from Atzil's with Fenella."

"Appreciated," Din said.

As Thomas disappeared into his room, Din returned to his laptop to finish at least one more paper before meeting Fenella, but his mind kept wandering to his dinner plans.

It was just a simple meal between friends, right?

No, they were more than that, or at least, they had the potential to be.

He tried to focus on the student's essay on his screen, but it failed to capture his attention. Instead, his mind wandered to Fenella—the way she'd looked in that flowery sundress at the café, how her walls had seemed to lower slightly during dinner with Ingrid and Atzil, the softness in her eyes when they'd said goodnight.

And that almost-kiss...

Din had replayed that moment countless times in his mind. He'd leaned in, certain she wanted it too, only to have her turn at the last second, his lips finding her cheek instead of her mouth. But it hadn't felt like rejection—more like caution, a silent request for more time.

Time he was more than willing to give her.

For fifty years, he'd carried her memory with him, a ghost, a what-if that had never found resolution. He could be patient now that she was real and present in his life again. What were a few weeks or months more compared to the half-century he had already waited, without even realizing he had been in standby mode?

He couldn't have known that she'd appear like a phoenix from the ashes of his memories, perfect and immortal, and yet he'd kept thinking about her and comparing every woman he'd dated to her.

Closing his laptop, Din rose to his feet and walked over to the bathroom for a quick shower. As the hot water pounded him from three pulsating shower heads, he planned the dinner he was going to prepare. Nothing too elaborate—simplicity had its own charm. Thomas's menu was perfect, but he needed to check what vegetables were available.

Did Fenella have a sweet tooth? He couldn't recall. Perhaps some fruit and cheese to finish the meal would be safest, provided that Thomas had the stuff in his fridge.

Regrettably, the village didn't have a grocery store, and he didn't have time to make a shopping trip to the nearest supermarket.

Stepping out of the shower, Din wrapped a towel around his waist and confronted his reflection in the steamy mirror. Like most immortals, he looked good, and he had better tools now to court Fenella properly than he'd had fifty years ago.

Perhaps he'd needed to go through the heartbreak of losing her once to become the male she needed him to be. He'd been prideful, rigid, unwilling or unable to communicate his feelings, because he hadn't been trained to find and court love.

It had all been about the conquest and moving from one woman to the next.

If he had stayed the same, he would have been ill-equipped to handle the complexities of Fenella's trauma, her wariness, her hard-won independence.

He dressed carefully, choosing gray, slim-fitting jeans and a burgundy button-down shirt. It was similar to what he'd worn the day before, just in different colors. He'd noticed Fenella's appreciative glance and decided not to fix what wasn't broken. A touch of cologne—not too much—and he was nearly ready.

Back in the living room, Din was surprised to find Thomas emerging from his bedroom.

"That was a short rest," he said.

"I don't need much." Thomas gave him a quick once-over. "Heading out so soon?"

"In a few minutes," Din confirmed. "Any last-minute advice for dealing with a woman who could either kiss me or stab me, and I'm not sure which is more likely?"

Thomas laughed. "Just be yourself, the guy who carried a torch for fifty years, and not the professor with a stick up his arse."

Din raised an eyebrow. "I don't have a stick up my arse." Much less so now than he had when he'd first met Fenella, at least.

"It's just a figure of speech. But seriously, academia has a way of making people rigid and overly analytical. Fenella doesn't need someone to lecture her. She needs someone who sees her as she is now, not who she was or who you wish she could be."

Din nodded. "I'm actually less rigid now than I was back then, but I will remember your advice about not lecturing. It's a good one."

"I have my moments." Thomas smiled.

After getting his phone and wallet, Din tucked them into his back pockets, and as he headed for the door, he paused with his hand on the knob. "Be careful tonight."

Thomas nodded. "Always am." Then, a mischievous smile returned to his face. "Make a couple extra steaks and save them for me for when I get back, will you?"

"Count on it," Din promised, then stepped outside.

The village was quiet at this hour, with most residents either working or resting before their evening activities. Din walked at a leisurely pace, enjoying the serene beauty of the surroundings. The pathways were lined with flowering shrubs, their blooms adding splashes of color to the carefully maintained landscape.

As he walked, he rehearsed how he might suggest dinner to Fenella. If he were too casual, it might seem dismissive of the significance, but if he were too formal, she might feel pressured. He needed to find that delicate middle ground.

Perhaps after their meeting with Atzil, he could suggest dinner as a way to celebrate. He had no doubt that Atzil would hire her.

He could frame it as a practical alternative to the limited dining options in the village, rather than a romantic gesture.

Unless Fenella signaled that she wanted more.

Yeah, dream on.

Din shook his head at his own thoughts. He was overthinking this, analyzing it like one of his archaeological sites—layer by layer, looking for meaning in every fragment.

Thomas was right. Fenella didn't need that version of him.

She needed someone real, someone present, someone who could match her directness with his own.

As he neared Shira's house, a strange sense of calm settled over Din. Yesterday's nerves had largely dissipated, replaced by a quiet confidence. Not arrogance—never that—but the steady certainty that he was exactly where he was meant to be, doing exactly what he was meant to do.

23

FENELLA

On the way back from the clinic, Jasmine had insisted that Fenella and Kyra stop by her house and go *shopping* in her closet. Her excuse was that she needed to get rid of some of the old stuff to make room for new, but Fenella knew that her newly discovered cousin was just being generous.

Jasmine wanted Fenella to have nice things for her so-called dates with Din and for her job interview.

Still, Fenella wouldn't have taken anything if Jasmine hadn't threatened not to let her and Kyra walk out of the closet unless they were each carrying an armful of clothing.

Fenella had chosen the few items that Jasmine had claimed were too short or too small or just no longer wanted, and out of the pile she'd taken, she'd opted to wear a simple white blouse and a pair of dark jeans for her job interview.

As the doorbell rang, her heart gave a little jump, and she gave herself a final once-over before hurrying to answer it.

When she pulled the door open, she had to catch her breath.

Din stood on the doorstep looking like he'd stepped out of a fashion magazine. He wore slim-fitting gray jeans that accentuated his long legs, paired with a deep burgundy button-down shirt that accentuated the rich tones in his dark hair. The sleeves were rolled up to his elbows, revealing strong forearms, and he'd left the top button undone—just casual enough to make her wonder what lay beneath.

"Hello," he said, a slight smile playing at his lips. "Are you ready to go?"

"I am." She stepped outside and pulled the door closed behind her. "You look nice."

"Thank you." His gaze traveled over her with quiet appreciation. "You look lovely. Beautiful."

They fell into step alongside each other, their arms occasionally brushing as they walked. Fenella was bursting to share her news, the excitement fizzing inside her like champagne.

"You're in a good mood," Din observed. "You're practically bouncing."

"I've had an interesting morning," she said. "You'll

never believe what Bridget discovered when she ran genetic tests on the samples she took from me."

Din gave her a curious look. "Do tell."

"I'm related to Kyra and Jasmine." The words tumbled out in a rush. "We share the same maternal lineage—some ancestor from the Caucasus Mountains about seven or eight hundred years ago."

Din's eyebrows rose. "That explains why the three of you look alike. But it is unexpected."

"It's absolutely mad." She couldn't keep the smile off her face.

"Well, congratulations. Do you think it's a good family to be related to?" he asked, his tone teasing.

Fenella laughed, the sound bubbling up from somewhere deep inside her. "Who knows? Jasmine's an actress, Kyra's a rebel fighter, and both of them have these weird paranormal abilities they channel through strange objects." She waved a hand dismissively. "I have none of that. I'm the boring relative."

"I don't think so." Din's eyes crinkled at the corners. "I'd say that you are the most fascinating of the three."

"Thank you." She flipped her long hair over her shoulder. "I don't know if Bridget told the Clan Mother yet, but even before the revelation, the goddess thought it was significant that Kyra and I were found together. She told Kyra that it wasn't a coincidence and that it must mean that my help was needed to find Khiann. She thinks I should work with Kyra and Jasmine to look for him."

Din stopped walking, his expression shifting to something more somber. "Khiann is dead. He has been dead for over five thousand years."

She frowned. "The Clan Mother thinks that Khiann is in stasis, buried under the sands in the Arabian Desert."

Din shook his head. "According to clan lore, he was beheaded by Mortdh. I wasn't aware that assumption has changed."

"Well, apparently it has," Fenella said. "I don't know all the details of how and why, but it has something to do with Syssi's visions."

"Ah." He nodded. "That piece of information explains it. I'm surprised that the news hasn't made it to Scotland yet."

Fenella suddenly feared that she'd said too much. "Maybe I shouldn't have said anything about that, so please, don't tell anyone."

"I won't," he promised. "I'm happy to hear that there is a chance Khiann might be found. I've always felt sorry for the Clan Mother and how lonely she seemed despite her warm smiles and the love she showed all of us. Never finding a true love mate is sad but finding him and losing him is tragic."

She looked at Din from under lowered lashes. "You're a romantic, aren't you?"

He smiled. "Why do you say so?"

"Because only romantics believe in fated mates and all that crap."

He looked offended. "Fated mates are real, and you've met them. Kyra and Max, Jasmine and Ell-rom, Syssi and Kian, and many others. Those matings are unlike what you are familiar with from the human world. When immortals meet their one and only, they know. It's a connection that feels deep from day one. There's a recognition on a soul-deep level. It transcends physical attraction or compatibility—it's a matching of essences."

There was so much conviction in his voice, such passion, that Fenella didn't feel like she should say anything to dispute it. She hadn't expected this level of romanticism from him.

"That's a lovely sentiment," she said noncommittally.

"Just think about it. Jasmine and Ell-rom—two people from entirely different species, and yet Jasmine felt the pull of Ell-rom's soul across continents, and when they met, their souls recognized each other instantly. Do you think it was a coincidence? Just consider how incredibly improbable that was for them to find each other. Talk about star-crossed lovers."

"Well, when you put it like that, it's hard to argue with."

He looked relieved that she stopped trying to argue against the existence of fated mates. "I think there's a reason I couldn't forget you for fifty years," Din said, his eyes never leaving hers. "Why no other woman ever measured up, why I felt compelled to come running the moment I heard you'd been found."

Fenella looked away, her chest tight with emotions she wasn't ready to acknowledge. "That's a lovely sentiment," she repeated, trying to keep her voice light. "But fifty years is a long time to build something up in your imagination. The reality of me is bound to disappoint."

"I'm a historian and an archaeologist, Fenella," Din said. "I deal in facts and evidence, not imagination or wishful thinking. And the evidence is that despite having only met you briefly half a century ago, I've been unable to shake the connection I felt to you—even when I believed you were human and therefore lost to me forever."

His words resonated in a way that both thrilled and terrified her. Part of her wanted to believe, to surrender to the possibility that something cosmic and beautiful had drawn them together across time and space. But the skeptical part balked at the notion.

"I don't know if I can believe in destiny," she admitted. "Not after everything I've been through. Chaos rules. Trust me on that."

"I'm not asking you to believe just yet," Din said.

"It's okay to be skeptical. But just to be open to the possibility."

"I suppose I can suspend disbelief for the time being," she conceded.

Din's lips curved into a smile. "That's progress."

As they resumed their walk toward the bar, Fenella studied Din from the corner of her eye, trying to reconcile the passionate believer in cosmic love with the overly serious, scholarly guy she'd first taken him for.

"Does Max know that you are such a romantic?" she asked.

He laughed. "I don't think he does but given how hard and fast he fell for Kyra, I'd say that he's a romantic himself."

"Good point."

As they rounded a bend in the path, Fenella caught sight of their destination and stopped in her tracks, a delighted laugh escaping her. "Oh my God, it actually looks like a hobbit hole!"

The Hobbit Bar was built into the side of a gentle hill, its façade covered in lush grass and wildflowers. A perfectly round wooden door, painted a cheerful green, served as the entrance, with a brass knob positioned exactly in the center. Small round windows peeked out from the hillside, warm light glowing invitingly from within.

"I've never seen anything like it," Fenella said.

"I think it was Syssi's idea to build it, but I'm not sure."

As they neared the round door, Fenella's anticipation mounted. This place looked magical, a fantasy brought to life. For the first time since arriving in the village, she felt like she might actually put down roots here, at least for a little while.

Din pushed the door open, and they stepped into a space that could have been lifted directly from the pages of Tolkien's imagination. The doorway was low, forcing Din to duck slightly, though Fenella had no such issues with her height. Wooden beams crossed overhead, from which hung bundles of dried herbs and lanterns that cast a warm, golden glow throughout the space.

The bar itself was a masterpiece of craftsmanship—a curved, polished oak counter that stretched along one wall, with shelves behind it holding an impressive array of bottles. Barrels served as tables, each surrounded by wooden stools that were sized just a bit smaller than standard to maintain the illusion of this being an actual hobbit establishment.

Atzil was already there, wiping down the counter that didn't need wiping.

He looked up at them, a smile breaking across his face. "Welcome to my humble establishment," he said, setting aside his cloth and coming to greet them. "What do you think, Fenella?"

"It's bloody brilliant," she said honestly. "I've never seen anything like it."

"I wish it were my idea, but it wasn't. It was Syssi's. I only offered to run the place. We can seat about seventy when it's full, which it usually is on weekends." He gestured around the space. "It's not large, but that's part of the charm."

Fenella moved toward the bar, running her fingers along the polished wood. "The craftsmanship is incredible."

"Thank you," Atzil said.

As Atzil went on to describe the things he'd built to Din, Fenella only half-listened to their conversation, her attention captured by the bar setup. The bottles were arranged by type and quality, and the glassware was sparkling clean and organized by style. It was a bartender's dream—efficient, well-stocked, and aesthetically pleasing.

"Ready to show me what you can do?" Atzil asked.

She grinned, rolling up her sleeves. "Absolutely."

"The bar is fully stocked," Atzil said, moving behind the counter and gesturing for her to join him. "Surprise me with three different drinks—one classic, one modern, and one of your own creation."

Din settled onto a barstool. "This should be entertaining."

Fenella walked behind the bar, feeling at home in the familiar territory even though it had been ages since the last time she'd bartended. She surveyed the bottles, cataloging what was available in her mind. The selection was impressive—top-shelf spirits from around the world, artisanal bitters, and there were also fresh fruits and herbs in refrigerated drawers beneath the counter.

"Right then," she said, cracking her knuckles. "Let's start with a classic."

She selected a bottle of rye whiskey, vermouth, and Angostura bitters. Filling a mixing glass with ice, she added the spirits and bitters and then stirred with a long bar spoon. After straining the amber liquid into a chilled glass, she expressed an orange peel over the surface and rubbed it around the rim before dropping it in.

"Manhattan," she announced, sliding the glass toward Atzil. "Classic, elegant, and simple. Too many bartenders rush the stirring and end up with a watery mess."

Atzil lifted the glass, inhaling the aroma before taking a sip. His eyebrows rose appreciatively. "Perfect dilution and temperature."

Fenella was already moving on to her second creation. This time she reached for gin, St-Germain elderflower liqueur, fresh cucumber, lime juice, and mint. She combined the cucumber and mint, added ice and the liquid ingredients, shook vigorously, and double-strained into a tall glass, garnishing with a cucumber ribbon and a mint sprig.

"Garden Party," she said. "A modern take on the classic gin smash, with elderflower for complexity and cucumber for refreshing crispness."

Din accepted the glass, taking a sip. "That's remarkable," he said, looking impressed. "I'm not typically a gin drinker, but this is balanced and refreshing."

"For my final offering," Fenella said, feeling a surge of confidence, "a creation of my own."

She selected a bottle of mezcal, along with Aperol, yellow chartreuse, lime juice, and a house-made ginger syrup she'd discovered in the refrigerated drawer. She combined the ingredients in a shaker with ice, shook vigorously, and strained the resulting coral-colored liquid into a rocks glass over a large ice cube. A final spritz of orange blossom water and a dried lime wheel garnish completed the presentation.

"I call this The Rover," she said, sliding the glass toward Atzil. "Named after my wandering lifestyle. The smokiness of the mezcal represents the fires I've warmed myself by in strange places, the bitterness of Aperol is for the hard lessons learned, the chartreuse adds mystery, and the ginger and lime bring brightness and hope."

Atzil took a thoughtful sip, his eyes widening. "The balance is impeccable. The progression of flavors tells a story. First smoke and bitterness, then herbal complexity, finishing with bright, spicy notes." He took another sip, nodding to himself. "You're hired."

Fenella blinked. "Thank you. That was easy."

"You clearly know what you're doing, and you have both technical skill and creativity. What more could I ask for?" He glanced at Din. "Frankly, she's much better than I am."

A wave of pure joy washed over Fenella, so intense that she acted without thinking.

Darting around the bar and launching herself at Din, she threw her arms around his neck. He caught her automatically, his strong arms wrapping around her waist as she clung to him in a moment of uninhibited happiness.

"I got the job!" she exclaimed against his neck, breathing in his warm, masculine scent.

Din's arms tightened around her, his low chuckle reverberating through his chest. "Congratulations," he murmured against her hair. "Atzil would have been a fool to turn you down."

The reality of what she'd done suddenly hit her, and she pulled back, though Din's hands remained at her waist. His eyes had darkened, the blue now just a thin ring around dilated pupils. Their faces were inches apart, and for a moment, Fenella thought he might kiss her.

Instead, he gently set her back on her feet, his hands lingering for just a moment before releasing her.

Atzil cleared his throat. "I think this calls for a celebration drink," he said. "Give me a moment."

He disappeared into the back room, leaving Fenella and Din alone in the bar. Fenella felt heat rising to her cheeks.

"Sorry about that," she mumbled. "Got a bit carried away with excitement."

"I quite enjoyed it."

Before she could respond, Atzil returned with a bottle of champagne and three flutes. He popped the cork and poured three glasses.

"To a new, wonderful partnership," he said, raising his glass.

"Partnership," Fenella and Din echoed, clinking their glasses together.

The champagne was excellent—dry and crisp with delicate bubbles.

"I can open the bar every night for you," Fenella said to Atzil, excitement bubbling up again. "I can do seven in the evening until two in the morning, or eight to three."

Atzil nodded. "That sounds reasonable for weekdays, although Guardians returning from missions might arrive even later, and they are usually my best customers. We might need to adjust based on demand, but it's a good starting point. Are you sure you can handle it on your own, though?"

"The bar I worked at in Scotland was twice this size, if not more, and the clientele was much less well behaved. I can handle a crowd of polite immortals with one arm tied behind my back."

"I don't doubt it," Atzil said with a smile. "Having the bar open every night will be a welcome addition to village life. There aren't many evening entertainment options."

Fenella walked back behind the bar, already feeling at home there. She ran her hands along the wooden surface, imagining the pub bustling with people, glasses clinking, conversation flowing, and maybe even a few lewd Scottish ballads sung by drunk Scotsmen. She'd missed those.

"When do I start?" she asked.

"How about this Friday?" Atzil suggested. "We need to work together for a few days until you get a feeling for the place, and it will also give me time to spread the word that we're extending our hours and to stock up on supplies."

"Perfect," Fenella agreed. "I can use the next few days to familiarize myself with your inventory and come up with a signature cocktail menu. Is there a dress code?"

Atzil shook his head. "None."

"Awesome. I can't wait to start."

24

KYRA

After so many years of living in constant danger, the tree-lined pathways of the village felt wonderfully serene to Kyra. She felt almost guilty for enjoying it and braced for the moment the universe would reverse course and plunge her back into chaos.

For today, though, she decided to enjoy the wonderful news of discovering another relative in Fenella, no matter how distant the connection might be. In the human world, Fenella's children could marry the children born to her or her sisters or to Jasmine, but in the immortal world that was taboo, and knowing who belonged to which matrilineal genetic chain was of utmost importance.

It wasn't a worry for today or anytime in the near future, but she wanted to tell her sisters about Fenella.

Would they be as happy about it as she was?

Rationally, a relation going back twenty-five generations could apply to half the population of a small town or an entire tribe of people who didn't travel far.

Standing in front of Yasmin's door, she rang the bell and waited.

The door was opened by Essa, Yasmin's eldest son, his solemn eyes brightening at the sight of her.

"Aunt Kyra." He stepped back to let her in. "Maman is in the kitchen."

"Thank you." She touched his shoulder briefly as she passed. The boy seemed to have aged years since his father's death.

"Kyra!" Yasmin walked out of the kitchen, wiping her hands on a dishtowel and managing to produce a smile. "I was just making tea. Soraya and Rana should be here soon as well."

Kyra's gaze followed Essa as he stepped out through the living room sliding doors to the backyard, where his siblings were. He was such a great help to his mother.

"What about Parisa?" Kyra settled at the kitchen island while Yasmin busied herself with the kettle.

"She said she will be a little late. Vrog is with her boys, showing them how to use the self-teaching software."

Kyra nodded. "How are you holding up?"

Yasmin shrugged. "Doing my best to be there for

the kids. Essa is such a great help. I don't know what I would have done without him."

The children had all experienced trauma, and each was processing it differently. "I actually have some news to share with all of you, but I can start with you if you'd like."

Perhaps it would cheer Yasmin up to know Fenella was a cousin.

Yasmin's eyebrows lifted. "Good news, I hope? We could use more of that."

"I think so," Kyra said. "Turns out that we are related to Fenella. Our common ancestress lived seven to eight centuries ago, but since we stem from the same female line, immortals consider us closely related, meaning that Fenella's children cannot marry any of ours."

"That's amazing," Yasmin whispered. "The world is so much smaller than we imagine."

The front door opened, voices filled the entryway, and a few moments later, Soraya and Rana walked into the kitchen.

"Kyra has news," Yasmin said as the two joined them. "About Fenella."

Kyra repeated her explanation as her sisters settled around the island, watching their expressions shift from surprise to wonder.

"So, we have more family," Rana said. "Our clan grows larger."

"Do you know if she has any siblings?" Soraya asked.

"I think she has two brothers," Kyra said. "But they must be old by now. She's seventy-three. And since her brothers couldn't transmit the immortal gene to their children, there's no point in seeking them out. She was very happy to discover that we are related and she's not alone."

Yasmin discreetly wiped at her eyes, hoping no one would notice, but Kyra did. She also noticed her sister's hunched-over posture, which spoke of bone-deep exhaustion, the kind that sleep couldn't help.

"What's going on, Yasmin?" Kyra put her hand on her sister's back. "Don't hold everything inside, trying to be brave. You have four sisters who are here for you."

The façade cracked. "It's so difficult. The children have nightmares. Rohan calls for his father every night, and I don't know what to say anymore." She set down her cup. "Cyra has become withdrawn. I can't reach her."

"It will get better," Rana said, though her tone lacked conviction.

Yasmin sighed. "I know. But sometimes I look at all of them—five children who need so much from me, and I wonder if I'm strong enough."

"You are not alone," Kyra reminded her. "We're all here. The whole clan is here. But you need to tell us what you need us to do. We can't just guess or assume."

"It's just not the same without him," Yasmin whispered, a tear finally spilling over. "Javad knew how to make Essa laugh when he became too serious. He knew exactly how many kisses Cyra needed before she would sleep. He..." She broke off, wiping her cheek. "I'm sorry."

"Don't apologize for missing him," Soraya said, reaching to squeeze her sister's hand. "You're entitled to your grief."

A small, tense silence fell over the kitchen.

"We met with Vrog today," Soraya finally said, breaking the silence. "He's the guy who's in charge of homeschooling in the village. He's such a nice man. The girls liked him immediately. He's half Kra-ell, but you wouldn't know except for how tall and skinny he is."

Kyra welcomed the change of subject. "How did it go?"

"He's brilliant." Soraya's expression became animated. "He used to run a college preparatory high school in China for English-speaking students. Now he's adapting the curriculum for our children."

"He designed programs specifically for the Kra-ell children who came to the village with only minimal English, if any," Rana added. "He's going to modify it for Farsi speakers as well. We can all use it so we can stop relying on these translating earpieces."

"I almost forgot to mention," Soraya said. "In the meantime, the children will be using this fascinating AI language teaching program. Arezoo has taken to it immediately. She says it's like having a conversation with a real person."

Kyra's interest was piqued. "I'd love to see it. Is Arezoo here?"

"She and her sisters are in the backyard," Soraya said. "They are showing the program to Essa. I'll call her."

She walked to the living room, opened the sliding door, and called out. "Arezoo! Kyra wants to see the language teaching program."

A moment later, Arezoo stepped into the living room holding a laptop, her long, dark hair pulled back in a ponytail.

"Hi, Aunt Kyra," she greeted with a bright smile. "This thing is amazing." She put the laptop down on the countertop. "You don't need it because your English is already perfect, but I'm learning so fast that I can't believe it."

"Show me," Kyra encouraged.

Arezoo sat beside her at the island, taking her mother's seat, and pulled up a program with a colorful interface.

"It's designed to feel conversational," she explained, navigating the menus. "You can choose different topics or just have an open dialogue. The AI learns your speech patterns and adjusts to your level. You can even talk to it instead of typing."

She demonstrated, speaking a phrase in English with a slight accent. The program responded naturally, offering corrections while maintaining the flow of conversation.

"It's quite sophisticated." Kyra was impressed. "And you are right. You seem to be picking up the language quickly."

"It helps that I studied some of the basics in school," Arezoo said. "But yes, this makes it easier. It's nice to have someone to talk to besides my sisters and cousins." She smiled sheepishly. "Someone who is always polite and complimentary."

Kyra studied her niece. Despite being surrounded by family, Arezoo was isolated—a young woman in a strange place, cut off from her group of friends and everything else familiar except her immediate family.

"It's hard to adjust to a new place," she said. "Especially when there are not many people your age here. But as soon as you learn enough English, you can enroll in college and meet many young people."

Arezoo's eyes brightened. "They will allow me out of the village?"

Kyra nodded. "This is just a transitory period. In time, you'll get your own car, and you will be able to go shopping in Los Angeles, see movies, and do all the fun stuff people your age do. Naturally, you'll be under compulsion not to reveal anything about immortals, and you won't be able to invite anyone to your house, but that's a small price to pay for all that this community gives you."

Arezoo blanched. "How am I going to pay for all these things?"

"From what I understand, the clan pays tuition, and all the expenses associated with higher education, and I'm pretty sure you'll get a stipend as well, but I'm nearly as new to this place as you are, so I'm not clear on all the details yet."

"We each got a credit card," Rana said. "We can order anything we want, and it gets delivered to the keep, and from there the Guardians bring packages here. I asked what the limit on our spending was, and the man who delivered the cards laughed, saying that I shouldn't worry about it. If I overspend, I'll get a warning on my phone."

"Interesting." Kyra frowned. "I need to tell Jasmine that. She got a credit card as well, and she's still waiting for someone to tell her to stop using it. Evidently, she hasn't gone over the limit yet, or she would have gotten a notification."

Arezoo gaped at them. "Are you serious? I need to order more clothes, more shoes, makeup, a straightening iron." She pulled her ponytail over her shoulder. "See how frizzy this is? I need to tame it."

Kyra laughed. "Go for it, girl."

Soraya shook her head. "We are guests here, and I will not buy anything above what's absolutely necessary. I will get a job, and you and your sisters should get jobs as well to pay for your things. I heard that babysitters are in high demand."

Arezoo's face fell, but she didn't argue with her mother.

Kyra herself still wasn't sure about what she was supposed to do in the village. Everyone had to contribute in some way, but Max encouraged her to take her time and figure out what she wanted to do.

Working for Eva's detective agency appealed to her, but she wasn't ready to take on a full-time job that would take her away from the village for days. Her relationship with Max was too new to take breaks from, and she'd just found her daughter, her sisters, and even a new cousin.

Besides, Max was more than happy to cover any and all of her expenses, which were relatively modest. She hadn't ordered anything new since returning from the mission, and now that Jasmine had forced her to take a small portion of the clothing in her overstuffed closet, Kyra wouldn't need to go shopping anytime soon.

She could allow herself to be a little spoiled for a while. It was okay not to be one hundred percent self-reliant at all times.

"Everyone has been so nice here," Arezoo said. "But I still feel shy about asking people if they need a babysitter. They don't know whether they can trust me with their kids. It's an awkward situation. Besides, I mostly stay home with my mother, sisters, and cousins."

"I know someone you should meet," Kyra said. "You've met her, but you were so out of it when we were rescued that you probably forgot about her. Her name is Drova, and she was part of the rescue team that got us out of that hellhole. She's a Kra-ell, a bit younger than you, but she's a powerful compeller, which is why she's training to become a Guardian despite her young age."

Interest sparked in Arezoo's eyes, but then her shoulders slumped. "What could I possibly have in common with a girl like that? And a compeller? I don't want someone to take my will away from me."

"She won't do that because it's against the rules to use compulsion on anyone unless it's to save lives." Kyra put her hand on her niece's arm. "Give it a try. If the two of you don't hit it off, then you don't, but maybe you will."

"Fine," Arezoo agreed grudgingly. "How do I go about meeting the Kra-ell girl?"

"I could arrange something if you'd like."

Soraya cleared her throat. "I'm not sure that's a good idea."

"Why not?" Kyra asked.

"I'm concerned about the influence." Soraya folded her arms over her chest. "I don't want Arezoo to get ideas into her head about joining the Guardian training program."

"She can't even if she wanted to," Kyra said. "Not as long as she's still human."

Soraya let out a relieved breath. "That's good to know."

"I'm not a child, Maman," Arezoo bristled. "I'm nineteen, and I'm not easily influenced by anyone. Stop worrying about me."

Soraya's expression softened. "I know, sweetheart, but I can't help it. You will always be my baby even when you have babies of your own."

Feeling a little emotional over the tender exchange between mother and daughter, Kyra decided to shift the conversation to another area of interest. "Have you met any immortals who caught your eye?"

Arezoo blushed. "Not really. As I said, I rarely leave the house."

"That's for the best," Soraya interjected. "She's not ready to date yet. It's too soon."

Kyra raised an eyebrow at her sister. "She's nineteen, Soraya. And the sooner she transitions to immortality, the better. You know that."

A tense silence fell as mother and daughter exchanged looks. Finally, Soraya sighed. "Yes, I know. But everything has happened so quickly. Is it wrong to want a little more time before my daughter takes such an important step? It's not something that should be rushed, you know. She needs to find true love."

"I would like to meet more people," Arezoo said quietly. "I don't know how to do it here."

"The gym is a good place to socialize," Kyra suggested. "And you could ask about a part-time job at the café. It's where everyone gathers, so you'd get to know most of the village residents while working there."

Hope brightened Arezoo's face. "Great ideas, Aunt Kyra. I need to do both." She glanced at her mother. "You just said that I need to find a job."

Soraya looked conflicted but nodded. "We could inquire about a part-time position at the café, but schooling comes first."

"Of course," Arezoo agreed quickly, as though afraid her mother might change her mind.

25

DIN

As Din and Fenella left the Hobbit Bar, he could practically feel her energy crackling. Getting hired had been like an injection of vitality for her, and for the first time since reuniting with her, he saw glimpses of the girl he used to know fifty years ago—full of life, smiling, and optimistic about the future.

His heart reacted. He hadn't realized how much he'd missed the girl she used to be and discovering that she was still somewhere in there made him hopeful.

"I'm so excited to work in a place that looks like it was plucked straight out of Middle Earth." She gestured animatedly. "Atzil seems like a nice guy, and if I prove to him that I can run the place without him, he will allow me to open the pub all week long. It could be my little queendom."

"He's lucky to have found you. The drinks you made were impressive. I had no idea you were so talented."

Fenella tossed her hair over her shoulder with a casual flick. "There's a lot you don't know about me, professor." The teasing lilt in her voice sent a pleasant warmth through his body. "Besides, I'm willing to bet that you've never ordered anything other than whiskey. All of you guys back home regarded cocktails as girly."

He chuckled. "True. It's probably the same here, and I'm surprised that Atzil didn't mention it. But given the selection of whiskeys on display, I suspect I'm right."

He wanted to bring up his dinner plans, but he didn't know how to do it without seeming like he was setting up the stage for seduction.

"Speaking of displays," Fenella said, tapping her lips with her index finger. "If you have time, I'd love to see the artifacts in the glass pavilion again, but this time with an expert by my side." She cast him a brilliant smile. "Would you like that? Or are you adamant about enjoying your break from teaching and don't want to look at one more dusty display until you have to?"

He feigned a frown. "And miss an opportunity to impress you with my knowledge? No way. Besides, I gave the display only a cursory look when I passed by it."

"Really? Why's that?" she asked teasingly. "I would think that you'd be interested to see what the competition was doing."

He had no reason to pretend like she hadn't been the only thing on his mind when he'd arrived at the village. "I was preoccupied with thoughts of you and in a rush to see you."

"Oh, that's sweet." Fenella threaded her arm through his and leaned her head against his bicep.

He could have started singing love ballads at that moment if he hadn't been too embarrassed. Fenella was letting him in and already treating him like a boyfriend. He hadn't expected to make so much headway in such a short period of time.

It's happening fast because we are fated to be together, a small voice in his head whispered.

"Fair warning, though," he said. "Once I start talking about archeology and the mysteries it uncovers, it's hard to get me to stop."

"I'll take my chances."

The glass pavilion that served as the village's central hub was quiet at this hour. Sunset was nearing, so the light wasn't as strong as it was midday, but it was still enough to illuminate the display cases containing Kalugal's artifacts.

"Let's start with an overview and then go back to whatever catches your interest, sounds good?"

Fenella nodded. "Perfect."

"Most of these are from Egypt," Din said as they

strolled along the wall. "Though there are some pieces from Mesopotamia, the Indus Valley, and pre-Columbian America as well."

Fenella stopped next to a case that contained a collection of small figurines. "These don't resemble the typical Egyptian artifacts I've seen in museums."

He was surprised that she'd even visited museums during her travels. Perhaps they had more in common than he'd assumed.

"Good eye. They're from pre-dynastic Egypt, before the unification of Upper and Lower Egypt around the third millennium BCE. The mainstream archaeological community tends to focus on the more 'iconic' periods—the New Kingdom with its grand temples and Valley of the Kings, or the Old Kingdom with the Great Pyramids."

He approached the case, pointing to a small statuette of a woman with an elongated head. "These depictions have always fascinated me. Conventional archaeologists attribute the elongated skull to artistic license or perhaps depicting a binding practice, but given what I know about the gods, perhaps some had naturally elongated heads, or had been genetically altered to have them, because it was fashionable at the time. Or it could have been a depiction of another alien species that had visited Earth at some point."

"You think it actually depicts an alien?" Fenella raised an eyebrow.

She studied the figurine with renewed interest. "That makes more sense than head-binding, which is the orthodox explanation."

Din shrugged. "It would have been easier to accept the head-binding explanation if there were no other anomalies throughout ancient Egyptian art that the orthodox narrative struggles to explain."

He walked to the next case, which contained several tablets covered in hieroglyphics. "Take these, for instance. They're from Abydos, dating to the reign of Seti I, around 1290 BCE. But if you look closely at these cartouches, they contain symbols that don't appear in standard hieroglyphic lexicons. For years, Egyptologists dismissed them as either errors by the scribe or later additions. But the carving technique is identical to the rest of the tablet."

Fenella leaned closer. "What do they say?"

"They reference 'those who came from the sky,'" Din translated. "And describe technology that sounds remarkably like spacecraft. Of course, mainstream archaeology interprets this as purely mythological language."

"But you know better." There was a hint of wonder in Fenella's voice.

Din nodded. "Humans gave divine interpretation to what they couldn't grasp, and the gods took advantage of that, playing into the narrative. According to the Clan Mother, their motives were benevolent. They wanted humans to develop a just and moral society, and to a large degree, they succeeded in doing so in Sumer. It's only after their destruction that things started to deteriorate, and humanity devolved instead of evolving. Regrettably, history is full of such circles. People erroneously assume that things will always get better and that their children and grandchildren will have it better. They fail to internalize what they learned from history, if they learned anything at all." He smiled at her. "I don't want to sound like a snob, but most humans are ignorant, yet they believe they know everything they need to know. It's very frustrating, especially for someone like me who does his best to teach them better."

As they kept walking from one display case to the next, Din pointed out curiosities that conventional archaeology struggled to explain—perfectly drilled holes in granite that would challenge modern diamond-tipped tools, pictures of precisely cut stones weighing hundreds of tons moved and fitted with millimeter precision, and artwork depicting what appeared to be advanced technology.

"This is one of my favorites," Din said, stopping before what must have been a replica of a relief carving from the Temple of Hathor at Dendera. "It's commonly called the 'Dendera Light' because of its resemblance to a modern light bulb."

The carving showed what appeared to be an

elongated bulb with a filament-like snake inside, supported by what looked like a cable connected to a box.

"Egyptologists insist it's a symbolic representation of a lotus flower with mythological significance. But considering the practical-minded nature of Egyptian art, that explanation never satisfied me. The gods possessed advanced technology, much more advanced than this, but they might have imparted a more primitive version to their human subjects."

Fenella studied the carving with skeptical interest. "So, the ancient Egyptians had electricity?"

"This particular device likely used some chemical reaction to create light."

"The ancients probably thought it was magic. It's like Clarke's Third Law," Fenella mused. "Any sufficiently advanced technology is indistinguishable from magic."

Din looked at her with pleasant surprise. "Exactly. I didn't know that you were a science fiction fan."

She shrugged, a mischievous smile playing at her lips. "As we already established, there are many things you don't know about me. Back in the day, when I was a young lass, there were no smartphones with endless entertainment options at the tips of my fingers. More often than not, the only thing I had were books to keep the boredom at bay, and I developed a liking for science fiction. I liked stories that took me away from the drudgery of this world, but fantasy didn't appeal to me because it was all about sword fights and magic. Science fiction opened windows into different possibilities, and instead of relying on magic, it relied on science, and it was much easier for me to suspend my disbelief."

"I completely get why you didn't like fantasy. Given what you have been through, you've become too jaded and sarcastic to suspend disbelief. Science providing different realities is easier for you to accept."

Fenella's expression turned guarded. "It wasn't all bad. I saw the world, experienced different cultures, and learned to rely on myself."

Din wanted to say more—to apologize properly for his role in her difficult life, to promise he'd make it up to her somehow—but he sensed that she wouldn't appreciate that. In fact, he regretted even bringing it up and spoiling her mood. Fenella was a proud woman, and she didn't want him to think of her as a victim.

She was a fighter and a survivor, and he'd better remember that.

Moving along, he stopped next to a display case containing small mechanical objects. "These are known as the Baghdad Batteries, though these examples were actually found in Egypt. Conventional archaeology dates them to around 250 BCE, during the Parthian period."

The artifacts consisted of terracotta jars containing copper cylinders that housed iron rods, with evidence of an acidic residue inside.

"When reconstructed with grape juice or vinegar as an electrolyte, they produce electricity. Mainstream archaeologists debate their purpose—some suggest they were used for electroplating jewelry while others think they had medical applications."

"And what do you think?" Fenella asked.

"I think they're downgraded versions of much more sophisticated power sources the gods used. Over generations, the technology was simplified and its original purpose forgotten, but humans continued making them based on inherited knowledge."

"They were trying to copy what the gods had."

"Precisely," Din agreed. "Much of ancient human civilization consisted of imperfect attempts to replicate the gods' technology and customs."

As they moved to the next display, Din was hyper-aware of how close Fenella stood, the subtle floral scent of her hair when she leaned forward to examine an artifact, the animated way her hands moved as she asked questions. The academic discussion was comfortable territory for him but underneath ran a current of something more primal—an attraction that had only kept intensifying the more time he spent with her.

"What about this one?" Fenella pointed to a small stone object that resembled a modern airplane.

Din smiled. "Conventional archaeology classifies it as a bird figurine or perhaps a weathervane, but its aerodynamic properties are remarkable. A larger model of this was built and tested in wind tunnels, and it displays genuine lift."

"So, it's a model airplane?"

"More likely a glider, but I believe it represents a flying machine of some kind. There are similar artifacts from ancient Colombia and other pre-Columbian civilizations that exhibit the same aerodynamic features."

Fenella shook her head in amazement. "It's incredible how much evidence of the gods' existence is hiding in plain sight."

"Humans see what they expect to see. The paradigm of gradual technological evolution is so entrenched that evidence contradicting it is rationalized away or ignored entirely."

"That's what makes it possible for immortals to live among them undetected," Fenella said.

"Exactly," Din agreed. "The human mind is remarkably adept at filtering out what doesn't fit its understanding of reality."

"Have you heard of the Piri Reis map?"

Fenella shook her head.

"It was created by an Ottoman admiral in the sixteenth century. What makes it extraordinary is that it shows the coastline of Antarctica without ice—something that shouldn't have been possible, as humans didn't discover Antarctica until the nineteenth century. Its coastline beneath the ice wasn't mapped until much later, using modern technology."

Fenella frowned. "Did it match?"

Din nodded. "The admiral claimed that he compiled the map from older sources, including some dating back to Alexander the Great's time, but I believe the ultimate source was the gods, who had aerial views of the earth and mapped it completely. That knowledge was preserved in ancient libraries and charts, but it was fragmented and degraded."

"So, the gods had satellite imagery?"

Din nodded. "Not only that, but carvings were also found in Sumer that look a lot like today's satellites. The technology was probably a little different, but the purpose was likely the same."

As the sunlight began to fade, casting longer shadows through the pavilion, Din realized they'd spent longer there than he'd expected. Fenella didn't look bored, for which he was thankful, but soon the place would become completely dark, and they needed to get home.

"I've been talking your ears off." He cast her a sheepish smile. "You should have stopped me."

"I enjoyed every moment." She took his hand, which sent a jolt of electricity through him.

It was time to mention dinner.

"Do you like ribeye steaks?" he asked.

She laughed. "Who doesn't? Why? Are you offering to cook some for me?"

Wow, that was much easier than he'd expected. Fenella had practically invited herself to dinner. Then again, she probably assumed that Thomas would be there. He needed to tell her they would be alone and allow her to bow out if she wanted.

"Thomas is out on a mission tonight, and he very generously offered the use of his kitchen and some excellent steaks from his freezer. I could cook for you, if you'd like."

"I'd like that very much." She offered him a bright smile. "Dinner sounds lovely, but do you actually know how to cook, or is this going to be an experiment?"

Din laughed, the tension draining from his shoulders. "I can manage a decent steak and some sides."

"Well then, Professor MacDougal," she said, the use of his formal name sending an unexpected thrill through him, "lead the way to this promised feast."

26

KYRA

Kyra pulled out her phone and glanced at the time. "It's getting late. Do you know how long it will take for Vrog to be done with Parisa's boys?"

Max should be getting home any moment now, and the tension in the invisible thread connecting them was slowly growing taut. She kept busy during the days he worked at the keep, but any separation that was longer than a few hours was difficult. She'd even offered to join him in the dungeon, but he'd refused, saying that confidential stuff was happening and only Guardians were allowed there. Kian had had to clear her previous visit to the dungeon, and there was no reason for her to be there again.

He was probably trying to protect her from the ugliness of his job, but she'd seen enough during her lifetime to harden her soul and not let things like that get to her.

Soraya shook her head. "Vrog doesn't work with a timetable. He takes as long as each child needs."

"That's commendable," Kyra murmured.

The sound of small feet in the hallway drew her attention, and a moment later Cyra appeared in the kitchen, her dark curls tousled from sleep, clutching a well-worn stuffed rabbit. She spotted Kyra and hesitated, her expression turning shy.

"Hello, little one," Kyra said softly. "Did you have a good nap?"

Cyra didn't answer, instead looking to her mother with solemn eyes.

"Come here, *habibti*," Yasmin said, opening her arms.

The child crossed over to her and climbed into her lap, burying her face against her mother's shoulder.

Yasmin stroked her daughter's hair with a concerned expression. "She's been like this since we met the Clan Mother," she said to Kyra. "Withdrawn, quiet. Not like herself at all."

"Children process things differently, I guess." Kyra watched the little girl. "I can't claim authority on the subject. I don't remember Jasmine's childhood."

She yearned to take the little girl and clutch her to her own breast, but Cyra needed her mother, and she wouldn't appreciate a needy aunt taking her away from that soft bosom.

"Is something bothering you, sweetie?" Kyra asked.

The girl burrowed even deeper into Yasmin's shirt, hiding her face with the stuffed bunny.

"She sometimes gets like this. It happened even before…" Yasmin swallowed. "I think she has bad dreams but refuses to talk about them."

Kyra's gut twisted. Javad had been a good father and husband, and his kids loved him, so suspecting him of having done anything inappropriate was out of the question. But little Cyra's uncles hadn't been paradigms of male morality, and Kyra had heard her share of child abuse stories that involved relatives and were perpetrated against children as young as Cyra and even younger.

She moved closer, kneeling to put herself at eye level with the child. "Hello, Cyra. Do you remember me? I'm your Aunt Kyra."

The girl nodded, peeking out from her mother's shoulder with wide, dark eyes.

"Do you know that I'm a mighty warrior?"

The girl shook her head.

"Well, I am, and I will not let anyone hurt you. I promise. Do you believe me?"

Cyra looked at her from under her long, dark lashes, with eyes that were oddly penetrating for someone so young. Then she nodded.

"So, if there is anything that's bothering you, if anyone has done something bad to you or even made you uncomfortable, you can tell me, and I will make sure that it never happens again."

Unsurprisingly, Yasmin looked troubled by what Kyra was implying, but she didn't say anything.

Cyra glanced at her mother, who nodded encouragingly. "It's alright, *habibti*. You can tell Aunt Kyra anything."

"I have a spooky dream." Cyra's voice was barely above a whisper. "I see a beautiful doll, but it's not a girl, it's a man doll. I've never seen a man doll before."

"There are man dolls in America," Kyra said, keeping her tone light though her interest sharpened. "I can get you a few to choose from."

"There are?" Cyra lifted her head. "It was a very beautiful man, with glowing skin like the pretty lady." She paused, her small brow furrowing. "He was sleeping. He was so alone and lost."

A chill ran down Kyra's spine. Was *sleeping* Cyra's way to say dead?

"He was sleeping, but not sleeping," the girl said as if she'd read Kyra's mind. "He's so alone."

Yasmin looked alarmed, pulling Cyra closer. "It's just a strange dream, sweetness. Don't be frightened."

"I'm not afraid," Cyra said. "I'm sad for the beautiful man. We need to find him so the pretty lady can play with him. She misses him so much."

Kyra felt the warm weight of the pendant against her skin. This wasn't just a child's dream. Somehow, this four-year-old girl must have tapped into Annani's consciousness and seen Khiann through the goddess's loving eyes.

Given Jasmine's descriptions of a body in stasis after such a long time, Khiann was a little more than a skeleton now, not the beautiful man doll that Cyra had seen.

The other adults in the room had gone quiet, watching the exchange with varying degrees of concern and confusion.

"Thank you for telling me, Cyra," Kyra said, touching the child's hand gently. "That was very brave of you."

Cyra studied her face. "Can you find him, Aunt Kyra?"

"I'm going to try," Kyra promised. "Would it be okay if I asked you more about your dream another time? Maybe you could even draw a picture of what you saw?"

A child's drawing was not going to help them with more information about Khiann's whereabouts, but perhaps it would help Cyra process the dream.

The girl nodded, a flicker of her usual brightness returning to her eyes.

"Just one more question. How long have you been dreaming about the beautiful man?"

"After meeting the pretty lady."

So, Kyra's suspicion was probably right, and Cyra had the ability to tap into the consciousness of those around her. That would explain her earlier bouts of moodiness, as she might have been affected by others.

Still, Kyra wasn't an expert by any means, and her assessment might be completely wrong.

"Go wash your hands for dinner," Yasmin said, kissing the top of her daughter's head before setting her down. "Ask Essa to help you reach the sink."

As the child scampered off, Yasmin turned to Kyra with worried eyes. "What was that about?"

"I think your little girl has psychic abilities, which isn't really surprising given that Jasmine and I have a touch of those as well. I think that she tapped into the Clan Mother's mind. The goddess believes her husband, Khiann, is in stasis somewhere in the Arabian Desert, not dead as most believe, and she wants me and Jasmine and maybe even Fenella to find him."

"And you think my four-year-old daughter somehow saw him through the goddess's mind eye?" Yasmin sounded incredulous.

Kyra nodded. "It also might not have been the first time since you said she used to get moody like that on other occasions. You have to tell Vanessa about it and have her talk with Cyra. A young child like her must have difficulty processing adult issues she inadvertently gets exposed to by touching people's minds."

Yasmin shivered. "That's terrible. How do I shield her from that?"

"I wish I knew." Kyra sighed. "I hope Vanessa does."

"This has been just a bizarre day," Rana muttered. "First, we learn that we're distantly related to a Scottish bartender, and now my niece is having visions of an ancient god? What's next?"

Before Kyra could respond, the doorbell rang, and a moment later, Parisa walked in with her four boys and Max in tow.

Kyra's heartbeat accelerated, and a smile bloomed on her face. She rose to her feet and pulled Max into a brief embrace. "I'm sorry I wasn't home when you got there."

"I didn't get there. I met Parisa on the way, and she told me you were here, so I joined."

"Excellent. I'm glad that you did," Yasmin said. "We are about to have dinner."

He leaned in to kiss her cheek. "I don't want to impose. Kyra and I should leave."

"Don't you dare." Yasmin cast him a mock glare. "Family doesn't impose, and the more the merrier."

He flashed her one of his charming smiles. "Okay, if you insist."

"I do." Yasmin motioned for Soraya and Rana to join her in the kitchen, and the three started a well-coordinated dance of preparing a quick dinner for their not-so-small clan.

"How did you boys do with Vrog?" Kyra asked.

"He's great," Tyrus said. "I like studying on my own much more than going to school and listening to boring teachers."

Zaden seconded his brother's opinion with a nod. "Where is Essa?" he asked.

"Helping the little ones wash up for dinner," Yasmin said.

As the four boys headed down the corridor to search for their older cousin, Parisa turned to Kyra. "I'm worried about the older boys and their induction ceremonies. How exactly is it going to happen, and who is going to organize it?"

"I have no clue." Kyra shifted her gaze to Max. "Can you shed some light on that for us?"

"Certainly." He sat on one of the stools and pulled Kyra to him to sit on his knees as if it was the most natural thing to do. "But maybe we should do that after dinner with the boys present. I'm sure that they are just as curious as you are."

27

ANNANI

Annani made subtle adjustments to the flower arrangements Ogidu had set out and then put her sunglasses on before stepping out on the terrace.

Her backyard faced north, so the afternoon light wasn't harsh, but she still needed to protect her eyes. It was a small sacrifice to make to have these joyous occasions outside so she could enjoy the fresh air with several of her favorite ladies.

When Bridget had told her the marvelous news of her pregnancy, asking the Clan Mother to keep it confidential until she could share it with others herself, Annani had instantly insisted on hosting a small gathering.

A new life was always cause for celebration in her clan, every birth cherished with reverence.

Her faithful Odu appeared in the doorway,

checking as always to make sure that she was wearing her protective eyewear and wasn't too chilled or too warm. Satisfied with what he saw, he offered her a small bow.

"The fruit platters and the pastry selections are ready. The champagne bottles, regular and non-alcoholic, are chilling in their buckets. Should I arrange everything on the outdoor dining table?"

"Yes, please." She waved her hand. "Just cover everything with nets so the pesky bugs don't feast on it."

"I have found a better solution to the bug problem, Clan Mother." The smug look on his face was so human that it was startling.

"What is it?" she asked.

"It is called Fly Fans. They look like miniature windmills and are placed near food items."

"What a brilliant little invention. Does it create strong enough wind for the insects to be effectively repelled?"

"That is just one of the ways it deflects them." Ogidu blinked, which usually indicated that he was accessing information. "Their blades are made of soft plastic, so they are safe around children, but they are printed with metallic stripes, and as the blades spin, the stripes bend and scatter sunlight, creating a strobing effect to the flies' compound eyes. They steer away from such confusing visual signals."

"Ingenious." She smiled. "I love technology and inventions. They make life so much better for everyone. I commend you for your initiative to find those little windmills."

"Thank you." He dipped his head, his smile brighter than usual at the praise.

Annani sat down on one of the comfortable outdoor chairs and adjusted the folds of her flowing gown of pale aquamarine silk over her legs. She loved arranging small, intimate gatherings at her village home. She also loved the grand celebrations that included the entire clan, but there was something special about these smaller moments.

When the doorbell rang, Annani straightened and turned toward the glass doors that led to the living room.

Ogidu answered the door, and Annani smiled as she saw her eldest daughter enter.

"Alena, my dear girl." Annani rose to embrace her, breathing in her daughter's familiar scent. "You're the first. Punctual as always."

"I was curious." Alena returned the embrace. "You refused to tell me what this gathering is about. Can you tell me now?"

"Not yet, child. We need to wait for everyone else to arrive."

Alena chuckled. "You are the only one who calls me child. I kind of like it. Makes me feel less ancient." She settled into one of the cushioned chairs, her gaze taking in the spread that Ogidu and Oridu were still busy arranging. "What are those?" She pointed at the windmills.

"Fly repellents. Such a simple and yet ingenious invention."

Alena nodded. "I've seen something similar at Geraldine's. They were a little fancier, so I thought they were decorations."

"How is Geraldine doing? I have not seen her in a while."

"Fussing over little E.T., pestering Cassandra and Darlene to get pregnant because she wants more grandchildren, chasing Roni around with home-cooked food trying to fatten him up."

Annani laughed. "Sounds like she is having fun. And how is my sweet little Evander Tellesious?"

Everyone called Alena's fourteenth child E.T., and Annani wondered if the nickname would stick with him to adulthood. It was cute for a baby, but Evander Tellesious sounded majestic, and she liked it better.

"Growing up too fast," Alena said.

"He is only two months old."

"It is still too fast. I enjoy every moment with him. Orion wants more children, and I'm not opposed to the idea. I might ask Merlin to design potions for me, but I'll wait to see if it doesn't happen naturally. With how fertile I am, it just might."

Annani nodded. "I will beseech the Fates to grant you your wish." She shook her head. "Or perhaps I should not. We do not want to be greedy."

"I don't think wanting more children qualifies as greedy, no matter how many I have. Each child is a blessing, and I'm not taking anything from anyone else."

"True," Annani conceded. "Still, in many cultures, people get very superstitious about fertility, afraid it will be jinxed by those who are not similarly blessed."

The door chimed again, and a moment later, the terrace filled with Annani's guests. Amanda arrived with little Evie, the girl babbling happily as Annani snatched her from her daughter's arms.

"It is Nana's time to cuddle sweet Evie." She kissed her granddaughter's cheek.

"Nana." Evie reciprocated by planting a slobbery one on Annani's cheek.

Ella and Vivian arrived with the two nurses, Hildegard and Gertrude, who probably suspected why they'd been invited but kept their boss's secret close to their chests.

Morelle was next, and Syssi came shortly after.

"Sorry for being late," Syssi said. "Allegra was fussy about the dress she insisted on wearing to the playground, and I had to put my foot down because Kian could not handle her tantrum. If I left him to it, he would have allowed her to sit in the sandbox in a tulle dress and patent Mary Janes."

"What did you end up dressing her in?" Amanda asked.

"Jean coveralls. She was so sulky that I'm afraid she won't have any fun in the sandbox and will pout the whole time." Syssi sighed. "But I can't give in to her tantrums over outfits. She will never stop if I do."

"That is the trouble with strong-willed children," Annani said. "You have to walk a razor-thin line between allowing them room to grow and flourish while still providing guidance and maintaining authority."

A discussion about boundaries continued for a few minutes until the doorbell chimed again, announcing the guest of honor.

Bridget, usually the epitome of self-assurance, looked a little nervous as she slipped onto the terrace.

"Good afternoon, Clan Mother." The doctor dipped her head. "Thank you for hosting this gathering for me."

"You are most welcome." Annani inclined her head in return. "The stage is yours, Bridget."

The doctor turned to the other guests. "Hello, everyone. I know you're curious about why you are gathered here today, so without further ado, here it is. Turner and I have been blessed. I'm pregnant."

For a heartbeat, there was silence as the news

registered, and then the terrace erupted with exclamations of joy. Alena was the first to rise and embrace Bridget, followed quickly by the others.

"How wonderful!"

"When are you due?"

"How is Turner handling the news?"

"Do you know if it's a boy or girl yet?"

The questions came from all directions, and Bridget laughed, holding up her hands. "One at a time, please! I'm about eight weeks along, so it's very early days. Turner is over the moon—not that anyone but me can notice anything different about him. And no, we don't know the sex yet, though I know that Turner is hoping for a daughter."

"Does Julian know?" Ella asked.

Bridget nodded. "I told him this morning, the same time I told the Clan Mother, and I asked both to keep it a secret so I could tell you all myself."

"This calls for a toast," Annani said, lifting her glass and signaling to her Odus to distribute the champagne flutes. When it was done, and everyone held a glass, she continued, "To new life, to the growth of our clan, and to Bridget and Turner's joy. May this child be blessed with health, wisdom, and the love of our entire community."

"Hear, hear, and amen," came the chorus of voices as glasses clinked.

"I guessed it," Gertrude said with a knowing smile. "I haven't seen you so happy and glowing since you were pregnant with Julian. Why did you wait to tell us?"

Bridget shrugged. "I guess I wanted to make sure that it holds. You know how it is with pregnancies this early. Some are lost."

Gertrude nodded. "Better not jinx it."

Amanda settled beside her, reaching for Evie's hand. "Do you want to come to mommy, sweetie?"

Evie shook her head. "Nana."

"Traitor," Amanda murmured under her breath. "She likes you better than me, her own mother."

"That is the superpower of grandmothers." Annani kissed the top of Evie's head. "We have the privilege of always being nice, never raising our voices, and leaving all the parenting to our daughters and sons."

"The clan is growing," Syssi said. "With Kyra's extended family joining us, we've added quite a number of members in a short time."

"Have you met all of Kyra's family yet?" Amanda asked Annani.

"Yes, they came to visit me the other day. Lovely women, and the children are delightful. One of them, the little one named Cyra, was particularly drawn to me. She climbed right into my lap without hesitation. Naturally, I was delighted."

"Speaking of Kyra's family," Bridget said. "I have more good news that I almost forgot about in all the excitement. Turns out that Fenella is related to them.

They share a maternal ancestor from many generations back. It's quite remarkable when you think about it, this family that was spread across continents, finding each other under such improbable circumstances."

"The Fates at work, no doubt," Amanda said.

"Indeed," Annani agreed.

Bridget had informed her right after getting the genetic test results, so it was not a surprise for her. In fact, it had not come as such a big surprise at all since she had sensed that there was a connection between the three women.

"Actually, I intended to discuss something with you about Fenella." She turned to look at Amanda. "I believe that she was found along with Kyra for a reason, and that she might have an ability that will contribute to the effort of finding my Khiann. She is not aware of having any paranormal talents, but perhaps you should test her."

"Of course," Amanda said. "But Fenella is a little busy now, with Din coming to see her and applying for a job at the Hobbit Bar."

"I am sure she can find a few hours to get tested." Annani transferred Evie to her mother. "I am glad to hear that things are working out for her. She seemed a little lost when I saw her."

28

SYSSI

"I need a word with you." Annani motioned for Syssi to follow her inside the house after most of the guests had left.

Syssi had been expecting that, and she had already planned on summoning another vision about Khiann.

"I am worried about Queen Ani," Annani said as she closed the door to her home office. "She has been sent on a diplomatic tour of the colonies by the Eternal King, and you know what that means. Since she could not take Aria with her, we have not had contact. Is there any way you can check on her? Ask to see if she is okay?"

Syssi hadn't expected that. She'd known about Ani's trip, of course, Annani had told her about it, but she hadn't expected the goddess to request a vision about her grandmother.

"Of course." She sat on one of the small armchairs flanking a round table.

"I cannot help fearing for her life." Annani sat down on the other one. "The Eternal King might have discovered Ani's connection to the resistance or her communication with me and decided to get rid of her."

"I'm sure Aria would have known if anything happened to the queen. It would have been big news on Anumati, and she would have let Aru know."

Annani regarded her as if she'd just found a cure for cancer. "Why did I not think of that? Of course, Aria would have informed Aru. As long as there is no news, it is good news, right?"

Syssi nodded. "If you want me to summon a vision about Ani, I will, but I'd rather not muddy the waters, so to speak. We need to concentrate on Khiann. Last time I asked for a clue about his whereabouts, I got Kyra instead. I'm glad that I did, and I'm overjoyed that we could save her and Fenella and the rest of the family, even if it meant postponing the search for Khiann."

Kian's and Allegra's joint birthday party had had to be postponed as well, but that had been a small sacrifice to make.

They'd had a small celebration at home, with two cakes and two candles and lots of presents for Allegra, but the village-wide celebration had to be moved and was finally happening this Saturday, provided that nothing else came up.

"Kyra was a clue," Annani said. "And now we have discovered that Fenella is related to Kyra. There is a pattern forming, I am sure of it, I am just not sure what the Fates are trying to show us. All that my gut tells me for now is that Kyra, Jasmine, and Fenella need to combine powers to find Khiann."

"I agree," Syssi said. "And I'm certainly willing to try again."

"When would you be able to attempt another vision?"

"After Allegra's birthday party," Syssi said. "I'm so preoccupied with the preparations that I won't be able to focus solely on Khiann. I need a clear head and proper preparation if I'm going to get this right this time. In the meantime, Amanda can test Fenella, and maybe the results will give us additional clues."

"So, after the birthday bash?" Annani asked.

Syssi nodded. "I will probably need a couple of days to calm down, meditate, and bring myself to a receptive state."

"I appreciate the effort you are putting into this. I wish I could lend you my powers somehow."

"Maybe you can," Syssi murmured, an idea occurring to her. "We haven't tried this yet, but what if Morelle can siphon the power from you and channel it into me?"

"That is an interesting thought," Annani said. "She channeled the energy she siphoned from me and from Kian into inanimate objects, but maybe she can channel it into people. The problem of doing so is that it might be dangerous. As much as I want to find my Khiann, I do not want to lose you while trying."

"Right." Syssi rubbed her temple. "There must be a safe way to test this. I just can't think of any."

The Clan Mother leaned toward her. "There is. The same way that we are testing Ell-rom's ability."

"On humans?"

Annani shrugged. "We have Doomers in the dungeon. Morelle can test her ability on them."

Syssi was surprised that the goddess was so callous with the lives of those Doomers, but Annani had changed her outlook recently. Her optimism had taken a nosedive after the slaughter the Doomers had ordered in Mexico, and recent global events had only made it worse. The world was not heading in the direction of peace and prosperity. It was galloping in the other direction.

"Morelle is not as soft-hearted as Ell-rom," Annani continued. "She would have no qualms about testing her powers on those monsters."

Syssi wasn't sure of that, but she didn't want to contradict the Clan Mother. Annani probably knew her sister better than she did.

"You should ask her," she said. "See what her

opinion is on that. After all, it's her power, and she knows more about it than we do."

"I shall call her later," Annani said. "Now, I need your advice on what to get my son and granddaughter for their birthdays." She chuckled. "Not celebrating birthdays in the clan was a practical decision. It made things simple."

Syssi leaned back in the chair, glad that the conversation had shifted to lighter topics. "Allegra is easy. Just get her the frilliest dress you can find, and she will be ecstatic. Kian is a little harder to please."

She blushed when she thought about the private gift she'd gotten him. It was a gift that kept on giving—many nights of exquisite pleasure.

Annani regarded her with a knowing smile. "I will not ask what passed through your mind right now. I have a feeling that it is very naughty."

Syssi covered her flaming cheeks with her hands. "It's unfair that you can read me so easily."

Annani laughed. "Anyone can read every thought that passes through your mind. You are like an open book. But try to concentrate for a moment and give me an idea for a gift."

"Cufflinks?" Syssi tried. "A rare whiskey bottle, perhaps?"

29

FENELLA

Fenella perched on a bar stool next to the counter watching Din, who moved with the confidence of someone who knew his way around a kitchen. He'd donned an apron to protect his clothes from splatters, a sensible burgundy one that somehow made him look even more attractive. He'd also rolled up his sleeves to reveal muscular forearms dusted with dark hair.

There was something unexpectedly sexy about a man preparing a meal for the woman he wanted to impress.

She preferred it to him inviting her to a fancy restaurant, a show, or a concert. Those were nice, but the only effort they required was spending money, and Fenella appreciated sweat equity much more.

Sipping the glass of red wine he'd poured for her,

she savored the rich flavor while she observed him seasoning the thick ribeye steaks with salt and pepper. His movements were practiced, indicating that he had done that countless times before.

"Where did you learn to cook?" She swirled the wine in her glass.

Din glanced up with a smile that lifted the corners of his eyes. "Everyone knows how to cook a steak. That hardly makes me a chef."

"I don't know how to do it," Fenella admitted with a shrug. "Honestly, my culinary expertise is limited to putting together a killer sandwich, but that's about it."

"Really?" Din drizzled olive oil into a cast-iron skillet. "Not even eggs and toast?"

She laughed. "Of course, I know how to make those, but that's it. When I was young and living at home, my mom did all the cooking, and after I left, I lived mostly in dingy hotel rooms or rundown bedsits with shared kitchens. I've never felt the need to learn."

Din laid the steaks in with a satisfying sizzle when the skillet began to smoke slightly. The rich aroma of searing meat filled the kitchen, making Fenella's mouth water.

"Would you like to learn?" Din's attention was seemingly on the steaks, but she caught his quick glance her way.

Fenella snorted. "An old dog can't learn new tricks, as the saying goes. Or doesn't really want to."

"That's not true." Din flipped one steak with a pair of tongs. "Especially not for immortals. You have eternity ahead of you to learn whatever you want, try whatever interests you." He flipped the other.

For some reason, his encouragement had sounded condescending to her, which made her bristle. "Being a homemaker isn't exactly on my bucket list," she said with a forced laugh. "I don't have visions of myself in an apron, baking cookies and waiting for my man to come back from work."

The words tasted sour on her tongue. Unbidden, images flickered through her mind of herself in a comfortable home like this one, she and Din cooking together in the kitchen while a small child sat at the counter, watching them with smiling eyes.

She could work at the Hobbit Bar in the evenings while Din taught at some local university.

Right.

Dreams were for losers.

Fenella shook her head, banishing the fantasy. That wasn't her. It had never been her, and dreaming of domestic bliss was the last thing she should be doing.

"Who said anything about homemaking?" Din said. "I meant that you can do anything that interests you. Cooking is just one skill among millions you could acquire."

The steaks continued to sizzle as Din added a sprig of rosemary and several cloves of garlic to the pan, followed by a generous pat of butter. The aroma intensified, and Fenella's stomach growled audibly.

"So, what else have you done with your long life?" she asked, eager to shift the conversation away from herself. "Apart from becoming Professor Indiana Jones, I mean."

Din's laugh was filled with warmth. "I've tried my hand at many things over the centuries. When I was young, I joined the Guardian Force for a while. That's how Max and I became friends."

She had a hard time imagining him as a soldier, but perhaps that was because she'd always known him as a civilian. Then again, when she'd met Max, he hadn't been a Guardian either. He'd taken a long break and had returned to the force only recently. Still, there was something about Max that said military, and it was absent in Din.

He just wasn't a fighter.

Not that it detracted from his appeal. Max was a simple guy, and there was nothing wrong with that, but she was more attracted to Din's complexity.

Well, now she was.

Back in Scotland, she'd been attracted to Max's overflowing confidence and brawn.

"I can't picture you as a Guardian," she said. "You are more of a scholarly gentleman."

"You are correct." Din acknowledged with a wry smile as he basted the steaks with the fragrant butter. "I wasn't particularly good at it. I'm too much of a thinker, not enough of a doer in crisis situations. Max, on the other hand, was a natural."

"So, what happened?"

Din shrugged. "I realized my talents lay elsewhere and retired. After that, I became a bricklayer for a time."

"A bricklayer?" Fenella couldn't help the surprise in her voice.

Din's hands didn't look like they belonged to someone who'd done manual labor, though she supposed immortal healing would have erased any calluses immediately, so that wasn't an indicator.

"It was peaceful work," Din said, a faraway look in his eyes. "I loved creating something tangible and lasting with my hands. There was a quiet satisfaction in it that's hard to describe." He transferred the steaks to a wooden cutting board, covering them with foil, and added another two to the pan. "But it didn't require much thinking, and I've always had a thirst for knowledge."

"So, you traded trowels for textbooks?"

"Eventually, yes. I enrolled in university and tried different subjects until I found one that captivated me." He moved to a pot of boiling water she hadn't noticed before, dropping in what looked like finger potatoes. "That turned out to be archaeology."

"The perfect field for someone who's actually lived history."

"That's why I chose archeology and not history." Din chuckled. "I had to be careful not to reveal knowledge I shouldn't technically have. Even worse, if my account would be dismissed because it didn't follow the established orthodoxy."

She winced. "I would have hated being in a situation where I knew what really happened, but no one believed me. I would have been so pissed."

"I can imagine." He cast her an amused glance.

As he kept working, Fenella watched his strong, capable hands moving with purpose and assurance, and it was so bloody sexy it made her tingle, and she couldn't remember tingling in a very long time.

"What about you?" Din asked. "What else have you done during your travels?"

Fenella took another sip of wine before answering. "Nothing worth mentioning, I'm afraid. Waitressing, chambermaid work, things that paid cash with no questions asked about documentation." She chuckled. "I make it sound like all I did was work, but I also partied, went to clubs, and met interesting people. It wasn't all bad." She paused, wondering if she should mention it again. "I played poker, sometimes for money, sometimes for thrills, and oftentimes for both."

"So you said. Professional gambling?" Din looked impressed rather than judgmental. "That takes skill, especially since you probably couldn't enter your opponents' minds, right? You didn't acquire the ability after your transition."

"I didn't, but I have great intuition. I also have a good poker face, which I've had plenty of practice perfecting."

There was a brief silence broken only by the sounds of the gentle bubbling of potato water and the sizzling of asparagus spears Din had added to a second pan. Fenella found the domesticity of the moment calming.

"This is nice," she said quietly, almost to herself.

Din glanced up from draining the potatoes. "What is?"

"This." She gestured vaguely around the kitchen. "A guy preparing a home-cooked meal especially for me."

"I hope it lives up to your expectations." He placed a beautifully arranged plate before her—the steak perfectly medium-rare as she'd requested, accompanied by boiled potatoes, asparagus, and a small ramekin of what appeared to be béarnaise sauce. The presentation was as impressive as the smells were appetizing.

"This looks incredible," she said.

Din smiled as he sat beside her at the counter, close enough that she could feel the warmth radiating from him but not so close as to invade her space. "I like eating well."

She was a little disappointed that he hadn't served the meal in the dining room, complete with a white tablecloth and lit candles, but maybe it was better this way—just two friends sharing a meal, with no expectations and no pressure.

The first bite of steak melted in her mouth, rich and flavorful. Fenella closed her eyes for a moment, savoring it. When she opened them, she found Din watching her with an intensity that sent a pleasant shiver down her spine.

"Good?" he asked, his voice slightly lower than before.

"Extraordinary," she admitted. "You've been holding out on me, professor. This isn't just knowing how to cook a steak—this is culinary excellence."

Was she flirting with him?

It felt natural, even refreshing. There was something about Din that made her feel safe. Not just physically secure, but emotionally so—as if he would accept whatever she offered without demanding more than she was willing to give.

As they ate in companionable silence for a few minutes, savoring the exquisite meal and punctuating the quiet only with the clink of silverware against plates and appreciative murmurs, Fenella studied Din surreptitiously between bites.

She hadn't remembered him being so attractive,

and the truth was that he was becoming more and more handsome in her eyes the more time she spent with him. Maybe it was her growing affection for him that was changing the way she saw him.

He was handsome, but not in the conventional, flashy way like Max. Din's looks were subtler, more nuanced—the kind that revealed themselves gradually rather than all at once.

"Do I have sauce on my chin?" Din asked, catching her gaze.

"No." Fenella laughed. "I was just thinking that you're not at all what I expected."

"Is that good or bad?"

She considered for a moment. "Good. Definitely good. You aged well without aging."

A slow smile spread across his face, making her heart do that uncomfortable fluttering thing again. "Wine does get better with time, but fifty years is just a brief moment in the cellar for our kind."

"Speaking of wine," Fenella said, holding out her glass for a refill, "I think I'm going to need more if we're getting philosophical about immortality."

Din obliged, the rich red liquid catching the overhead kitchen lights as it cascaded into her glass, and as their fingers brushed during the exchange, Fenella felt a jolt of awareness.

There was chemistry between them— had been from the moment they'd reconnected.

As Din topped off his own glass, Fenella contemplated a possibility that would have been unthinkable just days ago. The wine was excellent, the food delicious, the company surprisingly engaging. The evening had taken on a decidedly date-like quality, so perhaps this night could lead to more?

She was good at the game of seduction—had played it countless times over the decades, though never with any emotional investment. With Din, it would be different. He wasn't some random guy she'd never see again after a night or two of mutual pleasure.

He was part of her world now, connected to her new clan family.

More significantly, though, Din was perfectly safe.

She didn't need to worry if there was a monster hiding under the pleasant exterior, and whether he harbored malevolent intentions. She could trust him to treat her right.

He also knew what she'd been through. Not the details, perhaps, but enough to understand why intimacy might be a little difficult for her, or maybe a lot. She hadn't tried anything since getting free, not even self-pleasuring. How could she fantasize about sex after what had been done to her?

On the flip side, depriving herself of pleasure would be like handing the monster a victory, and she wasn't willing to do that, no matter how hard she had to work to overcome her aversion to intimacy.

After all, if Kyra had managed to get over it in order to be with Max, Fenella could do that, too. She might not be a rebel fighter, but she was a warrior in a different way, and she wasn't going to hide and cower because she'd been hurt.

She'd been hurt so badly, though.

Thankfully, Din had never treated her as damaged or broken, only a little fragile and worthy of patience and respect.

He was offering her exactly what she needed, not just physical comfort but emotional safety, a way to reclaim what had been violently taken from her, to create new memories that might, in time, overlay the traumatic ones.

Din was speaking about some archaeological expedition in Turkey, his deep voice weaving a story about ancient temples and unexpected discoveries. Fenella wasn't fully following the details, too caught up in her own thoughts, but she found the cadence of his speech soothing.

When he paused to take a sip of wine, she made a decision. Reaching across the space between them, she placed her hand over his on the countertop.

Din stopped mid-sentence, his eyes meeting hers with a question in them.

"Thank you for dinner," she said. "It's been a lovely evening."

He looked alarmed. "Are you leaving already?"

"Not planning to anytime soon. We haven't had coffee yet." She winked.

His expression softened. "I thought we could have it on the terrace. There is a decent view of the mountains. I just need to figure out how to raise the automatic shutters."

"You probably need to turn off all the lights first, or they won't go up."

"That makes sense. I should make the coffee first, then."

"Yes, you should," Fenella said, but didn't remove her hand from his. Instead, she stroked her thumb lightly over his knuckles, a deliberate gesture that couldn't be misinterpreted.

Din's breath caught. "Fenella..." he said, his voice rougher than before.

"What?" she asked, feigning innocence though her heart raced.

"I don't want to misread the situation or rush you into anything you're not ready for."

His consideration only strengthened her resolve. Here was a man who wouldn't take advantage, who was putting her comfort above his own desires even when she was clearly signaling interest.

"I'm not made of glass, Din," she said, meeting his gaze directly. "I know what I want."

"You need to spell it out for me because I don't want to make mistakes." He turned his hand beneath hers so their palms met, fingers intertwining.

Fenella hesitated, not quite ready to put her nascent feelings into words. "Right now, I'd like you to kiss me. The way you wanted to do it last night. I chickened out, and I've regretted it ever since."

"Really?" His voice sounded husky.

"Yes, really," she admitted with a soft laugh. "I'd like to find out what it's like to be kissed by you."

He reached up with his free hand, brushing a strand of hair back from her face with a gentleness that made her heart ache. "Finding out sounds like a worthy endeavor," he murmured. "Very archaeological, in fact. Exploring unknown territory with careful attention to detail."

"Are you comparing me to one of your dig sites?" Fenella arched an eyebrow despite the warmth spreading through her body.

Din smiled, his thumb tracing the curve of her cheek. "More like a precious artifact that deserves to be handled with reverence."

"Smooth talker," she whispered, leaning slightly into his touch.

"Only stating the naked facts," he said, his face now inches from hers.

The word *naked* still reverberated through her mind as her eyes fluttered closed and Din's lips finally met hers.

The kiss was tentative at first, a gentle pressure that inquired rather than demanded. When she responded, parting her lips in invitation, he deepened the kiss with a controlled passion that sent electric shocks through her body.

One hand came up to cup the back of her neck, fingers threading through her hair as he angled his head to better fit their mouths together. Fenella made a small sound of approval, her own hands moving to his shoulders, feeling the solid strength beneath the fabric of his shirt.

He kissed her like he had all the time in the world, like each moment was to be savored rather than rushed through.

When they finally parted to come up for air, Fenella was momentarily at a loss for words, which almost never happened.

Din's eyes had darkened to a stormy blue, his pupils dilated with desire. "Was that what you wanted to find out?"

Fenella nodded, not quite trusting herself to speak yet. The kiss had affected her more profoundly than she'd expected, awakening sensations she'd thought were still deadened by trauma.

"I'm glad," Din said, brushing his thumb across her lower lip. "I've been wanting to find out what it was like to kiss you for half a century."

A laugh bubbled up from somewhere deep inside her. "Was it worth the wait?"

"Every second."

Fenella wanted to make a joke, something that would deflect the intensity of the moment with humor as she always did when emotions threatened to overwhelm her, but she just couldn't.

Not this time.

Perhaps it was the warmth in Din's eyes, or the way his hand still cradled her face as if she were precious.

Instead, she leaned forward and kissed him again, putting into action what she couldn't yet put into words. This kiss was less tentative, more exploratory, as Fenella tested the waters of her own responses. To her immense relief, there was no flashback, no sudden panic—only warmth and a growing desire for more.

When they separated this time, Din rested his forehead against hers for a moment, his breathing slightly uneven. "Should I still make that coffee?"

"Coffee can wait," she said, her fingers trailing along the collar of his shirt. "I'm more interested in exploring other options at the moment."

Din's eyes darkened further, but he didn't move right away. "I need you to know that there's no rush and you can take all the time you need. Whatever happens or doesn't happen tonight—I'm not going anywhere."

The simple promise, delivered without dramatic flourish, touched something deep within her. "I know, which is why I feel safe with you."

30

DIN

*D*in took Fenella's hand, trying to keep his touch reverent and light despite the desire coursing through him. He'd imagined this moment for so long, yet now that it was here, he felt almost overwhelmed by its significance. His heart raced as he looked into her eyes, seeing trust there that he'd done nothing yet to earn.

"Are you sure about this?" he asked again.

The words cost him, but he meant them. After everything she'd been through, the last thing he wanted was to rush her into something she wasn't ready for. Her needs came before his desires.

"I want you, Din."

The simple declaration made his heart soar. He leaned forward, carefully capturing her lips, gently at first, but when she pressed closer, parting her lips in invitation, he deepened the kiss and pulled her tighter against his body.

When they separated, he rested his forehead against hers, breathing in her scent—a heady mixture of something that was uniquely Fenella.

"You're incredible," he murmured.

"You're not so bad yourself," she said with a smile that transformed her face, her fingers threading through his hair.

Din let his hand travel from her face to her shoulder, then down her arm in a feather-light caress, cataloging each response, each subtle reaction. He felt her tremble slightly beneath his touch and paused, uncertain.

"You're trembling," he observed quietly, searching her face.

"It's been a long time," Fenella admitted, vulnerability flashing briefly in her eyes. "Since I've been with someone I actually wanted to be with."

The admission struck Din like a sledgehammer. He knew what had happened to her, at least in general terms. The thought of what she'd endured enraged him, but it also made his protective instincts flare.

It took such incredible courage for her to be here with him now, choosing to trust him even though she barely knew him.

He offered his hand. "Shall we move somewhere

more comfortable? The terrace has a lovely view, but perhaps not for what we have in mind."

Fenella laughed, a sound that delighted him each time he heard it. She accepted his hand, and he led her toward the bedroom, hyper-aware of her presence beside him, the warmth of her palm against his.

"It's a nice bed." She ran her hand over the carved post. "Mine is much simpler, Shaker style."

Din couldn't take his eyes off her, the way the overhead light outlined her profile, highlighted the curve of her neck, and the slope of her shoulder. "Yes," he agreed. "Very nice. Beautiful, in fact."

She turned to look at him, realizing that he hadn't been admiring the bed, and a slight blush crept up her cheeks.

Din found the sight unexpectedly charming.

This woman, who had faced untold hardships over decades and yet carried herself with such strength, could still blush at a simple compliment.

"Flatterer," she accused, though her eyes sparkled.

"Truth-teller," he countered, drawing her closer, his hands settling at her waist.

She lifted her hands and placed her palms on his chest, her touch warm through the fabric of his shirt. He was acutely aware of every point of contact between them, every subtle shift of her body, the rhythm of her breathing.

When he kissed her again, he took his time, exploring the softness of her lips, the sweetness of her mouth, memorizing each response, each small sound of pleasure.

He felt her smiling against his lips. "What's so amusing?" He brushed kisses along the corner of her mouth.

"Just thinking that immortality has its perks," she said. "No need to rush."

"None whatsoever," he agreed, trailing kisses along her jaw to the sensitive spot just below her ear, delighting in the way her breath caught when he found a particularly responsive area. "Though I've been told patience is a virtue, and I'm feeling decidedly virtuous at the moment."

Her laugh turned into a soft gasp as he explored the sensitive skin of her neck. "Not too virtuous, I hope."

Din chuckled, the sound rumbling up from his chest. "Just virtuous enough."

His hands moved to the buttons of her blouse, but he paused, waiting for her permission. When she nodded, he began to undo them one by one, taking his time, treating each new revelation as the gift it was. With each inch of skin exposed, he paid homage with his lips, his fingertips, memorizing texture and taste.

"You're treating me like I'm made of glass," she murmured, though her tone held no complaint.

"Not glass," Din corrected, helping her out of the

blouse, his breath catching at the sight of her. "Something far more valuable. Irreplaceable."

He saw something flicker in her eyes—surprise, vulnerability, perhaps even wonder—and he paused, concerned he'd somehow overstepped. "Too much flattery?"

Fenella chuckled. "No, I like it."

Din smiled, understanding what she couldn't quite articulate. He'd observed that tendency in her —the difficulty in expressing certain emotions directly, the deflection with humor or sarcasm. It made these moments of openness all the more precious.

With gentle hands, he guided her to sit on the edge of the bed, then knelt before her.

"What now?" she asked, a hint of uncertainty in her voice.

Fenella had been with an immortal male before, but Max had erased her memories of his bite, and Din didn't know whether she knew what to expect.

Had her friends told her?

Had she spoken with Kyra about the particulars of immortal sex?

How could he bring it up without ruining the moment?

Perhaps it could wait for later, or maybe he didn't have to say anything at all. She must know that he had fangs and what they were for, right?

Instead, he lifted one of her feet. "First, I'm going

to help you get comfortable." He removed her shoe, setting it aside carefully, then did the same with the other. His fingers found the arch of her foot, applying gentle pressure, massaging away tension.

"Oh," Fenella breathed, her head falling back. "That feels wonderful."

He smiled. "They say that the way to a man's heart is through his stomach, but they should add that the way to a woman's heart is through the arches of her feet."

She chuckled. "Wisdom for the ages, professor."

This was what he wanted—to care for her in all the ways she'd been denied for so long. She deserved to be cherished.

"Din," she said softly.

He looked up, meeting her gaze. "Yes?"

"Come here." She tugged on his shoulder.

He shifted up, settling beside her on the bed, and she turned to face him. Reaching up to trace the line of his jaw with delicate fingers that left fire in their wake, she planted a soft kiss on his lips. "Thank you."

"For what?"

"For being perfect." She leaned forward to kiss him again.

No one had ever called him perfect, and he knew that he was far from that, but for now, he was willing to accept the compliment without arguing. Heat was building in their embrace, an intensity that had Din fighting for control.

Fenella's hands found the buttons of his shirt, working them open with delicate fingers.

"Let me help," he murmured, assisting her until the shirt hung open. Her curious hands explored his chest, his abdomen, each touch sending sparks through his nervous system, but he held still, letting her explore for as long she needed.

"You're in remarkable shape for an academic," Fenella teased.

"Field work can be quite physical." His breath caught as her fingers traced a path down his stomach. "I also enjoy rowing at Strathclyde Park."

"That explains it," Fenella said with an appreciation that made his blood run hotter.

Din let his own hands wander, skimming over her shoulders, down her back, learning the curves of her body through the thin fabric of her camisole. When his fingers brushed the strip of skin between her top and her jeans, he felt her shiver and smiled.

"Cold?"

"Quite the opposite," she admitted.

With infinite care, Din guided her to lie back on the bed, stretching out beside her. They continued their exploration, trading soft kisses and tender touches as clothing was gradually set aside. He was hyperaware of her reactions, alert for any sign of discomfort or hesitation, but she remained relaxed in his arms, her responses growing more enthusiastic with each passing moment.

When he finally removed the last of what had been covering her, he was overcome with how beautiful she was. Her body was a perfect blend of strength and softness, but it wasn't just her physical perfection that affected him—it was the trust she was placing in him and the vulnerability she was allowing him to witness.

"You're so beautiful," he whispered, his gaze traveling over her with reverence, his fingers tracing the contours of her breasts.

"So are you." Her gaze traveled down his nude body, and as her eyes settled on his erection, they started glowing, and he wondered if they had ever glowed with desire for anyone else.

When the scent of her arousal hit him full force, he felt dizzy.

"I have to taste you," he groaned, leaning down to take one small nipple into his mouth and suck on it gently.

She arched her back. "Yes, please," she hissed. "Don't stop."

Fates, he felt like he'd passed through the veil and gone to heaven.

Moving with his immortal speed, he was between her legs in a split second, his shoulders spreading her thighs wide. "You're mine, Fenella," he growled as he licked between her wet folds, finding her entrance and spearing his tongue into her.

He didn't know what had possessed him to say that.

That wasn't what Fenella needed to hear from him.

She was a free spirit who didn't belong to anyone, and a stupid remark like that could ruin all the great progress he'd achieved so far.

Thankfully, she seemed too lost to pleasure and either hadn't heard him or decided to ignore it.

"Din—" she moaned his name as her body convulsed in a violent climax.

He sucked and licked, helping her ride the wave for as long as it lasted, and when she finally stopped shuddering, he kissed her folds one last time and leaned away to look at the bounty sprawled on the bed before him.

"Gorgeous," he whispered as he rose over her.

As his shaft nudged her entrance, he was adamant about going slow and making love to her tenderly and slowly, but when she lifted her hips to draw more of him inside her, his control snapped, and he surged into her, joining them.

Fenella gasped, but it didn't sound like distress. It was the sound of coming home.

The world around them receded into nothingness, and as he began moving, going faster and stronger than he'd ever dared with the humans he'd been with, she was right up there with him, taking everything he had to give and demanding more.

His immortal beloved.

With her hips lifting to meet him stroke for stroke, her nails scoring his back, and the heels of her feet digging into his buttocks, she was just as wild as he was, if not more.

As the pleasure built toward its inevitable crescendo, Din felt something profound happening between them—something beyond physical connection, something that resonated in the core of his being. The bond he'd always sensed was there, manifest now in their joining, stronger and more significant than he'd dared to hope.

When she turned her head and exposed her neck to him, he was relieved that she knew what was about to happen and welcomed it.

He licked the spot to anesthetize it and then sank his fangs into her flesh.

Fenella groaned, and as her release barreled through her once more, Din's own rushed through him in a powerful wave.

After licking the twin incision points closed, Din buried his face in the crook of her neck where he could keep breathing her scent in.

Five centuries of life and half a century of dreaming about Fenella hadn't prepared him for the intensity of the experience with this exquisite female. She was his one and only.

He was certain of it.

This hadn't been just sex or even lovemaking.

This had been a joining, not only of bodies, but of souls.

Lifting his head, he gazed at her blissful expression, and satisfaction washed over him for being the one who had put it there. He pressed a gentle kiss to her temple, careful not to wake her.

"Sleep well, *mo chridhe*," he whispered.

31

FENELLA

Fenella floated through a landscape of impossible colors and sensations, only vaguely aware that what she was experiencing wasn't real. Mountains of emerald and sapphire rose around her, rivers of liquid silver winding between them, the sky above shifting between shades of amber and rose that no earthly sunset could produce. She soared over this dreamscape without wings, feeling lighter than air.

She'd never known such profound peace, such complete contentment, her essence free to drift on currents of pure bliss.

A tiny part of her knew this was the effect of Din's venom—a biological response designed to create pleasure and bonding—but that knowledge didn't diminish the experience. If anything, it enhanced it.

Amid the swirling colors of her vision, she became aware of something anchoring her to reality—the soft, gentle pressure of lips against her face. Din was kissing her—her forehead, cheeks, eyelids, corner of her mouth—each touch feather-light and impossibly warm. Through the pleasant haze of her dream state, she felt the reverence in those kisses, the tenderness that went beyond physical desire.

It felt like love.

The thought should have terrified her, but instead, it tugged at something deep within her that had been dormant and was slowly stirring to life. As beautiful as the venom-induced euphoria was, the emotion conveyed in those simple kisses meant more to her than all the psychedelic wonders in her mind.

Din's kisses were real in a way the surreal landscapes were not.

Slowly, reluctantly, Fenella allowed herself to drift downward, back toward consciousness, drawn by the promise of that connection. It took tremendous effort to open her heavy eyelids, like swimming upward through layers of warm honey, but eventually she managed it, her vision gradually focusing on Din's face above her.

He was beautiful.

The strong line of his jaw that was softened by his smile, the intelligence that shone in his blue eyes, the subtle cleft in his chin that demanded to be kissed, the strands of dark hair falling across his forehead that she wanted to brush back with her fingers—all of it combined into a face that made her feel impossible things.

Scary things.

"Hello," she murmured, her voice sounding distant to her own ears.

Din's smile widened. "Hello to you, too." He leaned down to place a gentle kiss on her lips. "I'm glad to have you back."

"I never left." Fenella snuggled closer to press her nose against the crook of his neck, inhaling his scent —a complex mixture of sandalwood cologne and something uniquely him. "I felt your kisses." She pressed her lips to that warm spot that smelled so heavenly. "But it took me time to decide to come back. How long was I out?"

"A couple of hours."

"Really? That long?"

It'd felt like minutes. No wonder Din had woken her up. He must have been worried.

"Did you enjoy your venom trip?" he asked.

"Tremendously. I knew what it was from Jasmine and Kyra, but it exceeded my expectations."

Max must have bitten her when he'd induced her transition half a century ago, but he'd erased the memory of his bite, leaving behind only the memories of the pleasure he'd given her, but even that had faded over the years.

She watched with drowsy amusement as a look of smug satisfaction spread across Din's face. His expression reminded her of a cat that had not only gotten the cream but had convinced its owner to refill the crystal dish.

"There's plenty more where that came from," he promised.

"Oh, really?" Fenella arched an eyebrow. "Kyra and Jasmine also told me that immortal males don't need recovery time, but they can only generate enough venom for one bite a night."

"Is that a challenge?" Din's eyes were gleaming with playful intent.

Fenella couldn't suppress a yawn. "I'm too tired for challenges." Her body felt pleasantly languid, muscles relaxed in a way she couldn't remember ever experiencing.

Din's expression showed a flicker of disappointment, but he quickly masked it. "Immortal females don't need recuperating time either."

"That's right." She ran her fingers lightly over his chest, enjoying the warmth of his skin while mapping the contours of muscle and sinew. "We can go as many times as the males, or more. Although until meeting you, I had no desire for marathon sessions. Most men aren't worthy of a second round."

"What about me?" He tried for an amused tone, but she heard the vulnerability he was hiding.

"You are definitely worth a second and a third and maybe even a fourth round."

It was amazing how liberating this experience had been for her. It was like her ordeal had been painted over by the psychedelic trip she'd been on. She'd heard of a kind of mushroom that had a similar effect, curing people of traumas and addictions, and she wondered whether the venom and that mushroom shared the same chemical compounds, therefore providing similar healing.

"Thank the merciful Fates." His hand traveled down her back to cup her bottom. "You held me in suspense there for a moment."

She followed the path of her fingers with her lips, dropping gentle kisses across his skin. "You smell so good," she murmured, breathing him in. The scent was intoxicating—clean and masculine, with an underlying note that seemed to call to something primal within her. "And you taste good as well."

Din's breathing quickened as she moved lower, his hands coming to rest gently in her hair. The contact was light, undemanding—he wasn't directing her movements, merely connecting with her, and she appreciated the distinction.

"What are you up to?" His voice sounded strained.

"You'll find out." Fenella looked up and smiled.

She wanted to explore him, to discover what

brought him pleasure, to deepen this connection that had sparked between them in such a short time.

His shaft was impressively erect as if he hadn't recently climaxed, and as she rubbed her cheek against the velvety skin, his fingers threaded in her hair. She brushed her lips over the tip, and it twitched in welcome. When she took it into her mouth, his fingers tightened on her scalp. He tried to keep still, but his hips were churning despite his efforts at restraint. It encouraged her to get bolder. With one hand holding his shaft and the other clasping his buttocks, she took him deeper and circled her tongue around the hard length.

He pressed into her mouth, only slightly, but his ragged breathing spurred her to take him even deeper. She wanted him to give control over to her so she could take him as deep as he could go, but he refused, stubbornly never giving her more than what he thought she could handle.

"Come here." He pulled her up his chest and rolled on top of her. "That was amazing, but I'd rather not finish inside your mouth."

"Why not?"

"Because—" He thrust into her, and her eyes rolled back. "We both enjoy this more." He retreated and surged back in.

"Yes." She locked her ankles in the small of his back.

This time their lovemaking was less frenzied, and

as he dipped his head and kissed her, the kiss was slow and lazy, his tongue thrusting inside her mouth to the rhythm of his erection doing the same between her legs.

As Din moved above her, his eyes never leaving hers, the walls she'd erected around her heart were crumbling. Each touch, each kiss, each whispered endearment was a stone removed from her carefully constructed fortress. The sensation was terrifying and liberating in equal measures.

As the rhythm of their joining gradually intensified, Fenella raced toward another peak, but this time, instead of the physical sensations alone, it was the emotional connection that overwhelmed her, the safety she felt in Din's arms, the acceptance in his eyes, the way he seemed to see beyond her defenses to her wounded core.

When the moment came, it wasn't just pleasure that washed over her but a profound sense of belonging. For a brief, crystalline moment, Fenella felt herself not just physically joined with Din but emotionally entangled in ways that encompassed everything. Their hearts seemed to beat in unison, their breath mingled, and something ancient and mystical passed between them—a recognition, a claiming, a promise.

As they collapsed together afterward, bodies intertwined and breath gradually slowing, Fenella felt at peace. The restlessness that had driven her for decades, the constant urge to keep moving, to stay one step ahead of shadows real and imagined—all of it had quieted, at least for now.

It was terrifying and wonderful and strange—and despite all her instincts screaming that happiness was fleeting, that safety was an illusion, that attachment would only lead to pain—Fenella hoped that morning would be slow to arrive, giving them a few more hours together.

As sleep began to reclaim her, one last coherent thought drifted through her mind—perhaps this was what people meant when they spoke of coming home. Not a physical place but a feeling of rightness, of belonging, of being truly seen and accepted.

32

FENELLA

When Fenella woke up again, she immediately became aware of the solid warmth pressed against her back, the heavy arm draped over her waist, and the steady rhythm of breath against her neck.

Din.

She relaxed into the embrace, the events of the previous night flooding back, bringing with them a complex mix of emotions she was still too sleepy to untangle.

She shifted, and the arm around her waist tightened reflexively.

"Good morning," Din murmured, his voice rough with sleep. His lips brushed the nape of her neck, sending a pleasant shiver down her spine.

"Morning." She smiled, surprised by how comfortable she felt. Usually, she'd be halfway out the door by now, avoiding awkward morning-after conversations.

But Din was different.

Her instinct to flee was nowhere to be found.

She turned in his arms to face him. His dark hair was mussed and his blue eyes, though sleepy, were suffused with warmth that was directed at her.

"You're still here."

Fenella raised an eyebrow. "Did you expect me to bolt in the middle of the night?"

"I thought I was dreaming and that when I woke up, you wouldn't be here." The wry tone and the crooked smile betrayed his words as a lie.

She kissed him lightly. "You lie so beautifully."

He chuckled. "Okay, you caught me. I half expected you to sneak out during the night."

"I considered it, but I decided the bed was too comfortable to abandon."

That was a complete lie. She'd been out like a light and hadn't woken up until now. She had no time to consider it.

The dimple in his cheek appeared as he smiled. "I'll have to thank Ingrid for ordering quality mattresses for the village homes."

"The company wasn't half bad, either." Fenella kissed his jaw.

It felt strange to be this open with someone, but also nice.

Din reached up to brush a strand of hair from

her face. "Just 'not half bad'? I think I need to work on my technique."

Fenella rolled her eyes, but the teasing was comfortable, familiar ground. "Your technique is fine, professor. Top marks, even."

"High praise indeed."

"Don't let it go to your head." She poked his chest.

Din caught her hand, bringing it to his lips. "I won't. I'm your humble servant, my lady." He started kissing the tips of her fingers.

"You're quite charming in the morning," she said, trying to regain her footing. "Is this how you are with all your lovers?"

"I've never felt about anyone the way I feel about you."

The directness of his statement caught her off guard. There was no coy flirtation, no games—just honest emotions laid bare for her to see. It was terrifying and exhilarating in equal measure.

"We've just met," she reminded him. "Fifty years of fantasy about someone isn't the same as knowing them."

"True," Din acknowledged. "But these days with you have only confirmed what I suspected all those years ago—that there's something between us worth exploring."

Fenella wanted to deflect with a joke, to maintain the emotional distance, but the sincerity in his eyes made it difficult.

"I'm not the same girl you knew in Scotland," she said.

"And I'm not the same man I was then. We've both changed, evolved. I'd like the chance to know who you are now, and I hope you'll like who I am."

Before Fenella could respond that yes, she wanted that, her phone buzzed on the nightstand.

"It's probably Shira, wondering where I am." She reached for the device and frowned. "It's from Amanda."

"What does it say?" Din asked.

"Good morning, Fenella," she read out loud. "I hope I'm not disturbing you too early but given the fabulous news of you being related to Jasmine and Kyra, I thought the three of you should get tested together. Would eleven-thirty work? If yes, I will have someone pick you up and drive you to the university campus. Let me know as soon as you can." Fenella frowned at the screen. "What the bloody hell is she talking about? What testing?"

"Amanda is a neuroscientist, and she runs a research laboratory that is equipped to test paranormal abilities. She must believe that you have some latent abilities worth exploring."

Fenella scoffed. "The only 'ability' I have is staying alive and a decent poker face."

"Don't be so quick to dismiss it," Din said. "Intuition is often underestimated, but it can be a powerful tool and even a sign of some psychic ability."

"Don't you think I would have noticed if I had magical powers?"

He chuckled. "It's not magic, love. It's genetics. Many immortals and Dormants have enhanced abilities—precognition, telepathy, far-seeing, and other talents. Amanda has the proper tools to test you for most of them."

Fenella thought about all the times she'd had a feeling about a place or a person that had later proved accurate—the inexplicable urges to leave town just before trouble found her, the sense of unease about Din's travel mishaps.

Could there be something to it?

The times she'd gotten in trouble were when she'd decided to ignore her intuition because listening to it meant giving up on something she'd wanted.

"There is no harm in giving it a try," she finally agreed.

Din smiled. "It's also an opportunity to get out of the village. You were complaining about feeling cooped up. The university campus is over an hour's drive from here, and there is a lot to see on the way. The campus itself is also a nice place to visit."

That caught Fenella's attention. The prospect of seeing something beyond the village borders was enticing.

"I suppose it's worth the trouble if just for that." She typed a quick reply to Amanda, confirming the time and asking where exactly they should meet.

The response came almost immediately: *Excellent! Be at the underground garage at 10 AM. Transportation will be provided. Kyra, Jasmine, and Morelle will be joining you. Din can come if he wants.*

"Well, that's settled," Fenella said, setting the phone aside. "It seems I have a date with the boss's sister. Do you want to come along?"

The truth was that she was nervous about someone with the title of neuroscientist poking around her head.

"If you want me to, of course."

"I do." She looked at the timer on her phone. "It's just a little past eight." A slow smile spread across her face as she moved closer to Din. "It seems we have some time to kill before we need to get ready."

"I can think of a few ways to occupy that time," he murmured, his hand sliding along her waist.

"I was hoping you'd say that." Fenella closed the distance between them.

Two hours later, freshly showered and dressed in a simple blouse and jeans that somehow managed to look designer despite their casual cut, Fenella walked with Din toward the underground garage that served as the village's transportation hub.

"Tell me more about Morelle. I know that she's Ell-rom's sister, but not much other than that."

"I don't know much about her or Ell-rom, but I can tell you what I've learned so far. They are twins, and they are the Clan Mother's half-sister and brother. Their shared father had a dalliance with the Kra-ell queen before he was exiled to Earth and married Annani's mother. He didn't even know that the Kra-ell queen was carrying his children. She sent them to him with a large number of Kra-ell settlers bound for Earth, but there was a malfunction, and the ship arrived seven thousand years later than scheduled. The twins almost died because their stasis pods malfunctioned, and Jasmine found them in the nick of time. Morelle is mated to Brandon, who is the village council member in charge of media."

"Ell-rom is nice. Is Morelle like him?"

"I don't know." Din smiled apologetically. "As I said, I've never met her."

When they made it to the underground garage, Kyra and Jasmine were already there, along with two others Fenella didn't recognize—a strikingly beautiful woman with short dark hair who was nearly as tall as the guy standing next to her.

"Fenella." He offered her his hand, flashing a

smile that could light up the entire space. "I'm Brandon, and this is my better half, Morelle."

"It's a pleasure to meet you both," Fenella said.

As Brandon introduced Din to Morelle, a sleek cream-colored SUV pulled up, driven by Okidu.

The butler stepped out of the vehicle with a broad smile plastered across his face and opened the passenger door with a flourish. "Please take your seats, mistresses and masters."

The interior of the SUV was luxuriously appointed, with buttery leather seats and more legroom than seemed possible from the vehicle's exterior dimensions. Fenella settled in between Din and Kyra, while Jasmine, Morelle, and Brandon took the row behind them.

"How far is the university?" Fenella asked as Okidu started the vehicle.

"The drive will take about ninety minutes, depending on traffic," Brandon said. "It shouldn't be too bad now, but we will crawl on the way back."

As they emerged from the tunnel and the windows cleared, Fenella pressed closer to the window, drinking in the sight of the outside world. After the pristine beauty of the village, the urban landscape should have seemed ugly, polluted, but to Fenella, it represented freedom, possibility, and the familiar rhythm of human life.

"I've always preferred cities to the countryside," she said. "There's an energy to them, a vitality."

"And plenty of places to disappear," Kyra added shrewdly.

Fenella glanced at her. "That too."

33

SYSSI

"There you are," Amanda called from across the lab as Syssi walked in. "I was beginning to think you'd decided to stay in the nursery."

"Allegra wouldn't let me go," Syssi said. "She was fussy and clingy and generally unhappy."

It had been difficult to leave her child in the hands of others when she was in such a lousy mood, but Amanda needed her help, so she'd practically peeled the crying Allegra off her and handed her to Julia.

Amanda nodded. "We need to watch the new assistant. If the girls don't like her, she has to go."

"Let's give her a few more days," Syssi said. "She seems nice, and Julia says that she's great with the kids. Allegra just doesn't like changes, and she misses the old assistant." She swept her gaze over the empty lab. "Where is everyone?"

"I sent them home for the day so we can do the tests without having to hide what we are doing. I said that we're having a facility inspection."

"Again? The university management might start asking questions if you keep doing that."

Amanda waved a dismissive hand. "The clan funds my research, the official and unofficial. The university is happy to give me free rein as long as the money keeps flowing and my papers keep getting published. Besides, founding the nursery bought me a lot of goodwill with the administration as well, especially after the glowing news article about how accommodating and family-friendly the establishment here is. My 'innovative childcare solution' is now featured in all their recruitment brochures."

Syssi smiled. "I have to admit that it is pretty amazing to be able to pop in and check on Allegra anytime I want. I wish more employers provided solutions like that. Perhaps it would encourage more women to have babies."

"Definitely." Amanda leaned against one of the desks and crossed her feet at the ankles. "Young couples just can't afford to have kids anymore, and if nothing is done to help them, we will soon be like Europe with an old and shrinking population."

"It's already happening," Syssi murmured. "People are not having enough children to preserve current numbers."

Amanda sighed. "Too many problems and too few solutions. I'm starting to feel like my mother."

Syssi lifted her head. "What do you mean?"

"You know how she is always the bastion of optimism?"

Syssi nodded. "That's why your comment is so startling. Has that changed?"

Amanda nodded. "She's talking about moving back to the sanctuary. She only talks like that when she feels unsettled and seeks solitude."

"I didn't know that. Annani always seems so strong. The strongest person I know."

"She is strong." Amanda smiled. "But everyone has their moments of weakness, even the indomitable Annani. I see through her façade. She also sees through mine."

"Mothers and daughters have a special connection." Syssi thought about Allegra and how she felt that unique link between them, even during the pregnancy, and later how she drew on her daughter's power when she summoned visions.

"There is something to your theory about Jasmine, Kyra, and Fenella enhancing each other's abilities. It's like Allegra and me and my visions."

Amanda tilted her head. "What do you think gave me the idea? The fact that the three of them share a maternal lineage is too significant to ignore. The Fates don't arrange coincidences of that magnitude without purpose."

"But Fenella insists she doesn't have any special talents."

"Not everyone is as strongly talented as you, darling. Most people with abilities don't recognize them as such and chalk it up to good instincts or luck."

"What kind of ability do you think she might have?"

"I'm not sure." Amanda tapped her lower lip with a long finger. "That's why I wanted to clear the lab and test everything I can think of. And what's more interesting is how her ability might interact with Kyra's and Jasmine's when they're together. The synergistic effect. That's why I also asked Morelle to join us today."

Syssi frowned. "How is Morelle going to help? You're not planning to have her siphon and redirect powers without proper safety protocols, are you?"

"Of course not," Amanda said, though the slight hesitation in her voice suggested she'd at least considered it. "It's more of a hunch, really. Morelle's ability to manipulate energy flows might help her identify patterns we can't detect with our equipment. Remember how she detected the flaw in the mantel stone?"

Syssi shivered at the memory. "I will never forget that. We almost lost Darius."

Kalugal's little boy had been sitting right under that piece of stone that had detached from the fireplace mantel. If Morelle hadn't been there to redirect the stone's trajectory by siphoning power from Annani, he would have been killed.

"She must have felt the vibrations," Amanda said. "Maybe Fenella vibrates too and Morelle can feel that. I won't have Morelle redirecting her power to another person without testing how it works first."

Amanda hadn't said how she was going to test that, but Syssi didn't need her to spell it out for her.

Leaning against one of the lab tables, she let her thoughts drift to Morelle's twin and his clandestine training. Kian had justified using Ell-rom's death-ray power on the worst of humanity's monsters as a necessary evil, saying that these people who had hurt children and would continue to do so given the chance deserved the death sentence. But the moral implications of using them as target practice for the twins still weighed on her.

"You're thinking about Ell-rom, aren't you?" Amanda asked, reading Syssi's expression with uncanny accuracy.

Syssi sighed. "Ell-rom is killing people for target practice."

"Monsters, not people," Amanda corrected. "The worst of the worst who don't even deserve to be called people."

"I know that." Syssi rubbed her temples. "I just worry about the effect it has on Ell-rom. He's a gentle soul who the Fates have dealt a nasty hand with that death-ray of his. I know that I wouldn't be able to do what he's doing without it destroying me from the inside out."

"Which is precisely why you're not the one who has been gifted with his talent." Amanda walked over to her and placed a comforting hand on her shoulder. "Ell-rom's Kra-ell heritage gives him a different perspective on justice and necessity. The same is true for Morelle."

"She seems more comfortable with the harsher aspects of her nature," Syssi agreed. "Her Kra-ell half is more prominent than her brother's."

"It's their dual nature that makes them so valuable to the clan," Amanda said.

"I suppose you're right," Syssi conceded. "But it still troubles me." She glanced at her watch. "We should probably check on the girls before everyone arrives."

"They're fine," Amanda assured her. "You need to give Allegra the chance to get used to the new girl."

Before Syssi could respond that it had been a while, the lab door opened, and Kyra and Jasmine entered, followed by Fenella with Din beside her.

Syssi was happy to see Din's hand resting protectively at the small of Fenella's back. It seemed like the couple who had been star-crossed for five decades finally had their stars in alignment.

Brandon and Morelle brought up the rear.

Even though it wasn't Morelle's first time in the

lab, she still scanned the equipment with the same interest. The woman had warrior instincts.

"Welcome, everyone," Amanda said. "Thank you for coming. I know it was short notice, but my mother is impatient to start the search for Khiann, and since you three ladies seem to be at the heart of that effort, we need to figure out how you will achieve that as soon as possible."

Fenella gave Amanda the thumbs up, but she looked far from enthusiastic or confident about the testing. Nevertheless, she looked around the lab with undisguised curiosity. "Nice setup you've got here. I'm getting a mad scientist vibe."

Amanda laughed. "I prefer *innovative*, but I'll take *mad scientist* as a compliment."

"What exactly are we doing here?" Kyra asked, with her hand resting on the pendant at her throat.

"I want to test all of your abilities and find out what Fenella's potential talent might be." Amanda motioned for them to follow her to the sitting area at the far wall of the lab. "I also want to explore how your talents might interact and whether Morelle can detect any interesting patterns that our machines cannot."

"I don't have any special powers," Fenella said.

She sounded part defensive and part apologetic, and Syssi felt for her. It wasn't fun to be placed in a position where she had no idea how to perform what was expected of her.

It wasn't fair of Annani to put such pressure on the woman, especially so soon after her rescue from a nightmare, but the Clan Mother was growing desperate for some reason.

Perhaps she could feel that Khiann's time was running out, in the same way Jasmine had felt that she needed to find her prince. She'd saved the twins days before they would have died.

"Most abilities aren't as dramatic as they appear in fiction," Amanda said. "Some manifest as heightened instincts, gut feelings, or inexplicable knowing. Once identified, they can be practiced and focused until they become a useful tool and not just a curiosity."

"Like my pendant," Kyra said, touching the amber stone. "It has taken me a while to feel the subtle clues it provides me with, and sometimes I still get them wrong."

"Exactly." Amanda turned to Morelle. "I know you are wondering why I invited you along."

Morelle nodded. "I thought that my talent needed to remain a secret."

Amanda waved a hand. "It does, but security be damned when my mother demands results, right? Not even Kian would dare say anything." She leaned forward, lacing her fingers over her knee. "Since you can siphon energy from paranormally talented people, I figured you can sense who has power you can tap into and who doesn't. Perhaps you could check Fenella and figure out if she has any reserves of power."

Morelle shifted on the simple plastic chair. "I'm not sure I can do that. I've been practicing, but it is still mostly instinctive."

Amanda nodded. "All I ask is that you pay attention when I test Fenella. You might sense surges in power."

"I can try," Morelle said.

"Let me give you a quick tour of the facility." Amanda rose to her feet. "Morelle has seen everything already, so you can skip it if you want."

"I will join you." Morelle stood up. "I was fascinated by all the sophisticated equipment the first time I was here, but I didn't retain much. I'd love another round."

"You're more than welcome," Amanda said.

As she led them through the laboratory, explaining various pieces of equipment, Syssi fell into step beside Morelle.

"Thank you for coming," she said quietly. "Amanda had something different in mind for testing your power, but she realized that it wasn't safe. We might have to try it the same way we are testing Ell-rom's abilities."

Morelle nodded. "Annani believes these ladies hold the key to finding Khiann, and I know how desperately she wants him found. I'll do anything to assist in any way I can."

Syssi didn't know whether she should be relieved that Morelle agreed to test her powers on the scumbags in the dungeon or be troubled by it.

"I keep thinking how terrible it must have been for you to wake and find that thousands of years had passed," she said instead.

Morelle shrugged. "Ell-rom and I expected to wake up in a different world, and we did. It didn't make much difference that this new world was much more advanced than the one we'd expected. And as for the passage of time, we didn't feel it. In deep stasis, there are not even dreams."

They reached the main testing area, where Amanda was showing Fenella one of their newest pieces of equipment.

"This is our pride and joy. It's a custom-built neuroimaging system that combines functional magnetic resonance imaging with electroencephalography. It allows us to observe neural activity in real time, mapping both electrical patterns and blood flow."

Fenella's eyes crossed. "In English, please?"

Amanda laughed. "It lets us see which parts of your brain light up when you're using your abilities. Even the ones you don't know you have."

"How exactly do you plan to trigger these supposed abilities?" Fenella asked.

"That's where it gets interesting," Amanda said with a smile that had those 'mad scientist' vibes

Fenella had mentioned. "We've developed a series of tests—some standard cognitive assessments, others specifically designed to elicit paranormal responses."

"Like what?" Fenella asked.

"Card guessing, remote viewing, precognitive timing tests." Amanda lifted a deck of cards. "But also some less conventional methods involving emotional triggers and adrenaline responses."

Fenella raised an eyebrow. "You're not going to electrocute me, are you?"

Amanda put a reassuring hand on her shoulder. "Nothing so dramatic, darling. Though I can't promise it won't be occasionally startling."

"What about the three of us together?" Kyra asked. "How are you going to test that?"

"We'll begin with touch. I will test you separately and then while holding hands or concentrating on the same outcome together."

"Where do we start?" Fenella asked.

"We'll start with the basics," Amanda said, guiding Fenella toward a chair positioned in front of a computer screen. "Let's establish a baseline for each of you individually, then we can explore what happens when you work together."

As Fenella settled into the chair, she cast an uncertain glance at Din, who gave her an encouraging nod.

Syssi wondered what they might discover.

The Clan Mother's instincts were rarely wrong.

If she believed that Kyra, Jasmine, and Fenella were the key to finding Khiann, then they were, or at the very least, they were an essential component of the effort to find him. And if they actually found Annani's long-lost husband after five thousand years, it would change everything, not just for the Clan Mother, but for their entire immortal community.

34

AREZOO

Arezoo took a sip of water from the cup she'd collected at the serve-out bar. Her mother had given her the clan credit card that was good for use at the café, but Arezoo felt bad about using it.

She didn't like feeling like a charity case, but that was her reality.

They were getting everything they needed for free, and her mother was only using the card for necessities.

After her meeting with Drova, Arezoo was going to ask for a job in the café, and if she got it, she would finally have some spending money and buy that straightening iron she desperately needed.

Some eyeliner and mascara would be nice too.

Not that it would help much. She was considered pretty back home, but here she was as plain as a broom. The immortals were all so perfect that it was hard to look at them, and they all looked the same age.

How was she supposed to interact with them and find a boyfriend?

Solve one problem at a time, her mother used to say.

First, she would meet Drova and thank her for taking part in the rescue mission that got her and her sisters out of the clutches of that monster, and then she was going to ask the tall, beautiful woman behind the counter for a job.

Aunt Kyra had arranged this meeting with Drova, insisting that the two young women might "find common ground."

Arezoo doubted it. What could she possibly have in common with a seventeen-year-old Kra-ell warrior?

Arezoo had spent her life focused on doing well in school and watching over her sisters and cousins. She had never held a weapon in her life unless it was a kitchen knife or a spatula.

Scanning the café again, she wondered if she would recognize Drova from that chaotic night of their escape. Her memories were fragmented—flashes of gunfire, shouted commands, the acrid smell of smoke and fear. She remembered a very thin, tall girl with an injured shoulder, leaning on an even taller female who looked a lot like her.

That was probably Jade, Drova's mother and the leader of the Kra-ell residing in the village.

As a shadow fell across her table, Arezoo looked up to see the girl she'd just been trying to reconstruct from memory.

Tall and thin, with huge dark eyes and a long ponytail of perfectly straight, glossy black hair. Definitely Kra-ell, and unmistakably a warrior from her uniform to her stance.

"Arezoo?" she asked, her voice surprisingly soft despite her intimidating appearance.

"Yes." Arezoo stood, extending her hand. "Thank you for meeting me."

Drova reached out and grasped her hand with surprising gentleness. "Your aunt and my mother decided that we should get to know each other since we are close in age." She glanced at the plastic cup with water on the table. "I'm going to get myself a juice box. Can I get you anything?"

Arezoo felt her cheeks reddening. "No, thank you. I'm fine with just water." She patted her rounded tummy. "I'm trying to lose weight."

Drova gave her a quizzical look as if she didn't know what Arezoo was talking about, but then nodded. "I'll be back in a minute."

As the Kra-ell walked away, Arezoo released a breath and sank into her chair. What had possessed her to say that she was trying to lose weight? Of course, the warrior girl wouldn't understand why someone would struggle with maintaining a slim figure. Not just because the Kra-ell were almost comically thin, but because the immortals they lived among were all perfect.

That could be her after the transition. She would never have to worry about a few extra pounds or annoying pimples that popped up whenever she was stressed or got her period.

Drova returned with a strange-looking juice box and settled across from her. Arezoo tried not to stare as Drova punctured it with the straw and took a sip of the dark red liquid inside. It looked like tomato juice, but the picture on the front was of a red flower.

"Does it gross you out?" Drova asked.

"No, why?"

Drova shrugged. "Humans and immortals get grossed out by us drinking blood. This is artificial, and someone in the clan came up with the brilliant idea of preserving it in what looked like juice boxes and serving it in the café."

Arezoo swallowed.

Of course, it was blood. What else would a pure-blooded Kra-ell drink?

"It's a good idea. Makes it more discreet."

Drova nodded, and an awkward silence stretched between them.

"I wanted to thank you for rescuing us," Arezoo said. "I remember that you were injured."

"Yes." Drova touched her shoulder. "I wasn't at my finest on that mission. I lost my voice amplifier and then got myself shot. My shoulder is almost back to normal, but it's still not perfect. Kra-ell don't heal as fast as immortals."

Another awkward silence fell between them, and Arezoo searched desperately for something to say, some common ground to establish. What could possibly bridge the gap between a sheltered human girl and a Kra-ell warrior?

She remembered her mother's advice about getting people to talk about themselves. "My aunt mentioned that you are training for the Guardian Force. What's that like?"

Drova grinned. "I love it. It's intense. Combat drills, weapons training, strategy sessions, you know, the standard stuff."

Arezoo had no clue. "That sounds challenging."

"Not really. It's what I was born to do." Drova shrugged. "The Kra-ell are warriors by nature."

"What about school? Did you graduate early?"

She could have finished all the requirements at seventeen. It wasn't that hard.

Drova shifted in her seat, her posture stiffening. "I was given a pass. I'm not good at studying. Physical activity comes more naturally to me than the academic stuff."

"I see." Arezoo didn't want to say anything that

would sound offensive. "Not everyone likes studying."

"It's not that I don't like it," Drova admitted after a moment. "I just can't focus. My mind drifts, and I get restless. Reading makes my head hurt. I learn better by doing than by reading about doing."

Something clicked in Arezoo's mind—the same pattern she'd observed in students with learning difficulties during her volunteer work at the literacy center in her former high school. "Have you always had trouble focusing on written material?"

Drova frowned. "I suppose. Schooling in the compound was limited to the very basics. My mother taught us mostly by telling us stories, but the majority of time and effort was spent on combat training."

Arezoo frowned. "What compound?"

Drova trained those strange, large eyes on her. "You are not the only one who was rescued and freed. My people were also enslaved, and the enslaver was my father." She grimaced. "I'd rather not talk about it."

Arezoo briefly closed her eyes, then opened them and sighed. "My father is not a nice man either, and I perfectly understand why you prefer not to talk about yours."

Drova snorted. "Mine was a monster, but let's not get into my-daddy-is-worse-than-yours."

"Agreed." Arezoo laughed, suddenly feeling much

more kinship with this alien girl than she'd thought possible only minutes ago. "But back to your learning difficulties, it sounds like something I might be able to help you with if you are interested. I wanted to become a special education teacher, so I know a thing or two about learning disabilities."

"A what?" Drova's eyes narrowed.

"It's just a difference in how your brain processes written information," Arezoo clarified quickly. "It's actually quite common, even among brilliant people. Some of the most successful humans in history had similar challenges."

"Kra-ell don't have learning disabilities." A defensive edge crept into Drova's voice. "We're just genetically more suitable for warfare."

Arezoo realized that she'd inadvertently offended her. "Different species might have different learning styles. Vrog is one of your people, and he's an educator. Hasn't he mentioned anything about alternative approaches that might work better for you?"

Drova shrugged. "He gave me the standard stuff every kid here needs to know to pass the equivalency test."

Perhaps Vrog wasn't aware of learning disabilities?

"I met Vrog when he came to our house to design a curriculum for me and my sisters." Arezoo took a small sip of water to wet her throat. "He mentioned that he used to run a school for exceptional students, but he didn't actually have a background in education. He was in technology before opening the school. He might not recognize different learning needs."

"It doesn't matter," Drova said with a dismissive wave of her hand. "Being a Guardian is what I was born to do. I'm a fighter, and with my rare compulsion ability, I'm an asset to the Force. I don't need to be good at math or history."

"If you ever change your mind, I'd be happy to help you. There are techniques that might make it easier for you to absorb information."

Drova looked at her with a frown. "Why? What's in it for you?"

"That's what I was studying to do—help people learn in ways that work for them. I enjoy doing that as much as you enjoy training to be a guardian. Besides, I could use a friend in the village."

Drova took a sip of her drink, making a slurping sound that was kind of gross. "I'm not sure I'd make a good friend for you. I don't socialize much outside the Kra-ell community."

"Why not?" Arezoo asked.

"There are only a few young immortals and humans in the village, and they are too young for me. I also have a history with them that is not a good one."

"What do you mean?"

"I was stupid," Drova admitted. "When my

compulsion ability first started to emerge, I thought I was invincible. I compelled the kids to steal things for me and to sabotage equipment. I thought I was being a big-time rebel, that I would lead the Kra-ell to leave the village and live independently." She shook her head. "I'm grateful to Kian for going easy on me when it was discovered."

Arezoo was surprised by such blunt honesty. Most people would have glossed over their past mistakes or made excuses. "That's remarkably forthright of you to admit."

"I take responsibility for my actions," Drova said with a shrug. "If I don't try to hide it, no one can throw it in my face."

"That's smart," Arezoo said. "I respect that, and I think you're incredibly brave. Not just because of your honesty, but because you took part in the rescue mission that got me, my sisters, and my cousin out. I envy you for being such a fierce warrior."

Something shifted in Drova's expression—pride breaking through her stoic exterior. "It's just a job. Kra-ell become fighters at a young age. That's what we're born to do."

"Still, it's admirable," Arezoo insisted. "I'd like to find my own purpose here. I need a job, actually. I don't want to rely entirely on the clan's generosity."

"What kind of job are you looking for?" Drova asked.

Arezoo glanced at the woman behind the counter. "I was told that working in the café is a good idea. That and babysitting."

"Wonder is always looking for help," Drova said. "Do you want me to ask her for you?" She was already on her feet.

"It would be great if you could introduce me." Arezoo stood as well and followed Drova to the counter.

"What can I do for you, ladies?" the beautiful, dark-haired woman asked.

"Wonder, this is Arezoo," Drova said. "She's looking for a part-time job, and I know that you are always looking for help."

Wonder turned her kind gaze to Arezoo. "Any experience serving coffee?"

"No," Arezoo admitted. "But I'm a quick learner, and I'm willing to work hard."

Wonder smiled. "You can start tomorrow, and we'll see how it goes. Be here at seven in the morning."

"Really?" Arezoo couldn't contain her surprise. "Thank you! I won't disappoint you."

"I know you won't."

As they stepped away from the counter, Arezoo turned to Drova with a grateful smile. "Thank you for that. I didn't expect it to be so easy."

Drova shrugged. "It's nothing. There is plenty of work in the village for those who are not too discriminating. Cleaning houses can get you the big bucks for now, but those types of jobs are not going to be available for long. The robots they are building in the underground will be doing those."

Arezoo's eyes widened. "Robots?"

"Yeah. Do you want to see? I can give you a tour."

"Yes, please!"

35

FENELLA

Fenella sat in an uncomfortable chair in Amanda's laboratory, electrodes stuck to her temples like some ridiculous science fiction prop. The whole setup reminded her of a low budget film about mind control, complete with blinking monitors and hushed, technical conversations she couldn't quite follow.

"Try to relax," Amanda said, adjusting something on her tablet. "Tension can interfere with the readings."

"I'm perfectly relaxed," Fenella lied, gripping the armrests tighter. "Nothing more soothing than having my brain probed by aliens."

Amanda chuckled. "When you are one of those aliens, it's not so bad, right?"

As Fenella cast the ridiculously beautiful

professor a glare, she caught Din giving her an encouraging smile from his position in the rear of the room.

Another professor. No wonder they were teaming up against her.

"The electrodes don't read your thoughts," Syssi explained. "They just measure electrical activity in different parts of your brain."

"That's supposed to be reassuring?" Fenella arched an eyebrow.

Amanda chuckled. "It's completely noninvasive. I promise you won't feel even the slightest discomfort. And remember, you can stop anytime you want."

Fenella sighed and tried to loosen her shoulders. She didn't have any special abilities. But these women, her newfound relatives, seemed convinced otherwise, and she didn't have the heart to quash their enthusiasm.

"Let's start with something simple." Amanda positioned herself behind a computer screen that Fenella couldn't see. "I'm going to show Kyra a series of geometric shapes. She won't say anything, but I want you to try to pick up on what she's seeing."

"Telepathy?" Fenella scoffed. "You're joking."

"Just give it a try," Jasmine encouraged. "Clear your mind and see if any shapes pop into your head."

Fenella rolled her eyes while Kyra seated herself across from her. At Amanda's nod, Kyra's hand closed over the pendant at her throat, and her eyes grew distant.

Five minutes of silence followed, during which Fenella thought of juicy steaks, red wine, cocktail recipes, and the tile pattern in Shira's bathroom—anything but geometric shapes.

"Anything?" Amanda asked finally.

"Unless you were hoping I'd telepathically pick up on Kyra's thoughts about vodka martini variations, the answer is no."

Amanda made some notes. "That's fine. Let's try something else." She tapped her tablet, and the monitor in front of Fenella lit up with a simple game interface. "This will display a shape, but there's a three-second delay between when the computer selects the shape and when it appears on the screen. I want you to try to guess what's coming."

"Precognition?" Fenella sighed but nodded. "Fine."

The first shape—a red triangle—appeared without warning. Fenella hadn't had even an inkling it was coming.

"That's all right," Amanda said. "Let's try again. Focus on the blank screen."

Shape after shape appeared—circles, squares, stars, hexagons—and Fenella punched the keys more to appear as if she was cooperating than because she was sensing what shape was coming next. After twenty minutes, she was too frustrated to continue and had developed a headache.

"This is pointless," she muttered. "I told you I don't have any special abilities."

"Let's see how Kyra does," Amanda suggested, gesturing for Kyra to switch places with Fenella.

Relieved to be free of the electrodes, Fenella walked over to where Din was sitting and sat on the chair next to him.

He reached for her hand and clasped it. "How are you doing?"

"Not good. My head is about to explode."

"Ready?" Amanda asked, and Kyra nodded, her fingers wrapping around her pendant.

The first shape hadn't even flashed on the screen when Kyra punched a key and spoke. "Green circle."

The green circle appeared.

"Blue square," Kyra said confidently, and sure enough, a blue square followed.

"Yellow star... Red hexagon... Purple triangle..."

Kyra identified shape after shape with perfect accuracy, her expression calm and focused, fingers never leaving the amber pendant at her throat.

"Show-off," Fenella muttered, but there was no real heat behind it. Instead, she felt a twinge of something like envy. Not for the ability itself, but for the confidence with which Kyra wielded it.

After a few minutes, Kyra started to make mistakes, and Amanda stopped the experiment.

"Incredible readings," Amanda said, studying her

tablet, then moving to another station. "Jasmine, you're up next." She waved her over.

Jasmine settled into the chair with an ease that suggested she'd done this before. Instead of a shape-guessing task, Amanda provided her with a sealed envelope that had something written on top of it.

"Those are coordinates," Amanda said. "Try to describe the location."

Jasmine closed her eyes, and after several moments of silence, she opened them. "Sydney Opera House," Jasmine said with a hint of uncertainty in her voice. "Am I right?"

"I don't know," Amanda said. "If I knew what was inside, you could have picked it up from my mind, which could have confused the results, but since those envelopes are prepared ahead of time by my assistants, I have no idea what is inside them. You have to open the envelope to find out."

Jasmine did as instructed and pulled out a postcard depicting the opera house.

"Look at that." Amanda grinned. "Just as I suspected, that was far viewing. The ability to perceive distant objects or locations."

"Wow. I had no idea," Jasmine said. "I thought it was the scrying stick."

"It helped you focus," Amanda said. "Now let's see what happens when you work together. Did you bring the stick with you?"

Jasmine nodded. "It's in my purse."

"Go get it," Amanda instructed.

After Jasmine got her stick, she and Kyra sat side by side. Kyra's hand was on her pendant, while Jasmine's fingers were wrapped around her stick. They joined their free hands, forming a connection.

"Let's try something more challenging," Amanda said, producing a new envelope. "This contains coordinates to a location that's not a major tourist attraction. See if you can describe what's there."

The women closed their eyes, their clasped hands tightening. The air in the laboratory seemed to thicken, an almost tangible energy building around them. Fenella felt the fine hairs on her arms stand up.

"A temple," Jasmine murmured. "Ancient... crumbling... half-buried in sand."

"There's a false wall," Kyra continued, her voice distant.

"Darkness..." Jasmine's voice grew softer.

They fell silent simultaneously, their eyes opening as they released each other's hands. Both looked slightly dazed.

"That was..." Kyra began.

"So much more powerful than when we worked separately," Jasmine finished.

"Excellent," Amanda said with a grin. "The neural synchronization patterns are extraordinary. Your abilities aren't just adding together—together they're amplified exponentially."

"What did we see?" Kyra asked.

Amanda gestured at the envelope. "Open it and find out."

As Kyra lifted the picture to show everyone, it depicted exactly what they had described—a burial chamber in some desert location. Kyra turned it around to read the inscription on the back of the photograph. "This is a tomb site in China."

"It's exactly what the Clan Mother suspected," Syssi said. "There is a resonance between you."

Fenella shifted uncomfortably, acutely aware that she was supposed to be part of this magical family circle. The only problem was that she apparently didn't have anything to contribute.

"So where do I fit into this?" she asked.

Amanda turned to Morelle, who had been observing silently from Din's other side. "What do you sense?"

Morelle switched seats and sat next to Fenella. "May I?" She extended her hand.

"Sure." Fenella clasped the female's slender hand.

Morelle held on for a long moment before letting go. "There's definitely power there. I can sense it, and it calls out to me." She smiled. "I'm like a vampire smelling blood. When I sense power, I want to absorb it."

Fenella shivered at the predatory gleam in the female's eyes. Morelle hadn't been joking. She looked like she was hungry and wanted to drink up what she'd sensed in Fenella.

"Can you tell what kind of power it is?" Amanda asked.

Morelle shook her head. "To me, they all seem the same. Power is power."

Fenella frowned. "So, I supposedly have some mysterious power that no one can identify, and I can't access? That's helpful."

"We just haven't found the right trigger yet," Amanda said, undeterred. "Let's try a different approach."

For the next hour, they subjected Fenella to a battery of tests. She tried to bend spoons with her mind, which was utterly ridiculous, predict the order of a shuffled deck of cards, which was embarrassing, and guess the contents of a locked box, which was as pointless as all the rest.

Each failure only added to her frustration.

"This is a waste of time," she finally snapped, tearing off the electrodes for the third time. "I don't have any magical powers."

"Morelle sensed something in you," Kyra insisted. "And the Clan Mother believes you're meant to help us find Khiann."

"Based on what? The fact that we share a great-great-great-grandmother from eight centuries ago?" Fenella stood, pacing the small space between monitors. "That's hardly a mystical connection, or any connection for that matter. I bet most of the residents of my little town in Scotland have more recent shared ancestors."

Kyra watched her for a moment, then unclasped her pendant from around her neck. "Try this," she said, holding it out. "Maybe it will help you focus your power like it does for me."

Fenella stared at the amber stone with its etched symbols. "What am I supposed to do with it?"

"Just hold it," Kyra said. "Sometimes an object can help focus abilities."

"That's actually not a bad idea," Amanda said. "If your abilities are similar, the pendant might serve as a catalyst."

Fenella sighed but took the pendant, if only to humor them. The stone was warm from Kyra's body heat, smooth except for the etched symbols that caught against her fingertips.

"Now what?" she asked.

"Just concentrate on it," Kyra instructed. "See if you feel anything."

Fenella stared at the amber, feeling faintly ridiculous. But just as she was about to hand it back and suggest they call it a day, something changed. The warmth of the stone seemed to intensify, spreading up her fingers into her palm. The laboratory around her grew distant, sounds muffling as if she were underwater.

And then—images.

A darkened room, men with guns, the acrid smell of blood and gunpowder. The pendant burned hot against her skin as bullets flew overhead.

A mountain pass, snow blinding in the sunlight, the pendant growing warm in warning as hidden snipers took position.

A concrete room, a young girl tied to a chair, her eyes wide with terror. The pendant was vibrating with urgency as Kyra cut through the ropes.

The visions came faster, one bleeding into the next—fragments of missions, moments of danger, split-second decisions. Fenella gasped, overwhelmed by the flood of memories that weren't hers.

The pendant slipped from her fingers, clattering to the laboratory floor, and Fenella staggered backward, would have fallen if Din hadn't moved with immortal speed to catch her.

"Bloody hell," she whispered, her heart racing. "What was that?"

Kyra bent to retrieve the pendant, examining it for damage. "What did you see?"

"Your bloody life," Fenella said shakily. "Is the pendant okay?"

"It's fine. Nothing got damaged." Kyra pulled the string over her head and tucked the stone under her shirt. "What did you mean by my bloody life?" She imitated Fenella's accent.

"Gunfire. Rescues. Places I've never been. Things I've never done." Fenella ran a trembling hand through her hair. "It was like the pendant was showing off, letting me see everywhere it had been with you and how it had helped you."

Amanda's face broke into a delighted smile. "Psychometry," she said, typing rapidly on her tablet. "The ability to obtain information about a person or event by touching objects associated with them."

"Brilliant," Jasmine breathed. "That's why the Clan Mother thinks you are the key to finding Khiann. If you could touch something of his..."

"You might be able to see where he is now," Kyra finished.

Fenella shook her head, still dizzy from the intensity of the visions. "That's not how it worked. I didn't see where the pendant is now—I saw where it had been in the past. It was its history, not its present."

"But Khiann is in stasis," Syssi pointed out. "For him, there is no present—only the moment he was placed there. His 'now' is still five thousand years ago. The problem is that we don't have anything of his that he carried with him when the earthquake happened. Whatever he had is buried with him."

Din put his hand on Fenella's shoulder. "Are you all right?"

"I'm fine," she said automatically, then reconsidered. "Actually, no. I feel like someone just force-fed me a decade of someone else's memories."

"That's essentially what happened," Amanda said.

"Your brain processed years of sensory information in seconds. It's no wonder you're disoriented."

"Can any of you do this?" Fenella asked, looking around at the others. "Get visions from touching objects?"

They shook their heads.

"Each of us has different abilities," Jasmine said. "Kyra has precognition, I have far-viewing, and you have psychometry."

"But together we are stronger." Kyra's eyes were bright with excitement. "Together, we might be able to find Khiann when none of us could do it alone."

"I don't really see how." Fenella sat heavily in the nearest chair. "And how come it has never happened to me before? I've touched plenty of objects that belonged to other people. I never got any impressions from their lives."

"Maybe it has to be a special object," Syssi said. "We should have you talk with Jacki, Kalugal's wife. She has the same type of talent. They are in Egypt right now, but they are coming back for Kian and Allegra's birthday on Saturday."

"Those visions hit me like a freight train," Fenella murmured.

"The shared lineage must be the key," Amanda said. "That could be another reason why it never happened to you before. You need Kyra and Jasmine to resonate with you." She shook her head in wonder. "The Fates have outdone themselves this time."

"So, what now?" Fenella asked, still feeling light-headed and overwhelmed.

"Now we practice," Kyra said. "Together and separately. We hone our abilities until the Fates provide us with the missing piece we need to find Khiann."

36

AREZOO

*A*rezoo hadn't expected the café to be buzzing with activity at seven-thirty in the morning, with patrons forming a long line to the counter, and Wonder and Aliya working at a pace that seemed inhuman.

Well, to be fair, neither of them was entirely human. Both were part aliens, and not even from the same species.

Not for the first time, Arezoo wondered if she was dreaming, and this was an elaborate fantasy that her mind had created.

"Don't look so terrified," Wonder said, glancing over at her while simultaneously brewing espresso, steaming milk, and taking an order from a tall, intimidatingly handsome immortal in workout clothes. "The chaos will subside once the morning rush is over."

Arezoo nodded, not really knowing what to do or say. So far, she'd been busy staying out of the way of Wonder and Aliya's well-coordinated dance, hoping someone would tell her what to do.

"Here you go, Henry." Wonder handed the guy a cup. "Extra shot of espresso, just the way you like it."

Henry offered Arezoo a friendly nod. "New recruit?"

"This is Arezoo," Wonder confirmed. "She just started today."

"Welcome to the village." He smiled. "Don't let these two work you too hard."

"I want to work hard," Arezoo said, hoping the translating earpieces were not messing up the communication for her.

She'd learned that literal translations from English to Farsi and the other way around often didn't convey the same meaning.

As Henry walked away, Wonder gestured toward the growing line. "Just watch me for a little while, and once you get the hang of it, I'll let you start taking orders." She offered her a dazzling smile that was nearly blinding.

Wonder was a tall, dark-haired beauty with olive-toned skin just like Arezoo's, but she was so much more beautiful that it was disconcerting to look at her and make the unflattering comparison.

Arezoo secretly hoped that the transition would transform her into a stunning beauty like her new boss, but she knew that, realistically, that wasn't possible. The starting point was too far off.

Aliya was also gorgeous and a little intimidating. She was only half Kra-ell, but the Kra-ell side was definitely winning. Her big, dark eyes could barely pass for human, and she was tall and incredibly thin like the pureblooded Kra-ell.

How were they so strong with those long and lean limbs of theirs?

Nature was indeed wondrous, and conventional wisdom wasn't always right.

"Ready to try the register?" Wonder asked during a brief lull.

Arezoo nodded. "I think so. It looks easy."

No one used cash in the village. The only form of payment was the clan-issued credit card, and people just tapped it against the display after Wonder or Aliya entered the ordered items. The touch screen was intuitive, with pictures of the various drinks and food items making it easy to navigate.

A monkey could have done that after watching them do it for five minutes.

"It is," Wonder said. "I'll handle the coffee while you take orders and Aliya serves the tables. Just call out the orders clearly so I can hear them over the machines."

The register was not a problem. It was the interactions with the customers that were stressful.

Everyone was nice, and they were patient with

her, but Arezoo had never worked with customers before.

"You're doing well." Aliya leaned against the counter during a brief pause in the rush. "Getting used to all these new faces isn't easy, and remembering everyone's names is even harder, but you will eventually be able to greet everyone by name." She leaned closer to whisper in Arezoo's earpiece. "Do you know what mnemonics are?"

Arezoo nodded. "Things that help you remember other things."

"Exactly. I try to find something about each person's appearance that will remind me of their name. I made a game out of it."

"That's smart," Arezoo said.

"Wasn't my idea. It was Vrog's. He's my mate, you know."

Arezoo's eyes widened. "I didn't know that. He's very nice."

Aliya smiled, which looked kind of strange on her Kra-ell face. They didn't smile much. "I know, right? He's the nicest male. He also gave you a compliment, saying that you were smart and that you should go to college."

"I want to," Arezoo said. "I want to become a teacher for special needs kids."

Remembering her talk with Drova, she wanted to ask Aliya if she was aware of other Kra-ell with learning disabilities, but she didn't feel comfortable asking her a question like that so soon. Maybe later, when they became friends, she could ask her, or better yet, she could ask Vrog the next time he came over to check on her and her sisters' progress with the self-learning program he'd designed for them.

Aliya tilted her head. "Can women get higher education in Iran?"

Arezoo felt her cheeks heat up. "Yes. We are not as backward as some of the other countries in our area."

"I'm sorry if I offended you." Aliya pushed away from the counter and turned around to face the new group of customers heading their way.

Soon, Arezoo was back to the whirlwind pace of taking orders and calling out drink specifications to Wonder, who worked the espresso machine like she had four arms instead of two.

Sometime after ten in the morning, the rush had finally subsided, leaving only a handful of patrons scattered among the café's tables. Arezoo's feet ached, and her cheeks hurt from smiling, but she felt accomplished.

She hadn't messed up any orders, and she'd only fumbled a few words here and there.

"Take a break," Wonder said. "Grab something to eat and drink and sit down."

"Thank you," Arezoo said.

She selected a blueberry muffin from the display

case and poured herself a cup of tea before sinking onto a stool behind the counter.

"Have the two of you been working here for long?" she asked to start a conversation.

Wonder laughed, the sound like water over stones. "Not at all. This whole village is quite new."

"What did you do before that?"

"I was a bouncer in a nightclub." Wonder poured herself a coffee and joined Arezoo at the counter.

That was an odd occupation for a woman, but Arezoo didn't want to offend Wonder by saying that.

"Do they have a nightclub in the village?" she asked instead.

"No, but I wish they did. There is a shortage of recreation options in the village. I worked in clubs before I discovered that I wasn't the only immortal in the world. I was very effective thanks to my strength."

Arezoo frowned, remembering what she'd been told about immortals belonging to one of two camps. They were either affiliated with the clan or with the Doomers, and there were no lone wolves out there.

"Forgive me for asking, but how come you were alone?"

Wonder cradled her cup. "I didn't know any immortals other than myself existed. I entered stasis five thousand years ago when an earthquake swallowed my caravan, and I woke up a few years ago when a water pipe burst near the place I was buried in."

Arezoo tilted her head. "Is water what's needed to revive someone from stasis?"

Wonder nodded. "It's that simple. The thing is, I was buried in the desert, where there was no rainfall, so I stayed in stasis for five thousand years. When I woke up, I found myself in a brand-new world, still nineteen, which was the age I was when I entered stasis, and with no memory of who and what I was."

Arezoo couldn't imagine how terrifying that had to have been for Wonder. "What did you do?"

"I dug my way out like a deranged mummy and scared the life out of anyone who saw me. I stole a burka from a clothesline and covered myself until I gained enough muscle and fat not to scare people."

"That's incredible," Arezoo murmured. "Did you have a family? Did you try to find them?"

A shadow passed over Wonder's face. "At first, I didn't remember who I was. The Fates helped me find my way to the clan, and I got reunited with my childhood best friend, the Clan Mother. Seeing her revived my memories, and I learned that everyone back home was dead. Later, I discovered that my sister Tula lived."

Arezoo's head was spinning. Wonder was the Clan Mother's best friend? How?

She had so many questions she wanted to ask the woman, but didn't feel comfortable asking yet.

"I'm glad your sister survived. Are you two close?"

That was an innocent enough question that shouldn't be difficult to answer, but the shadow over Wonder's face grew darker.

"We were very close, but it's not possible now. Anyway, I found a new family, and my new home is here with my mate and my best friend."

There was one more question that was just burning in Arezoo's mind, and she couldn't help but ask it. "I guess that you weren't named Wonder at birth. Did you adopt the name because you couldn't remember your own?"

Wonder nodded. "Back in Egypt, a child called me Wonder Woman because I resemble the actress who played the character in the movie, and when it happened again, I decided it was a good name and adopted it."

"What's your real name?"

Wonder grimaced. "I was called Gulan, and I always hated it. It was a name that befitted a servant girl, and I no longer felt like it fit me."

Arezoo nodded, thinking that she would have liked to change her name as well. She wanted something that sounded American, like Judy, Sally, or Nancy.

Her mother would never agree to her actually using a different name, but perhaps when she went to college, she could tell everyone that she preferred to be called something else.

"The name Wonder fits you well," Arezoo finally said. "It gives me food for thought on the kind of name I will adopt one day."

"What's wrong with Arezoo?" Aliya asked. "I think it has a nice sound to it."

"I want a new beginning," Arezoo whispered. "A completely new beginning. And this name ties me to a country and people I don't want to belong to. People who allowed themselves to be conquered by an alien ideology that stripped them of their dignity. The ancient Persians and their proud empire are gone, and they shouldn't have gone down in history that way."

The two women looked at her with twin puzzled expressions, clearly having no clue what she was talking about. The truth was that she'd surprised herself with those words, which could have gotten her hanged in Iran.

"Well, enough about reinventing ourselves," Wonder said. "It's time for the next lesson. Let me show you how to make a proper cappuccino."

37

ANNANI

Annani held the delicate gold necklace in her hands, fingers tracing the ancient filigree with a tenderness born of five millennia of longing. Every curve and swirl of the precious metal was as familiar to her as her own heartbeat. Khiann had gotten it for her after they were married, one of many pieces of jewelry he had bought for her.

Over the years, she had been forced to sell many of those precious gifts to sustain her growing clan, but she had kept a few she wasn't willing to part with.

"Even the best craftsmanship in the world cannot produce beauty that does not pale beside yours, my love," he had whispered as he fastened it around her neck.

She wore the necklace only on special occasions, but over five thousand years, that had amounted to countless moments and memories for Fenella to access. The question was whether Fenella could access Khiann through it, and the answer was, probably not.

The necklace had been in his possession for only a short time before he had given it to Annani, so he could not have imparted too many memories onto it, and even if he had, those were memories from before the disaster that had claimed his body, but hopefully, not the spark of life retained within it.

"Will this suffice, Clan Mother?" Ogidu interrupted her reverie, standing beside the elegantly arranged tea service to await her approval.

Annani surveyed the spread with an appreciative smile. The delicate cucumber sandwiches, miniature pastries, and an assortment of teas were served in her favorite porcelain set. "It is perfect, Ogidu. Thank you."

"Shall I bring out a fruit platter as well?" he asked.

"Fruit is always a good idea," Annani said. "My guests might enjoy it."

When the doorbell rang a few moments later, and Oridu walked over to open the door to show her guests in, Annani carefully returned the necklace to its velvet-lined box and rose to greet the three ladies she had invited for a mid-morning tea.

She extended her hands in welcome. "Thank you for coming on such short notice." She motioned at the couch and armchairs. "Please, make yourselves comfortable."

"It's an honor to be invited to your home again, Clan Mother." Kyra dipped her head before taking a seat on one of the armchairs.

"Yes," Fenella agreed. "It's a great honor." Her gaze darted around the room. "You have a beautiful place."

"Thank you," Annani said. "It is not much different than all the other residences in this section of the village. I just added a few personal touches here and there."

Fenella seemed to be searching the walls for something. "I was told that you had a portrait of Khiann commissioned from a forensic artist. Is there a chance you can show it to us?"

The portrait hung in Annani's bedroom, and she did not like inviting anyone in there, but she had stored a copy in the gallery of photographs on her phone.

"Of course." Annani settled on the sofa and pulled out the device. "Do you want me to send you the picture?"

"That would be great. Maybe it will help us in some way." Fenella looked at Kyra and Jasmine. "The three of us should have it."

Annani nodded. "I should have thought of that. I am sending it to you all."

When their phones pinged with the incoming message, all three women immediately looked at their screens, and a moment later, a chorus of oohs and ahhhs ensued.

"He's beautiful," Jasmine breathed.

Fenella and Kyra nodded in agreement.

"Yes, he is." Annani's throat constricted. She turned toward Fenella and forced a smile. "I want to congratulate you upon the discovery of your remarkable talent."

Fenella shifted uncomfortably. "Thank you, Clan Mother, but I'm not sure *remarkable* is the word I'd use. The words 'invasive' and 'disorienting' come to mind."

"Psychometry can be overwhelming," Annani acknowledged. "Objects carry so much history, so many impressions. Learning to filter what you allow yourself to receive is a skill that comes with practice."

"So I'm told," Fenella said. "Though I'm not convinced it's a skill worth developing. Touching Kyra's pendant was like having someone force-feed me a decade of memories in seconds."

"I understand," Annani said. "But it might be the key to finding my Khiann."

Fenella's expression softened. "I'm more than willing to try. I just don't want to get anyone's hopes up."

Ogidu walked in with the tea tray, offering it first to Annani, then to each of the guests in turn.

"Try the cucumber sandwiches," Annani encouraged. "They are simple but delightful."

"They're delicious." Jasmine took a small sandwich. "I've always loved the ritual of tea, whether it was in the morning or in the afternoon."

"Tea and little sandwiches are very pleasant," Kyra agreed, her gaze focused intently on Annani. "But I suspect we're not here for just that."

Annani smiled. "I like your directness, Kyra, and you are quite right. I have asked you here because of Fenella's psychometric ability and what Amanda told me about the three of you working together." She set her teacup down. "When you touch objects, Fenella, you perceive their history, the moments and memories they have witnessed."

"In vivid, overwhelming detail," Fenella confirmed. "At least that's what happened with Kyra's pendant."

"The pendant has been with Kyra through many intense experiences," Annani said. "It is not surprising that it carries powerful impressions."

"Amanda said I should practice with simpler objects." Fenella put her teacup down on the coffee table. "Things with less dramatic histories."

"A sensible approach," Annani agreed. "But time is not a luxury we have in abundance. Not when it comes to finding my Khiann."

The three women exchanged glances, and Annani

could sense their unspoken communication—the subtle bond of shared blood asserting itself.

"Do you have something of his?" Jasmine asked.

"I do." Annani reached for the velvet box on the side table. "This is a necklace Khiann gave me shortly after our wedding." She opened the box, revealing the exquisite gold piece nestled against dark fabric.

"It's beautiful," Kyra breathed.

"And very old," Jasmine added.

"Five thousand years," Annani confirmed.

Fenella eyed the necklace with obvious apprehension. "And you want me to touch it and see if I can pick up anything about Khiann?"

"That is my hope, yes," Annani said. "But the truth is that I do not expect to miraculously find Khiann with its help."

"That's a relief," Fenella said dryly.

Annani smiled. "The necklace has been in my possession far longer than it was in Khiann's. I have worn it countless times throughout the millennia. I fear that any impressions you might receive will be of my memories, not his."

"That's kind of obvious," Fenella said.

"It still might provide some insight." Annani traced her finger over the delicate pattern. "Perhaps the necklace retains some impression of the moment Khiann presented it to me, or of him fastening it around my neck, and maybe that will give you the connection you need to where he is now."

Fenella's brow furrowed. "I don't know if I can control what I see. With Kyra's pendant, the visions just flooded in."

"I understand that, child. All I am asking you to do is try."

"Of course." Fenella straightened her shoulders. "I'm willing to try anything and everything to help you find Khiann."

That was said with so much conviction that Annani felt touched. Fenella was not motivated just by gratitude. It was about one woman feeling the pain of another and wanting to do everything in her power to alleviate it.

It was the essence of goodness.

Annani held out the box but hesitated before passing it to Fenella. This necklace was one of her most treasured possessions, a tangible connection to Khiann that had survived when so much else had been lost to time. Letting another handle it, even for such an important purpose, required an act of trust.

"Perhaps we should do this over the sofa," Jasmine suggested. "In case Fenella drops it like she did with the pendant."

"It's a valid concern," Fenella said. "My heart nearly shattered along with the pendant when I dropped it after the visions hit me."

"The sofa is a wise precaution," Annani agreed,

moving to sit beside Fenella. She placed the velvet box between them.

Fenella took a deep breath. "Alright. Let's do this."

"Perhaps I should hold your hand?" Kyra asked. "When we work together, our abilities seem to strengthen each other."

"That is a good idea," Annani said. "The shared maternal lineage creates a resonance between you three. It is why the Fates brought you here together."

Kyra moved to sit on Fenella's other side, taking her free hand, while Jasmine positioned herself on the floor before them, her hand resting on Fenella's knee.

Fenella stared at the necklace for a long moment, then slowly extended her hand. Her fingers hovered over the gold, trembling slightly. "Here goes nothing," she murmured, and closed her hand around the delicate chain.

The effect was almost immediate. Fenella's eyes widened, her pupils dilating as her gaze turned inward. Her grip on Kyra's hand tightened, and her breathing became shallow and rapid.

Annani watched, heart pounding, as emotions flickered across Fenella's face—wonder, confusion, and something that looked unsettlingly like fear.

What was she seeing?

What memories did the necklace preserve?

After what seemed an eternity but could only

have been seconds, Fenella gasped and released the necklace, letting it fall back into its velvet nest. She pulled her hand away as if burned, her face pale.

"Fenella?" Kyra sounded concerned. "Are you all right?"

"I—yes," Fenella managed, though she looked unsettled. "It was intense."

"What did you see?" Annani asked, trying to keep the desperation from her voice.

Fenella hesitated, her gaze darting away from Annani's. "Snippets, mostly. Fragments of your memories. But none of them seemed ancient. Nothing that would help locate Khiann."

Disappointment settled like a cold weight in Annani's chest. "I feared as much. The necklace has been with me too long, gathered too many of my memories."

"It was mostly you wearing it on various occasions," Fenella confirmed. "They all seemed pretty recent."

"Nothing from earlier times?" Jasmine pressed.

Fenella shook her head. "I'm afraid not."

Annani studied Fenella's face, noting the careful way she was choosing her words. There was something the woman was not saying, some vision she was deliberately omitting. Annani's curiosity was piqued, but she would not press.

"You should try again," Kyra suggested. "Maybe

focus specifically on the oldest memories, try to push past the recent ones."

Fenella's expression tightened. "I don't think it works that way. I don't control what I see—it just comes at me in a flood."

"With practice—" Jasmine began.

"Perhaps another time," Annani interrupted, seeing Fenella's discomfort. "A newly discovered paranormal ability can be an intense experience. We should not push too hard, too quickly."

Relief flickered across Fenella's face. "Thank you."

Annani carefully closed the velvet box, securing the necklace inside. "This was a worthy first attempt. I have other objects that we can try, but they will probably yield the same results. I only have Khiann's gifts. I do not have anything that was personally his."

"Which brings us back to the original problem," Kyra pointed out.

"Indeed." Annani sighed. "A circular conundrum."

"We'll find him," Jasmine said with a confidence that warmed Annani's heart. "Between my far-viewing, Mother's precognition, and Fenella's psychometry, we have abilities the Fates clearly meant to work in concert."

Annani smiled. "Your confidence gives me hope."

"Hope is dangerous," Fenella murmured. "But sometimes it's all we have."

Annani studied the three women before her—Kyra with her warrior's resolve, Jasmine with her mystic's intuition, and Fenella with her hard-won resilience. They were an unlikely trio, brought together across time and continents by the machinations of the Fates. Yet in them, Annani sensed a powerful potential, a convergence of abilities that might accomplish what had seemed impossible.

"Would you care for more tea?" Annani offered, deciding to lighten the mood.

"Yes, thank you," Fenella said.

"By the way," Kyra said as Ogidu poured more tea into her cup. "My little niece Cyra has an interesting ability. I believe she's able to tap into the minds of people she gets physically close to, and she tapped into yours, Clan Mother. After meeting you and sitting in your lap, she started dreaming about a beautiful doll man sleeping under the sand. She told me we have to find him."

Annani shivered. "Perhaps she shares your family's talent, and she somehow saw my Khiann? Maybe she can somehow lead us to him."

Kyra smiled apologetically. "She couldn't have seen Khiann as he is now. Jasmine told me what Ellrom looked like after seven thousand years in stasis. If Cyra saw the real Khiann as he is now, she would have seen a skeleton. Instead, she saw him the way you think of him, still as beautiful and perfect as you remember him, and she also absorbed the urgency you feel to find him."

It all sounded logical, but Annani's gut told her

there was more to it. The little girl could be the key to it all.

She had to see the child again.

38

AREZOO

After countless attempts, Arezoo finally produced a cup of coffee that was not pretty but drinkable. It was recognizable as a cappuccino, but not at the level the café's patrons were accustomed to.

"It takes time." Wonder clapped Arezoo on her back. "Don't get discouraged."

Aliya glanced at the tables. "Looks like we have a few customers who might need refills. Want to try taking orders tableside?"

Arezoo didn't want to get so close to the customers. The register was one thing—the counter served as a barrier—but walking among the tables meant direct interaction with the village's intimidatingly beautiful immortals.

"They don't bite," Aliya said with a crooked smile. "Well, not unless they are invited to do so."

Arezoo swallowed. Aliya's words evoked images that were as terrifying as they were arousing. She'd overheard Aunt Kyra talking with her mother and the other aunts, giggling about how wonderful sex with immortal males was. They hadn't known she was in the living room while they'd acted like a bunch of teenage girls, and she'd pretended she hadn't heard anything, but that conversation was etched in her mind.

"That wasn't helpful," Wonder chided, then turned to Arezoo. "You'll be fine. Just be polite and ask if they need anything. If they have questions you can't answer, say you'll check with me."

Arezoo nodded, tucking a small notepad and pen in her apron pocket.

The first table she approached was safe, with two females who seemed nice. They smiled when they saw her, asking for refills of their teas and ordering two more croissants with a warmth that eased her nervousness.

Table by table, Arezoo made her way around the café. Most patrons were friendly, some merely polite, but none were rude, and she slowly relaxed, growing more confident with each interaction.

Until she reached the back, where a man sat alone at a small table in the shade of a large canopy. A laptop was open before him, but his attention wasn't on the screen. Instead, his gaze was fixed on her with an intensity that made her skin prickle.

He wasn't conventionally handsome like many of the immortal males she'd seen around the village and the café. He was slightly built, with narrow shoulders and a lean face.

Not ugly, but not striking either.

There was something about his stare, though, that made her uncomfortable.

"Can I get you anything?" she asked, steadying her voice.

He continued staring for a moment before answering. "Black coffee, please. No sugar."

His voice was softer than she'd expected, and a little hesitant, which somehow made the intensity of his gaze all the more unnerving.

"Right away, sir," she managed, jotting down the order even though it was simple enough to remember.

As she turned to leave, she felt his eyes follow her, a physical sensation like fingertips trailing down her spine. She quickened her pace, returning to the safety of the counter.

"Everything okay?" Aliya asked.

"Yes," Arezoo said automatically, then reconsidered. "Actually, could you handle table 13 in the corner? The guy sitting there is making me uncomfortable."

Aliya glanced over. "Ruvon? He's harmless. Just a bit socially awkward, especially around females."

"Do you know him?" Arezoo asked.

"Everyone knows everyone here," Aliya reminded her. "It's not a big village. Ruvon is Kalugal's tech security specialist. He's actually quite nice once you get to know him. Sometimes he just stares like that into the distance, probably thinking deeply about something. He doesn't mean anything by it—he just isn't good with social interactions."

Arezoo barely heard anything after Aliya had brought up Kalugal. The name had come up several times since her arrival in the village—the former Doomer commander who'd defected with his men. Men who'd once been part of the same Brotherhood as the evil people who had abducted her and her sisters and cousin and who had killed Uncle Javad.

"That makes him even creepier," she murmured. "I have a very good reason to fear Doomers."

"He's a former Doomer," Aliya said. "Like all of Kalugal's people. They've been part of this community for a while now, and they are sworn to defend it along with the immortals just like all the Kra-ell are sworn to do. Besides, Ruvon is completely harmless. He was probably abused when he was a Doomer, and I wouldn't be surprised if that was why Kalugal took him under his wing. A scrawny guy like him would have gotten beaten up mercilessly in their training camp."

Now, Arezoo felt sorry for the man and ashamed for feeling such resentment toward someone who had most likely been a victim of those monsters as well.

"Black coffee for table 13," Wonder said, sliding a mug across the counter.

"I'll take it to him," Aliya offered.

Arezoo shook her head. "No, I'll—" she began, then stopped as an involuntary shiver ran through her.

Aliya couldn't be sure of any of the things she'd said. She'd been making assumptions based on the guy's social awkwardness and slight build. That didn't mean that he was harmless. He could be just as much of a monster as the fake doctor who had done unspeakable things to her aunt and to Fenella, and to a lesser extent to her and her sisters and cousin.

Arezoo was trying hard not to think about the things that had been done to them, leaving them hazy in semi-lucid, drugged memories, but she knew she'd been hurt. If the clan hadn't rescued them, they would have been forced into becoming breeding stock for immortal warriors.

"Actually," she said, setting the mug back on the counter with trembling hands. "Would you mind? I need a moment."

Aliya took the coffee. "Sure. No problem."

As the Kra-ell female delivered the coffee to Ruvon, Arezoo stepped into the tiny employee bathroom in the back of the hut and locked the door behind her. She leaned against the sink, staring at her reflection in the mirror.

Her face looked the same as always—the same dark eyes, high cheekbones, and determined chin. But the world around her had changed irrevocably. She'd thought that she'd left the nightmare behind, but the ghosts had chased her even here, to the immortals' hidden paradise.

Logically, she knew that Aliya was right at least about the former Doomers being sworn to protect the village. They wouldn't be living here among the immortals if they were up to no good. But Arezoo had a hard time believing that the evil they'd been a part of could be washed away with time and good behavior.

Another shiver ran through her, this one harder to control. She gripped the edge of the sink, forcing herself to take deep, even breaths. She couldn't afford to fall apart, not here, not now. Her mother and sisters depended on her to be strong. She had to adapt, to show them that they could all thrive in this new place.

But how could she feel safe knowing that men who had been born to the Brotherhood, raised with hate, and brainwashed with evil, walked the same paths, breathed the same air, sat at tables that she was expected to serve with a smile?

The gentle tap at the door startled her. "Arezoo?" Wonder asked. "Is everything all right in there?"

"I'll be out in a minute," Arezoo called, splashing cold water on her face. She dried her hands and face with a paper towel and unlocked the door.

Wonder still stood outside, concern evident in her expression.

"I'm sorry," Arezoo said. "I just needed a moment."

"No need to apologize," Wonder said gently. "Aliya told me about your reaction to Ruvon."

"It's fine," Arezoo lied. "I just need to mentally adjust to them being here and posing no threat."

Wonder studied her face. "Your family suffered at the hands of the Brotherhood. It's natural to be wary of anyone associated with them, even if they've changed allegiances."

"Have they, though?" Arezoo asked before she could stop herself. "How do you know that they have really changed?"

"I'd bet my life on it." Wonder put a hand on her chest. "But your feelings are valid, and no one expects you to be comfortable around them right away." She squeezed Arezoo's shoulder. "If you'd prefer not to serve any of Kalugal's men, just say the word."

The understanding in Wonder's voice nearly undid Arezoo's composure. "Thank you," she whispered. "I'm sorry to be so difficult on my first day."

"You're not being difficult," Wonder assured her. "You're being human. Well, mostly human." She smiled. "Take a few more minutes if you need them, then come back when you're ready. The afternoon rush won't start for another hour or so."

After Wonder left, Arezoo leaned against the wall and tried to reconcile her new reality. The village wasn't the perfect sanctuary she'd imagined. It housed victims—her and her family and others, and former perpetrators, Doomers, offering second chances to those who'd once served darkness.

She wasn't sure she was ready to extend such grace, especially to men who'd been part of that organization, but neither could she retreat. This was her new home, for better or worse, and she needed to learn to live with its reality.

39

FENELLA

Fenella studied her reflection in Shira's full-length mirror, adjusting the black blouse she'd 'purchased' from Jasmine's seemingly endless wardrobe. Paired with black jeans, it meant she was ready for her first night tending bar at the Hobbit.

"Not bad for a seventy-three-year-old," she murmured to herself as she struck a pose to admire her profile.

Her belly was flat, her breasts were perky even without a bra, although she was wearing one now, and her face was exactly the same as it was fifty years ago.

All thanks to Max.

Behind her, the bathroom door opened, releasing a cloud of steam as Din emerged with a towel wrapped around his waist. Water droplets clung to his broad shoulders, and his hair was slicked back from his face, emphasizing his strong jawline.

"Hello, beautiful," he said, his eyes traveling appreciatively over her body.

"Hello to you, too, handsome." Fenella stretched on her tiptoes and kissed his cheek.

She'd spent the night with him again, just as she had the night before. Waking up beside him in the morning was a nice treat, and it felt as natural as if they'd been doing it for years instead of days. Then he'd come with her to Shira's place.

Her roommate was working the midday shift in the library again, but she'd promised to do her best to stop by the bar and get a drink or two to support Fenella on her first night on the job. She'd also murmured something about a potential hookup with a guy she'd met in the library, so Fenella wasn't really expecting Shira to show up tonight.

Din pulled on a T-shirt. "Nervous?"

"Excited, not nervous." She watched him dress with unabashed interest. It was a luxury to enjoy such casual intimacy with a guy, the simple pleasure of admiring a lover's body without fear or reservation or the urge to bolt at the first opportunity. "For me, bartending is like riding a bicycle."

"Except, this time, the clientele is immortal," Din pointed out, zipping his jeans.

Fenella waved a dismissive hand. "Immortal, human—doesn't matter. Drinkers are drinkers the world over. They want their drinks made properly, a bit of conversation, and someone to listen to their troubles without passing judgment."

She took a final glance in the mirror, then grabbed her small purse from the bed—another acquisition from Jasmine's closet. "We should head out soon. I want to get there early and help Atzil set up for the evening."

Din nodded, running a hand through his damp hair. "Do you want to stop by Thomas's place first? I need to grab a dress shirt."

"The one you're wearing is fine."

"It's a T-shirt. I thought I'd wear a button-down."

Fenella raised an eyebrow. "Why? You're just walking me over there, right?"

Din's sudden interest in examining his shoe spoke volumes. Fenella narrowed her eyes.

"Din?"

"I thought I'd stay for a little bit," he said, attempting nonchalance. "To show support on your first night."

"A little bit, meaning what?"

"Until closing."

Fenella crossed her arms. "You want to sit at the bar all night and watch me work?"

"Why not? I spent decades thinking about you and the way you looked behind the bar. Now, I finally get a replay of my fantasy."

It was a nice sentiment, but Fenella wasn't fooled. "Try again. The truth this time."

Din sighed, finally meeting her gaze. "Fine. I want to make sure everything goes smoothly and that no one gives you any trouble."

"Trouble? In this village of perfect immortals with their perfect teeth and perfect manners?"

"Immortals can be assholes too," Din said. "Especially after a few drinks. Not everyone behaves themselves when they've had too much."

"And you're going to do what exactly? Defend my honor if someone gets obnoxious? I know how to handle drunk patrons, Din, and I've done that in places a lot rougher than a bar called 'the Hobbit' in an immortal commune."

"I know you can handle yourself," Din protested. "But this is your first night, and I just want to be there for you."

Fenella softened at the earnestness in his expression. "It's sweet that you want to protect me, but it's unnecessary. And if I'm being honest, a bit stifling."

"Stifling?" Din looked offended.

"Yes." Fenella slung the strap of the purse across her body, signaling it was time to leave. "Having someone hover over me is going to take some adjustment."

"I'm not hovering," Din protested as they walked down the hallway. "I'm being supportive."

"Supportive would be saying 'have a great first

night, I can't wait to hear all about it when you get home.' Hovering is planting yourself at the bar for seven hours to make sure no one looks at me wrong."

Din ran a hand through his hair, a gesture Fenella was beginning to recognize as a sign of frustration. "What's wrong with me wanting to be with you?"

"We've hardly been apart since you've arrived."

"And it's been wonderful."

"It has." Fenella surprised herself by agreeing. "But I also need space to breathe, Din. I don't need a babysitter."

She walked to the front door and checked her watch. Still plenty of time to get to the bar early.

"Look," she said, her tone softening, "you can come tonight and stay until closing, but just this once. It's important to me that I establish myself there on my own terms."

"Fair enough," Din conceded, though his expression suggested he wasn't entirely convinced. "Just tonight, unless you decide that you actually like having me around and keeping the drunks from harassing you."

Fenella wasn't sure she believed he would obey her wishes on that. There was something in his tone that hinted at future arguments over this boundary. For all the talk about fated mates she'd heard from Kyra and Jasmine, she and Din were still navigating the complexities of two fiercely independent people trying to forge a connection that wouldn't suffocate either of them.

Kyra and Jasmine both seemed completely in sync with their mates—unable to be apart for long without experiencing physical and emotional distress. They described it as a tether connecting them to their mates and pulling taut when the separation exceeded a few hours.

Fenella hoped that would never happen to her. She craved her space, her independence, and she couldn't imagine being attached to someone at the hip. She enjoyed Din's company, found him intellectually stimulating and physically irresistible, but she didn't feel like she couldn't breathe without him being near.

In her not-so-humble opinion, Kyra and Jasmine were the crazy ones and she was the normal one.

Then again, it was possible that her and Din's connection was not fated but something more mundane and, therefore, potentially more fragile.

40

FENELLA

"You're quiet," Din observed as they neared the bar.

"Just thinking about drink recipes," Fenella lied, pushing aside the jumble of thoughts that had been swirling in her head since they had left Shira's place and continued through the stop in Thomas's place for Din to change his shirt.

Tonight was about her return to bartending, not existential questions about fate and compatibility.

The Hobbit looked even more charming in the waning light, with soft illumination spilling from its round windows and creating golden pools on the path outside. It wouldn't last long as the shutters would go down as soon as it got dark outside, but for now, it looked very inviting.

Inside, the cozy space glowed with warmth, the wooden beams overhead strung with tiny lights. The huge bar dominated the floor, with plenty of stools for patrons who wanted to sit right next to it, but there was also ample seating available around small tables that were made from barrels topped with wooden round platforms.

"Fenella!" Atzil called from behind the bar. "Right on time. Come and let me show you the setup."

Din squeezed her hand before releasing it. "I'll find a table in the back where I will disappear into the shadows."

Fenella nodded and made her way to the bar, where Atzil welcomed her with a warm smile.

"Ready for your first night?" He handed her a tiny black apron with the bar's logo embroidered on the pocket.

"Yes, sir." Fenella tied it around her waist. "It's been so long since I've done this."

"It's like riding a bicycle," Atzil said, unknowingly echoing her earlier words to Din.

"Exactly." Fenella ran her hands along the polished wood of the bar, familiarizing herself with its contours.

For the next twenty minutes or so, Atzil guided her through which bottles were most popular and the drinks the Kra-ell favored.

"We get busier as the night goes on, with the peak usually around midnight. Most nights, I have to forcibly kick people out, or they would stay until it was daylight."

That meant people were enjoying themselves, and if it was up to her, she would have kept the bar open until it was daylight, the automatic shutters opened, and everyone went home without needing to be kicked out.

"Any troublemakers I should watch out for?" Fenella asked.

"Not really. The worst we get is Rogan waxing poetic about his lost love after his fifth whiskey, or Gunter trying to convince everyone to join in singing sea shanties. Anandur is a hoot, but he never comes without Wonder, and she likes to go to bed early, so there is that."

"Sounds very tame compared to some places I've worked."

"This is a pretty civilized crowd."

"What about the former Doomers?" she asked. "Do they behave themselves?"

"You forget that I'm one of those infamous former Doomers. Of course, they behave themselves here."

Fenella wanted the floor to open up and swallow her whole. How could she have forgotten that Atzil was Kalugal's chef? After all, that was the reason he couldn't open the bar during weekdays and why he was offering her the job.

"I was just joking," she tried to save the situation. "Naturally, they would behave in your bar or you would spit in their food. Right?"

He snorted. "That's right. They know what's good for them."

The door opened, and Ingrid entered, her platinum blonde hair gleaming like spun silver in the warm light.

"Well, hello." She walked over to the bar. "Good luck tonight, Fenella."

"Thank you."

Atzil bent over the bar and grabbed his mate for a quick kiss. "Are you going to stay tonight?"

"Just for a little bit." She cast an amused look at Din. "I'll keep him company for a few minutes." She turned around and headed toward his table, her high heels making clicking sounds on the wood floor.

As customers began to arrive, Fenella fell into the familiar rhythm of mixing drinks, making small talk, and ensuring glasses stayed filled. Her body remembered the dance of bartending—the exaggerated arm movements for dramatic effect, the multitasking, the art of listening while working. It felt good, purposeful, a reminder that some parts of her had survived intact.

Din remained at his table, now alone since Ingrid had moved to chat with other patrons. He nursed his beer, his eyes following Fenella as she worked. She tried not to let his steady gaze unnerve her, focusing instead on the growing crowd of customers.

"It would seem that word is getting around that we have a new bartender," Atzil commented as the bar began to fill. "People are curious to see you, and it looks like you'll have a busy first night."

"Good," Fenella said, expertly mixing a Manhattan for a dark-haired immortal who'd introduced himself as Graham. "I like being busy."

Graham took his drink with a nod of thanks. "I've heard that you possess an interesting ability. Psychometry. Is that right?"

Fenella shot a glance at Atzil, who shrugged apologetically. "Word travels fast in a small community."

"So I'm learning," Fenella said dryly. "And yes, apparently I can sometimes get impressions from objects I touch. Though it's not very reliable."

After the morning with the Clan Mother, she'd tested her ability on a variety of objects, but none evoked any visions of past events. She was starting to think that it was unique to necklaces and pendants that were worn close to the heart. Maybe that was the connection. Or maybe it was the antiquity of the objects that made the difference.

"Fascinating," Graham said, pulling out a pocket watch from his vest. "Would you mind trying it with this? I've had it for over two hundred years."

Fenella hesitated. Her experiences with psychometry so far had been overwhelming and intrusive—Kyra's pendant flooding her with violent missions, Annani's necklace revealing intimate glimpses of the goddess's personal life that Fenella had no right to witness.

The thought of another such invasion felt uncomfortable.

"I'm not sure that's a good idea," she said. "I'm still learning to control it."

"Just a quick try?" Graham pressed. "We don't get many psychometrics in the clan."

Other patrons had noticed the exchange and were now watching with interest. Fenella felt the weight of their curiosity like a physical pressure. She glanced at Din, who looked ready to intervene, and made a quick decision.

"Sure, why not?" she said, holding out her hand. "But I'm not promising anything."

Graham placed the watch in her palm, and as Fenella closed her fingers around it she braced for the rush of visions, the disorienting plunge into someone else's memories, but nothing happened.

The watch remained just a watch—cold metal against her skin, ticking steadily but revealing nothing of its history. No visions, no impressions, not even a hint of emotion.

Relief mingled with embarrassment as Fenella returned the watch. "Sorry. I've got nothing."

"Perhaps it needs more time," Graham tried.

Fenella shrugged. "Like I said, my so-called talent is not very reliable."

"Try mine," called another patron, sliding a ring across the bar.

Fenella picked it up, again feeling nothing beyond the physical object. "Sorry. Nothing here either."

A line began to form as more customers produced objects for testing—keys, jewelry, even a dagger that an intimidating Kra-ell warrior slid down the counter toward her.

None of them triggered any psychometric response.

"Performance anxiety, maybe?" Atzil suggested quietly as Fenella handed back yet another object with an apologetic smile.

"Or it's just not working consistently," she said. Then, struck by inspiration, she added in a louder voice, "Though I'm getting some rather interesting impressions from this glass."

She held up a tumbler she'd just washed, pretending to study it intently. "Hmm, yes. Very interesting indeed."

"What do you see?" asked the glass's previous owner, a burly immortal named Dan or Derek. She didn't remember.

Fenella put on a serious expression. "This glass has witnessed you thinking about a truly spectacular dance performance you did in your kitchen earlier, wearing nothing but socks and headphones."

A ripple of laughter spread through the crowd as Dan's face reddened. "That's ridiculous! I've never—"

"The glass doesn't lie," Fenella said solemnly. "And you have quite the moves, buddy."

More laughter erupted, and Fenella's lips curved into a mischievous smile. "Who's next?"

For the next hour, the game continued. Patrons would hand her an object, and Fenella would invent increasingly outlandish visions about their owners. An elegant pen revealed a secret passion for romance novels. A wristwatch disclosed a tendency to talk to houseplants. A dollar coin exposed a childhood habit of hiding vegetables in potted plants to avoid eating them.

The bar filled with laughter as Fenella's fabricated revelations grew more creative. Even Din seemed amused, his earlier overprotectiveness relaxing as he watched her work the crowd with ease.

"You are a natural entertainer," Atzil commented as he helped her mix an order of vodka cocktails for a group of Kra-ell.

"I've missed this more than I realized," Fenella admitted.

The night passed in a blur of activity—mixing drinks, inventing ridiculous psychometric 'readings,' and falling into easy conversation with the village residents. Fenella hadn't felt this alive in decades.

Even the knowledge that some of the patrons were former Doomers couldn't dampen her spirits.

Din remained at his table, occasionally ordering another beer but otherwise content to watch from a distance.

Fenella appreciated that he'd given her the space to establish herself, even if his continued presence suggested he wasn't entirely comfortable with her handling the rambunctious patrons who were getting progressively drunker.

As midnight approached, the crowd showed no signs of thinning. If anything, the bar had grown more packed as word spread about the entertainment.

The place was bursting at the seams, with people standing between tables and along the walls because there was no more room to sit.

"Read mine next!" called a woman Fenella recognized from the café, sliding a pencil across the bar.

Fenella picked it up, making a show of closing her eyes and concentrating. "Oh my," she gasped. "This pencil has seen things. Scandalous things."

"What kinds of things?" the woman asked, playing along.

"It seems," Fenella said dramatically, "that this pencil has been used to write some rather spicy letters to a certain Guardian whose name rhymes with 'Rex.'"

The woman's mouth dropped open in pretend shock. "How did you—"

"The pencil doesn't lie," Fenella said with a wink, returning it to its cackling owner.

Atzil laughed, shaking his head in admiration. "You're going to be very popular around here."

"I aim to please," Fenella said, already mixing the next order.

She was working nonstop without even taking a potty break, and yet she felt energized rather than drained.

This was what she'd needed—purpose, connection, a place where her skills shone, and her company was enjoyed.

She was having the time of her life.

41

DIN

Din nursed his third beer, watching Fenella work behind the bar with joy and confidence that made his chest swell with pride.

She belonged here.

Her hands never hesitated as she poured drinks, mixed cocktails, and bantered with customers. This was the woman he'd spent fifty years dreaming about, the one who could light up a room and cheer everyone up just by being herself.

She'd vanished for a while, had been buried beneath layers of trauma and wariness, but tonight she had resurfaced in her full glory.

This was the Fenella he remembered—vibrant, quick-witted, her eyes sparkling with mischief as she teased the patrons. When she laughed, the sound carried across the crowded room, bright and uninhibited.

She was radiant.

"Earth to Din," a familiar voice said, breaking through his reverie.

Din blinked, turning to find Max standing beside his table with Kyra at his side. He hadn't even noticed them enter the Hobbit.

"Mind if we join you?" Max asked, pulling one of the barrel-shaped stools from a nearby table that must have been vacated while Din had been daydreaming.

"Please do," Din said.

"She looks like she's having oodles of fun," Kyra said as she settled onto the stool Max brought for her.

"She was always magnetic behind a bar."

"I remember," Max said with a smirk.

Din chose to ignore the reminder that Max had enjoyed Fenella back then. Their renewed friendship was too fresh to test with old rivalries. Besides, Max was happily mated now, his days of competing for female attention long behind him.

Fenella approached their table, a tray of drinks balanced expertly on one hand. "Well, well," she said, looking from Din to the newcomers. "The cavalry has arrived."

"We came to cheer you on," Kyra said. "Though it looks like you don't need it. The place is packed."

"Word travels fast about a new bartender who can read your deepest secrets from your pocket lint,"

Fenella said, distributing the drinks—beer for Max, a whiskey for Kyra, and a fresh beer for Din that he hadn't even ordered yet.

"How are you holding up?" Din asked.

"Fabulously." Fenella's eyes sparkled with amusement. "No one's been handsy, belligerent, or insulting. The toughest challenge was keeping up with the orders."

"The night is still young," Max said.

That earned him an elbow in the ribs from Kyra. "Don't jinx it," she warned.

"It wouldn't be a proper first night without at least one minor catastrophe," Fenella said, not sounding concerned in the slightest. "Though this crowd seems too well-behaved for anything even a little dramatic."

Din reached for her hand and pulled her to sit on his knee. "Your psychic act is a hit."

Fenella laughed. "I'm simply communicating what the objects tell me. It's not my fault if people's possessions are shockingly indiscreet about their owners' embarrassing habits."

"Right," Din drawled, not fooled for a moment. "What about Markus practicing naked yoga on the roof of his house?"

"His tie was very forthcoming about it," Fenella insisted with mock solemnity. "Practically begged me to tell everyone."

Their banter was interrupted as the door swung

open, and Jasmine and Ell-rom walked in. The Kra-ell royal looked somewhat out of place in the rustic, Tolkien-inspired setting, his regal bearing and ethereal features marking him as distinctly alien despite his immortal-style beauty and casual attire. Yet no one paid him much attention. The village inhabitants had grown accustomed to him and his sister and all the other Kra-ell hybrids and purebloods living among them.

"Looks like a family gathering," Fenella observed as the couple made their way toward their table. "Should I expect the sisters and all thirteen kids next?"

"God, I hope not," Kyra said. "We're still working on public outings with them. Arezoo's the only one who's ventured out on her own so far."

"She's enjoying working at the café," Jasmine said as she and Ell-rom pulled more stools to the table.

"Like aunt, like niece," Fenella said with a wink. "Now, much as I'd love to stay and chat, duty calls. Holler if you need anything."

As she rose to her feet and returned to the bar, Din couldn't tear his eyes away from her. The sway of her hips, the confident set of her shoulders, the way she flicked her hair over her shoulder as she laughed at something someone said—every movement was mesmerizing.

"You've got it so bad," Max teased.

"Is it that obvious?" Din asked.

"You look like a starving man staring at a feast," Ell-rom said bluntly.

Din winced. "I'm trying to keep a low profile. She already thinks I'm smothering her."

Kyra frowned. "Did she say that?"

"She called it stifling. I wanted to stay here with her tonight to make sure no one gave her trouble, and she told me that I was hovering."

"Well, what would you call sitting here in the corner all night long?" Jasmine asked.

Din started to deny it, then reconsidered. "I worry about her. After everything she's been through..."

"She's not made of glass," Kyra said gently. "Trust me on this. The worst thing after suffering a trauma is being treated like you might shatter at any moment."

"I know." Din ran a hand through his hair, a habit when frustrated. "I just want to protect her."

"And she appreciates it," Jasmine assured him. "But she also needs space to find herself again. To remember who she was before all the bad stuff happened."

Din nodded toward the bar where Fenella was now entertaining a group of Guardians with an elaborate tale involving one of their watches. "She seems to be doing a fine job of that on her own."

"Just be there when she wants you," Max said. "Give her room when she doesn't."

Din nodded. "When you are right, you're right."

"So, when do you go back to Scotland?" Ell-rom asked, changing the subject.

Din tore his gaze away from Fenella. "I took two weeks off for a so-called family emergency, but..." He hesitated, the decision crystallizing in his mind as he spoke. "I don't think I'm going back. Not permanently, anyway."

"What about your students?" Jasmine asked. "Your research?"

"The term ends in a few weeks. My assistant can administer the final exams, and I can grade them remotely." Din took a sip of his beer, considering his options. "After that, I could request a sabbatical."

"And then what?" Max pressed. "You'll move to the village?"

"Where else? But I haven't discussed any of it with Fenella yet. I still need to see where this is going. If things don't work out between us, I'll be on the first flight back to Scotland. I wouldn't be able to tolerate seeing her with someone else."

Max looked away.

"It's going to work out between you," Jasmine said. "But don't make any rash decisions. Let things unfold naturally."

Din couldn't argue with that logic. He was contemplating major life changes based on a relationship that was barely a week old. Yet it didn't feel new—it felt like the continuation of something that had started half a century ago, been interrupted, but never truly ended.

"It would be foolish of me to burn bridges," he said. "That's why I was thinking about finishing the academic year remotely and waiting with the request for a sabbatical. But I can't wait too long."

A burst of laughter drew Din's attention back to the bar, where Fenella was now entertaining a group of patrons with another hilarious 'psychic reading' of a pencil.

"She's brilliant," Jasmine said, wiping tears of mirth from her eyes. "She's transformed her inconsistent psychometric ability into entertainment, turning a potential liability into an asset."

"She's always been quick on her feet," Din said, pride swelling in his chest.

He watched as Fenella moved on to her next victim, a guy who handed over a ring with dramatic reluctance. She held it up to the light, narrowed her eyes, and gasped theatrically.

"This ring has witnessed a secret talent," she announced to the delighted crowd. "Our brave Guardian here has a hidden passion for..." She paused for effect, "competitive ballroom dancing! In cowboy boots!"

The Guardian's face contorted with a mix of horror and amusement. "That's absurd!"

"The ring never lies," Fenella insisted, her expression perfectly serious despite the mischief dancing in her eyes. "I'm quite impressed with your tango, though your foxtrot needs work."

The Guardian's friends howled with laughter, clapping him on the back as he shook his head in good-natured denial.

"She's found her perfect audience." Max chuckled. "Immortals who've lived long enough to appreciate a good tall tale."

Din nodded, his eyes never leaving Fenella as she continued her performance. This was the woman he remembered—the bright spark of life that had drawn him to her all those years ago, the wit and warmth that had haunted his dreams ever since.

And in that moment, watching her shine amidst the laughter and camaraderie of the village pub, Din realized he was falling in love with her all over again, not with the memory or the fantasy he'd carried for fifty years, but with the actual woman before him—complex, wounded, resilient, and utterly captivating.

The Fenella of his memories had been a sketch, a partial impression based on limited interaction. The real Fenella was a masterpiece—layered, textured, more vivid and more complicated than he could have imagined.

He still had so much to learn about her, though.

She kept so much bottled up that she was not ready to share with him yet. The decades she'd spent wandering, the traumas she'd endured, the strengths she'd developed along the way—these were all parts of her story he had yet to discover. But he knew with absolute certainty that he wanted that chance, wanted to uncover every facet of who she had become.

42

FENELLA

"Last call!" Fenella shouted over the noise of the crowd, her voice hoarse from hours of conversation and laughter.

The announcement was met with a chorus of groans and protests.

Despite the late hour, the Hobbit remained packed, the atmosphere electric with conversation and periodic bursts of song.

"Come on," a guy called from the corner. "One more round!"

"You've had enough, Niko." Fenella laughed.

He'd been one of the most enthusiastic participants in the impromptu singing contest that had broken out an hour earlier. Max had won it hands down.

"You heard the lady," Atzil announced. "Time to go home. We're closed, but the good news is that we are open tomorrow, and you are all invited to return."

The complaints grew louder, but they were good-natured.

People were just reluctant to end the fun and accept closing time, which Fenella regarded as a great success. A bar emptying on its own was a sign that the atmosphere needed a boost.

"Will Fenella be here tomorrow?" someone shouted from the back.

"You can count on it," she said. "It was a pleasure serving you all tonight, and, hopefully, I will see you all tomorrow."

That seemed to mollify some of the more reluctant patrons, who began shuffling toward the door. Others required more persuasion, with Atzil 'helping' them politely but firmly out the door.

"I had no idea immortals could get so drunk," Fenella said. "Or sing so many lewd Scottish ballads. I don't remember them from when I was working back home."

"They make up new ones as they go." Din walked over to the bar and sat down on one of the recently vacated barstools. "You were amazing tonight."

Fenella rewarded the compliment with a broad smile. "I had fun."

"Evidently." Din leaned over the bar and kissed her cheek. "Ready to go home?"

She shook her head. "There's a lot of cleanup to

be done before Atzil and I can call it a night. But you don't have to stay and watch me cleaning." She grabbed a rag and walked around the bar.

"No, but I can help." Din started rolling up his sleeves.

"You don't have to do that."

"I want to. The sooner it is done, the sooner you can go home."

Atzil returned from depositing two particularly inebriated patrons outside.

It was good that no one was driving home, or it would have been dangerous to just kick them out like that.

Fenella wouldn't be surprised if she found them sleeping on benches along the way.

Might actually do them some good.

"Finally." Atzil flipped the sign on the door to 'Closed.' "Successful first night, I'd say."

"Indeed," Fenella agreed. "But I'm going to be feeling it in my muscles tomorrow. Being immortal doesn't help with that."

Atzil started collecting empty glasses and beer bottles from the tables. "First night's always the hardest." He turned to Din. "I don't remember hiring you."

"I volunteered."

Atzil grinned. "I won't say no to free labor."

Fenella watched Din with a mix of appreciation

and fondness as he worked in tandem with her and Atzil.

They'd gotten into a rhythm, with Atzil clearing tables, her wiping them down, and Din piling the stools on top to clear the floor for mopping.

For an archaeology professor, he seemed remarkably at home with menial work.

"Your mate's handy to have around," Atzil said as Din ducked into the back room to grab a mop.

"He's not my mate," Fenella said automatically, then reconsidered. "We are just getting to know each other."

Atzil raised an eyebrow, but before he could come up with a retort, Din appeared with the mop and went to work.

"How much did we make tonight?" Fenella asked. "If you don't mind me asking."

"More than usual for a Friday," Atzil said. "Your psychic act was quite the draw."

"It wasn't an act," Fenella insisted with mock seriousness. "I was merely communicating vital information from inanimate objects."

"Right," Atzil drawled. "And I'm a hobbit who's very tall for my kind."

"The look on Karin's face when you 'revealed' her secret underwater knitting hobby..." Din chuckled, pausing in his mopping. "Priceless."

"She does have very pruney fingers," Fenella said. "The evidence was right there for anyone to see."

"And Marcus with the ballroom dancing?" Atzil added. "He nearly fell off his stool."

"Maybe because it was true. His pupils dilated when I revealed it as if he was surprised that I found out his secret hobby."

Atzil's booming laughter echoed in the emptiness of the bar. "I'll take the trash to the incinerator." He hefted two large bags. "You two finish up in here."

As he left through the back door, Fenella was left alone with Din for the first time in hours. She watched him as he finished mopping, looking as fresh and as put together as he had been at the start of the night. The guy had a gift for looking composed no matter the circumstances.

"Thank you for helping." She broke the silence. "I'd forgotten how exhausting a night of bartending can be."

Din looked up, a smile warming his features. "I'm more than happy to help. But tell me the truth. What was more tiring, the entertaining or the actual bartending?"

"Equal measures." Fenella leaned against the counter.

"You were amazing," Din said, and there was something in his tone that made her cheeks heat up. "The queen of the night. You had them eating out of your hand."

"It's just part of being a good bartender," Fenella said, deflecting the compliment. "Half of what people pay for is the show. Some bartenders do that with fancy bottle acrobatics, which I do well, and some tell jokes or make up stories about what they supposedly heard from former customers."

He chuckled. "I didn't know those were made-up stories. I thought they were real. Still, I'm sure that not everyone can invent outrageous stories on the spot like you do."

"I surprised myself. I guess the years of constantly changing identities and reinventing myself helped me develop a talent for storytelling."

Din's expression softened into something that looked dangerously like sympathy. "Thankfully, you don't have to do that anymore. You are finally safe."

"Who says I feel safe?" she murmured.

The words emerged more honest than she'd intended, hanging in the air between them. Fenella hadn't meant to reveal that persistent feeling that safety was an illusion that could shatter at any moment, even here, even in the immortals' village.

Shit happened, and it usually didn't come with warning bells, and even if it did, people tended to ignore the sounds until it was too late.

Din set the mop aside and walked over to her. "The village is the safest place you could be in, and people here care about you."

Fenella knew he meant it kindly, but something in his certainty pricked at her. "I had people who cared about me in Scotland, too," she said. "That didn't stop what happened. I've gotten immortality out of it, but at what price? The years I could have spent with my family that I can never recover, the endless roving and fear of being discovered."

"I'm sorry. I didn't mean to sound dismissive of your concerns."

His immediate acknowledgment of her perspective disarmed her, the apology easing the defensive tension that had begun to build. "It's fine. I know the village is safe, but that doesn't mean nothing bad can ever happen here. You have all these security measures in place for a reason."

He nodded. "Good point. Perhaps a better way to state it is that the village is as secure as it gets, but there are no guarantees that nothing bad will ever happen here."

The sound of the door opening startled her, but it was only Atzil.

"All done?" he asked.

"The bar's clean, glasses are stacked in the dishwasher, and Din has mopped the entire floor."

"Excellent," Atzil said. "We make a good team."

"We do," Fenella agreed.

Atzil clapped her gently on the back. "Time to go home, girl. Tomorrow is another day."

Outside, the night air was cool and refreshing after hours in the warm, crowded bar. Stars blanketed the sky above the village, more visible now than on any of the previous nights.

"Well, I'm off to collapse in bed for a few hours." Atzil locked the door behind them. "You did a great job tonight, Fenella. I'll see you tomorrow at seven?"

"I'll be here," she confirmed.

He offered his hand to Din. "Thanks for the free labor. You're invited to volunteer every night."

Din chuckled. "I just might."

Wasn't going to happen, but Fenella was too tired to argue with Din about it now. It could wait for the morning.

"I'm looking forward to more psychic revelations tomorrow," Atzil said with a grin. "Goodnight, you two."

As he walked away and Fenella was left alone with Din, the adrenaline that had sustained her throughout the evening started to ebb, leaving exhaustion in its wake. Without thinking, she leaned against him, her head finding a comfortable spot on his shoulder.

"Tired?" he asked, his arm coming around her waist.

"Completely drained," she admitted. "But in a good way."

They started toward Shira's place at an easy pace. The village was quiet at this hour; most residents had long since retired for the night, and surprisingly, there were no drunks sprawled on the benches they were passing by.

"I've been thinking," Din said.

"A dangerous pastime," Fenella murmured.

He chuckled. "Perhaps. But necessary."

Something in his tone made her glance up at his face, trying to read his expression in the dim light of the moon and stars. "What about?"

"I'm in love with you, Fenella."

The declaration stopped her in her tracks. She pulled away to look at him, searching his expression to see if he expected her to tell him that she loved him back.

"I don't need you to say it to me," he added quickly. "That's not why I'm telling you. I just wanted you to know where I stand. You can take all the time you need."

A jumble of emotions tumbled through her. Part of her wanted to flee from the intensity of his declaration, while another part yearned to believe in the possibility he was offering and grab on to it.

"You claimed to be in love with me fifty years ago," she said finally, resuming their walk. "But it couldn't have been true then because you didn't know me. Don't fall into the trap of falling in love with the notion of love. We are just getting to know each other, and one day this relationship could blossom into love, but we are not there yet."

She was acutely aware of how painful it must be for him to hear, but one of them needed to be the voice of reason, and it seemed that the task had fallen to her.

"You're right," Din admitted, falling into step beside her. "What I felt then wasn't really love. It was infatuation, fascination, desire—but not love. I didn't know you well enough."

"And you do now?" Fenella challenged.

"I know you better now. And every new facet I discover only deepens my feelings for you." He paused. "But I know you're nowhere near ready to say those words back to me, and that's okay. I can wait."

Part of her wanted to deflect with humor or sarcasm, her usual defenses against emotional vulnerability, but Din deserved better than reflexive deflection.

"It's been a very long time since I allowed myself to get close enough to even try to feel anything."

"I understand," Din said, and she believed he did. "There's no rush."

They walked a bit further in silence, the path winding between the village's charming homes and lush greenery.

"The birthday party tomorrow should be fun," Fenella said to defuse the tension that had settled between them. "Jasmine says half the village has been involved in planning it and that everyone is going to participate."

"Immortals don't usually celebrate birthdays, but it's Allegra's first, and since she was born on Kian's two thousandth birthday, Syssi decided that a joint party was the way to go. Perhaps it will become a new village tradition." Din reached for her hand. "We are still writing our customs and traditions. Perhaps there will be a new one based on your fake readings. It could be a competition for who can make up the most outlandish stories."

"It could be fun." She sighed. "The truth is that I don't know what I want yet. I'm still figuring out who I am now, and if this latest cycle of reinventing myself will be the last."

He gave her hand a gentle squeeze. "Finding a safe haven doesn't mean that you have to stick to whatever role you want to play right now. You can keep reinventing yourself as many times as you want. Take me, for example. I wasn't always defined as a stuffy professor."

"You're not a stuffy professor." She turned to him, wound her arms around his neck, and stretched on her tiptoes to plant a soft kiss on his lips. "You are the hunky professor all the female students fantasize about."

He took over the kiss, deepening it, and when they came up for air, he rested his forehead against hers. "I only care about the fantasies of one feisty bartender. No one else's."

Later, when Fenella was standing under the spray in the shower, she thought about Din's declaration of love and how it complicated things. Surprisingly, she didn't feel the urge to run from the complication as she would have expected. Instead, she was cautiously circling it, examining it from different angles, considering possibilities she'd long since abandoned.

She had a job she loved, a newfound family to get to know, and a man who looked at her like she was the answer to a question he'd been asking for centuries. It wasn't a bad position to be in, all things considered.

The future, for once, held more promise than threat. And that, perhaps, was the most surprising development of all.

COMING UP NEXT
The Children of the Gods Book 96
Dark Rover's Gift

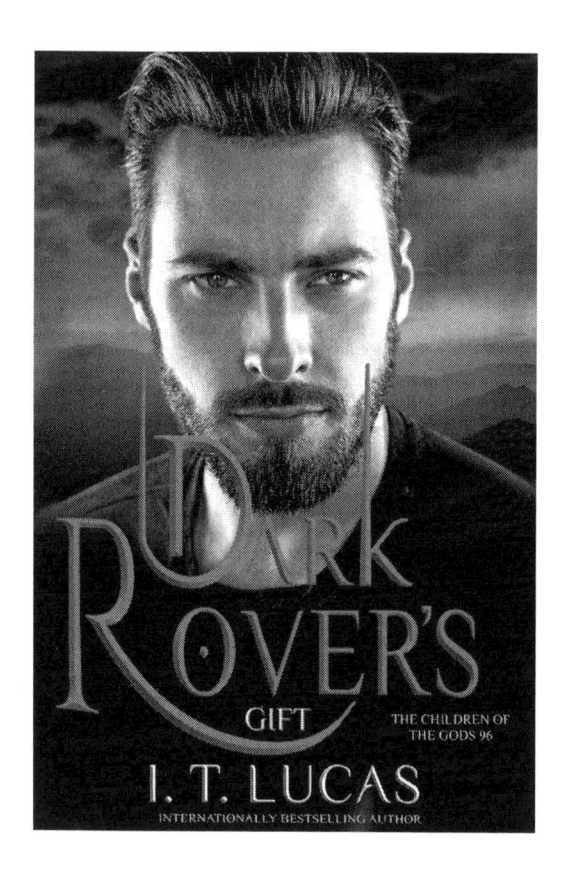

Fenella has led the life of a nomad, wandering the world, relying solely on herself, and encountering hardships that left deep emotional scars. Now, safe in the immortals' village, she uncovers an unexpected connection and a hidden talent that may inspire her to finally put down roots.

NOTE

Dear reader,

I hope my stories have added a little joy to your day. If you have a moment to add some to mine, you can help spread the word about the Children Of The Gods series by telling your friends and penning a review. Your recommendations are the most powerful way to inspire new readers to explore the series.

Thank you,

Isabell

Also by I. T. Lucas

THE CHILDREN OF THE GODS ORIGINS
1: GODDESS'S CHOICE
2: GODDESS'S HOPE

THE CHILDREN OF THE GODS
DARK STRANGER
1: DARK STRANGER THE DREAM
2: DARK STRANGER REVEALED
3: DARK STRANGER IMMORTAL

DARK ENEMY
4: DARK ENEMY TAKEN
5: DARK ENEMY CAPTIVE
6: DARK ENEMY REDEEMED

KRI & MICHAEL'S STORY
6.5: MY DARK AMAZON

DARK WARRIOR
7: DARK WARRIOR MINE
8: DARK WARRIOR'S PROMISE
9: DARK WARRIOR'S DESTINY
10: DARK WARRIOR'S LEGACY

DARK GUARDIAN
11: DARK GUARDIAN FOUND

12: Dark Guardian Craved
13: Dark Guardian's Mate

Dark Angel
14: Dark Angel's Obsession
15: Dark Angel's Seduction
16: Dark Angel's Surrender

Dark Operative
17: Dark Operative: A Shadow of Death
18: Dark Operative: A Glimmer of Hope
19: Dark Operative: The Dawn of Love

Dark Survivor
20: Dark Survivor Awakened
21: Dark Survivor Echoes of Love
22: Dark Survivor Reunited

Dark Widow
23: Dark Widow's Secret
24: Dark Widow's Curse
25: Dark Widow's Blessing

Dark Dream
26: Dark Dream's Temptation
27: Dark Dream's Unraveling
28: Dark Dream's Trap

Dark Prince

29: Dark Prince's Enigma
30: Dark Prince's Dilemma
31: Dark Prince's Agenda

Dark Queen

32: Dark Queen's Quest
33: Dark Queen's Knight
34: Dark Queen's Army

Dark Spy

35: Dark Spy Conscripted
36: Dark Spy's Mission
37: Dark Spy's Resolution

Dark Overlord

38: Dark Overlord New Horizon
39: Dark Overlord's Wife
40: Dark Overlord's Clan

Dark Choices

41: Dark Choices The Quandary
42: Dark Choices Paradigm Shift
43: Dark Choices The Accord

Dark Secrets

44: Dark Secrets Resurgence
45: Dark Secrets Unveiled
46: Dark Secrets Absolved

Dark Haven
47: Dark Haven Illusion
48: Dark Haven Unmasked
49: Dark Haven Found

Dark Power
50: Dark Power Untamed
51: Dark Power Unleashed
52: Dark Power Convergence

Dark Memories
53: Dark Memories Submerged
54: Dark Memories Emerge
55: Dark Memories Restored

Dark Hunter
56: Dark Hunter's Query
57: Dark Hunter's Prey
58: Dark Hunter's Boon

Dark God
59: Dark God's Avatar
60: Dark God's Reviviscence
61: Dark God Destinies Converge

Dark Whispers
62: Dark Whispers From The Past
63: Dark Whispers From Afar
64: Dark Whispers From Beyond

Dark Gambit
65: Dark Gambit The Pawn
66: Dark Gambit The Play
67: Dark Gambit Reliance

Dark Alliance
68: Dark Alliance Kindred Souls
69: Dark Alliance Turbulent Waters
70: Dark Alliance Perfect Storm

Dark Healing
71: Dark Healing Blind Justice
72: Dark Healing Blind Trust
73: Dark healing Blind Curve

Dark Encounters
74: Dark Encounters of the Close Kind
75: Dark Encounters of the Unexpected Kind
76: Dark Encounters of the Fated Kind

Dark Voyage
77: Dark Voyage Matters of the Heart
78: <u>Dark Voyage Matters of the Mind</u>
<u>79: Dark Voyage Matters of the Soul</u>

Dark Horizon
80: Dark Horizon New Dawn
81: Dark Horizon Eclipse of the Heart
82: Dark Horizon The Witching Hour

Dark Witch
83: Dark Witch: Entangled Fates
84: Dark Witch: Twin Destinies
85: Dark Witch: Resurrection

Dark Awakening
86: Dark Awakening: New World
87: Dark Awakening Hidden Currents
88: Dark Awakening Echoes of Destiny

Dark Princess
89: Dark Princess: Shadows
90: Dark Princess Emerging
91: Dark Princess Ascending

Dark Rebel
92: Dark Rebel's Mystery
93: Dark Rebel's Reckoning
94: Dark Rebel's Fortune

Dark Rover
95: Dark Rover's Luck
96: Dark Rover's Gift

PERFECT MATCH

Vampire's Consort

KING'S CHOSEN
CAPTAIN'S CONQUEST
THE THIEF WHO LOVED ME
MY MERMAN PRINCE
THE DRAGON KING
MY WEREWOLF ROMEO
THE CHANNELER'S COMPANION
THE VALKYRIE & THE WITCH
ADINA AND THE MAGIC LAMP

TRANSLATIONS

DIE ERBEN DER GÖTTER
DARK STRANGER
1- DARK STRANGER DER TRAUM
2- DARK STRANGER DIE OFFENBARUNG
3- DARK STRANGER UNSTERBLICH

DARK ENEMY
4- DARK ENEMY ENTFÜHRT
5- DARK ENEMY GEFANGEN
6- DARK ENEMY ERLÖST

DARK WARRIOR
7- DARK WARRIOR MEINE SEHNSUCHT
8- DARK WARRIOR – DEIN VERSPRECHEN
9- Dark Warrior - Unser Schicksal

10-Dark Warrior-Unser Vermächtnis

LOS HIJOS DE LOS DIOSES

EL OSCURO DESCONOCIDO
1: EL OSCURO DESCONOCIDO EL SUEÑO
2: EL OSCURO DESCONOCIDO REVELADO
3: EL OSCURO DESCONOCIDO INMORTAL

EL OSCURO ENEMIGO
4- EL OSCURO ENEMIGO CAPTURADO
5 - EL OSCURO ENEMIGO CAUTIVO
6- EL OSCURO ENEMIGO REDIMIDO

LES ENFANTS DES DIEUX
DARK STRANGER
1- DARK STRANGER LE RÊVE
2- DARK STRANGER LA RÉVÉLATION
3- DARK STRANGER L'IMMORTELLE

THE CHILDREN OF THE GODS SERIES SETS

Books 1-3: Dark Stranger trilogy—Includes a bonus short story: **The Fates Take a Vacation**

<u>Books 4-6: Dark Enemy Trilogy</u> —Includes a bonus short story—**The Fates' Post-Wedding Celebration**

Books 7-10: Dark Warrior Tetralogy

Books 11-13: Dark Guardian Trilogy

Books 14-16: Dark Angel Trilogy

Books 17-19: Dark Operative Trilogy

Books 20-22: Dark Survivor Trilogy

Books 23-25: Dark Widow Trilogy

Books 26-28: Dark Dream Trilogy

Books 29-31: Dark Prince Trilogy

Books 32-34: Dark Queen Trilogy

Books 35-37: Dark Spy Trilogy

Books 38-40: Dark Overlord Trilogy

Books 41-43: Dark Choices Trilogy

Books 44-46: Dark Secrets Trilogy

Books 47-49: Dark Haven Trilogy

Books 50-52: Dark Power Trilogy

Books 53-55: Dark Memories Trilogy

Books 56-58: Dark Hunter Trilogy

Books 59-61: Dark God Trilogy

Books 62-64: Dark Whispers Trilogy

Books 65-67: Dark Gambit Trilogy

Books 68-70: Dark Alliance Trilogy

Books 71-73: Dark Healing Trilogy

Books 74-76: Dark Encounters Trilogy

Books 77-79: Dark Voyage Trilogy
Books 80-82: Dark Horizon Trilogy
Books 83-85: Dark Witch Trilogy
Books 86-88: Dark Awakening Trilogy
Books 89-91: Dark Princess Trilogy

MEGA SETS
The Children of the Gods: Books 1-6
INCLUDES CHARACTER LISTS
The Children of the Gods: Books 6.5-10

Perfect Match Bundle 1

CHECK OUT THE SPECIALS ON ITLUCAS.COM
(https://itlucas.com/specials)

FOR EXCLUSIVE PEEKS AT UPCOMING RELEASES &
A FREE I. T. LUCAS COMPANION BOOK

Join my *VIP Club* and gain access to the VIP portal at itlucas.com

To Join, go to:

http://eepurl.com/blMTpD

Find out more details about what's included with your free membership on the book's last page.

TRY THE CHILDREN OF THE GODS SERIES ON
AUDIBLE
2 FREE audiobooks with your new Audible subscription!

FOR EXCLUSIVE PEEKS AT UPCOMING RELEASES &
A FREE I. T. LUCAS COMPANION BOOK

Join my *VIP Club* and gain access to the VIP portal at itlucas.com

To Join, go to:

http://eepurl.com/blMTpD

INCLUDED IN YOUR FREE MEMBERSHIP:

YOUR VIP PORTAL

- Read preview chapters of upcoming releases.
- Listen to Goddess's Choice narration by Charles Lawrence
- Exclusive content offered only to my VIPs.

FREE I.T. LUCAS COMPANION INCLUDES:

- Goddess's Choice Part 1
- Perfect Match: Vampire's Consort (A standalone Novella)
- Interview Q & A
- Character Charts

If you're already a subscriber and you are not getting my emails, your provider is sending them to your junk folder, and you are missing out on important updates. To fix that, add isabell@itlucas.com to your email contacts or your email VIP list.

**Check out the specials at
https://www.itlucas.com/specials**

Made in the USA
Middletown, DE
18 May 2025